SHADES of WICKED

By Jeaniene Frost

JEANIENE FROST

SHADES *of* WICKED

A Night Rebel Novel

AVONBOOKS

An Imprint of HarperCollins*Publishers*

First Avon Books mass market printing: November 2018
First Avon Books hardcover printing: October 2018

Print Edition ISBN: 978-0-06-286876-3
Digital Edition ISBN: 978-0-06-269559-8

FIRST EDITION

18 19 20 21 22 LSC 10 9 8 7 6 5 4 3 2 1

To all the readers who asked—
and asked, and *asked*—
when Ian would finally get his own book.
grins
The answer is NOW. I hope you love it.

Acknowledgments

As always, my first thanks go to God. Fifteen years ago, I was praying to finally finish writing an entire book because I'd never been able to, at that point. Today, I'm writing the Acknowledgments page in my seventeenth published novel. You bet I still consider all this to be a real-life miracle that I will always be grateful for.

The saying "it takes a village" applies to publishing, too. Thanks so much to my wonderful editor, Erika Tsang, for your excellent work on this and all my other books. Thanks also to Pamela Jaffee, Caroline Perny, and the rest of the fabulous people at Avon Books, for everything you've done to get my novels into readers' hands. Thanks of course to my amazing agent, Nancy Yost, for far too many things to list here. Thanks also to Ilona Andrews and Melissa Marr, both for your invaluable feedback on this book and for something even more invaluable—your friendship these past twelve years. Of course, I also can't thank readers enough, either. I'm grateful to every single one of you who gave my books a chance, and I'm doubly grateful to readers who told a friend/family member/total stranger via reviews or blog posts. Reader word of mouth is the wind beneath every book's wings. If a book flies, it's because of you, readers.

Last, but definitely not least, I have to thank my family. Mom, I'll always miss you. Dad, you're still my hero. Jeanne and Jinger, other relationships might come and go, but sisters are forever. Matt . . . fifteen years ago, I was complaining that I'd never see any of my words "in print" because I'd never finish a book. You told me you'd calligraphy one of my poems onto our living room wall so I could see my words "in print" every day. You've probably forgotten about that. I haven't. For that and a million other reasons, "I love you" doesn't even begin to cover it.

SHADES
of
WICKED

Chapter 1

$\mathcal{T}$his had better be the right whorehouse.

It didn't look like the seedier brothels I'd recently been to. This three-story structure could pass as the meeting place for an elite social club. Despite its unexpected prettiness, if I had to wade through another flesh-fest only to turn up empty-handed again, I wouldn't be responsible for what I did to my quarry when I finally found him.

To vent my aggravation over weeks of fruitless searching, I kicked the door open. Politeness had been wasted at the last several establishments anyway. No smart proprietor willingly gave up a well-paying client, and I'll say one thing for the bordello-loving vampire I was after: He obviously paid well.

To my surprise, I didn't see anyone in the elegant foyer. Brothels usually had several prostitutes lingering around the entryway to welcome new customers. I was further surprised when I didn't hear sounds of carnal activity coming from the upper floors of the house. I pulled out my mobile and checked the GPS pin. Yes, this was the right place. What's more, it certainly *smelled* like sex, once you got past the choking scents of various perfumes and colognes.

But where was everyone?

Faint vibrations in the floor made me stride toward the hallway. Ah, so the party must be downstairs. I followed the strongest scents of perfume until I found a staircase that descended two floors. It ended at a locked door that I also kicked in. No point in being dainty now.

Noise blasted out. The basement must have been soundproofed for me to miss it before. Now, I wished I couldn't hear what was going on. A boisterous chorus assaulted my ears, repeating over and over. *Thunder and Blazes*, the favorite opening song of the former Barnum and Bailey circus.

And I had walked into a circus, I saw now, although one without any real animals. About a dozen naked women and men frolicked on the ground, doing woefully inadequate impressions of the creatures their full body paint represented. *No work ethic*, I thought when three faux lions appeared more interested in petting each other than in more realistic fights for dominance, and don't get me started on how they ignored the two faux gazelles that walked by them.

The dozen or so prostitutes dressed in clown suits showed more dedication for their roles. They emerged from a fake car in the far corner of the room, some falling forward in rolling somersaults once they exited, some tripping each other with comedic exaggeration, and some blowing up balloons into explicit body parts that they then graphically connected.

An eruption of fireworks yanked my attention to the other side of the room. They were going off around what looked like a throne, haloing its occupant in a blaze of sparks, fire and smoke. The mini pyrotechnic display was so bright, I couldn't make out the enthroned person's face, but when he called out, "Act Eight will now begin!" I heard a distinct English accent.

Then the smoke cleared enough to show a tall man wearing a blue circus-ringleader jacket. The smoke still concealed him from the waist down, but I didn't need to see more to know I'd finally found my target. The vampire who'd blazed a trail through a dozen whorehouses in only two weeks had a face as beautiful as an angel's, not to mention that his fire-and-umber hair was as distinctive as his looks. When he got off the throne, revealing he wore nothing beneath the ringleader jacket, I realized those weren't Ian's only notable attributes.

For a moment, I stared. What vampire in his right mind would pierce himself with silver *there*?

I was the only one shocked by the silver piercing through the tip of Ian's cock. Everyone else stopped what they were doing and rushed toward him. Even the glitter-covered acrobats leapt from their swinging perches near the ceiling, gracefully landing near the pile of limbs that now formed around the red-headed vampire.

It wasn't enough that I had to be burdened with a vampire so mentally deficient that he'd willingly given himself a case of perpetual cock burn. He also had to be depraved enough to indulge in carnival-themed orgies. I wasn't about to find out what the rest of Act Eight entailed. I made my way to the growing flesh pile and began flinging people aside, taking care not to throw them too hard. Their heartbeats meant they were human, so they couldn't heal the way my kind could.

"What's this?" Ian asked in an annoyed manner when I reached the bottom of the bodies. Then he let out an appreciative noise when I yanked him up with none of the care I'd shown the other people.

"Why, hallo, my strong blonde sweeting." Now he didn't sound annoyed at all. "Are you the surprise I was promised?"

Why not let him believe that? "Sure," I said. "Surprise." And I grabbed him by the cock. I had one more thing to verify before I went any further.

Ian chuckled. "That's the spirit, poppet."

I dropped to my knees. I wasn't about to do what he thought. Still, this act allowed me to zero in on my goal with the least amount of resistance from him. Once I got a good look at the smoke-colored brands near the base of Ian's groin, I released him. Only one demon branded people with these particular markings, and it was the same demon I'd been after for thousands of years.

"Ian," I said as I straightened. "Say good-bye. We're leaving."

He laughed outright. "I don't think so. You might be lovely, but two's lonely, while a dozen is a party."

I gave a disparaging look around. "No great loss. The clowns were fine, but none of your faux animals fought each other or even *attempted* to jump through the fire rings."

At that, he gave the animal-painted prostitutes an accusing look. "You didn't, did you?" Then, his eyes suddenly narrowed as he looked back at me. "Wait a moment. I know you."

We'd only officially met once before, so I hadn't thought he'd remember me. Someone with his tendencies had to have crossed paths with vast numbers of blonde women.

"Veritas, Law Guardian for the vampire council," I confirmed. Then my hands landed on his shoulders. "And as I said, you are coming with me."

His eyes changed from their natural vivid turquoise into glowing, vampiric emerald. "Leave it to a Law Guardian to try and ruin a perfectly good orgy. Sorry, luv, I'm not going anywhere. Now, take your hands from me before I remove them."

He couldn't mean that. Merely striking a Law Guardian was enough to garner a death sentence, if the council was in a testy mood. Only the vampire council itself was above us in undead society. That's why I ignored his threat and tightened my grip.

"There's no need for empty threats—"

The next thing I knew, I was thrown several meters away. I blinked, more startled by his quickness than by his reckless disregard for the punishment his actions merited.

"No need?" he repeated, contempt edging his tone now. "I remember the last time I saw you. I'd say your complicity in the murder of my friend's daughter more than qualifies as a need."

She isn't dead.

The words rang in my mind, a comfort I drew on whenever I thought back on that awful day. But if Ian didn't know that the child's supposed execution had been nothing more than a clever ruse . . .

"That was the council's decision, not mine," I said, my voice roughening from the memory. I'd nearly lost my position as Law Guardian arguing against the girl's execution, but fear and bigotry had made the council unmovable. At least they hadn't succeeded in taking her life as they'd intended to.

Ian snorted. "Sleep better telling yourself that, do you? You make *my* sins look forgivable, and that takes some doing."

"Enough." How dare he judge me? "Now, come."

His brows rose, as if he couldn't believe I'd spoken to him the same way some people called their dogs. Well, if he insisted on acting like a beast, I'd treat him like one.

"All of you, leave," Ian said to the prostitutes, who'd been watching us with more boredom than interest. They'd probably thought our exchange was more role-playing. "My compliments for the day's entertainment, but now it's over. Go," he stressed when some of them hung back instead of joining the ones that began to file out the door.

I bit back a disbelieving laugh. "Are you getting them out of the way because you're intending to *fight* me?"

Ian flashed a smile that increased the intensity of his unusual beauty. "You must not have done your research if you thought I'd come willingly."

The silver from his piercing must have gotten into his bloodstream and damaged his brain. That was the only explanation. "I'm more than four thousand years older than you."

"Really?" he said with mock surprise. "Here I was thinking you didn't look a day over twenty, little Guardian."

I'd been older than that when I was changed into a vampire, but his guess was a common mistake. People put far too much emphasis on appearances. "Is 'little Guardian' supposed to be insulting? If so, do better."

"Not being insulting," he replied in an easygoing tone. "But if you're half my weight, I'd be surprised."

Yes, I currently looked more delicate than formidable. Even if that were true, it wouldn't help him. With age came strength, and I had thousands of years on him. "Stand down, Ian, and I won't punish you for attacking me."

"Why don't you try begging me to stand down?" he suggested. "Make your plea interesting enough, and I might consider it."

I was done negotiating. I plowed into Ian hard enough to shatter the bones in his upper body. To my surprise, he did nothing to block the blow. Instead, he flung me upward with a strength he should never have had. I hit the ceiling with such force, I went all the way through. For a stunned moment, I stared at him through the hole my body made in the floor.

"Stop now and perhaps you're the one who won't get punished," he said in a pleasant tone.

I suppressed the urge to immediately charge him again. *Never underestimate an opponent twice, if you're lucky enough to survive the first time.* My vampire sire, Tenoch, had taught me that. Following Tenoch's advice had saved my life many times, so I pushed back my urge to retaliate.

Ian was wrong—I *had* done my research on him. It hadn't revealed anything unusual except for a voracious sexual appetite, an open disdain for rules, and a penchant for collecting the rare and expensive. My previous assault should have left him on the ground, not whistling along to that awful circus tune while looking more bored than concerned.

Maybe his unusual strength came from the demon brands? They did more than act as a leash between Ian and the demon who'd seared them onto him. Over time, those brands would also endow Ian with some of that demon's strength and power. Ian had only been branded for a few weeks though. Not nearly long enough for him to manifest parts of the demon's strength or abilities.

I'd find out his secret later. Right now, I needed to take him down, and thankfully, I had some surprises for him, too.

I gave Ian a level look. "My turn."

His smile grew into a grin. "Come and get me, little Guardian."

Chapter 2

I didn't jump down through the hole above him, which was what he would have expected. Instead, I made a new hole in the floor on the other side of the room. Ian leapt back to avoid my instant grab, then kicked me during the split second my back was turned. I sprawled forward, but even as he pounced, I spun away, leaving him to hit the floor instead of me. Then I jumped onto his back and clamped my legs around him to hold on.

He began to buck at once. I tightened my grip until his ribs broke. He didn't slow. I began to whack the back of his head, using strength I normally kept dormant.

His head rocked from the blows, though he still bucked hard enough to throw us both around the room. Those demon brands might not be the source of his bewildering strength, but they must be causing him to heal even faster than a vampire's normal swift regeneration. Soon, I was gripping him just to keep from being thrown off. Then he began to fly, smashing me against the walls, the ceiling, and the floor, all while bucking like a crazed, rabid bronco.

My bones began to break and my head rang after being repeatedly bashed against various hard surfaces. If he were anyone else, I would kill him, but I needed Ian alive. And cooperative. Maybe his brains hitting the floor would help with that last part.

I whacked his skull even harder to force him to the ground and hold him there. It took a lot of effort, which was why I kept punching his head while shoving his body against the carpet. I couldn't allow him to get enough leverage to start flying again. If he did, I might have to reveal powers I'd rather he not know about and . . . wait. What was that sound?

I stopped hitting Ian to listen more closely. It almost sounded like . . . no. He couldn't be.

"Are you *laughing* at me?"

He was, and now his chuckles sounded louder since they were no longer competing with the noise from our fight. I also realized that the long, hard object I'd felt near my foot was *not* a concealed weapon. He wasn't just amused by my attempts to beat his skull open—he was *aroused* by them!

"Your bouncing up and down on my back plus all this rough chafing is *really* doing the trick," Ian said, still chuckling. "Soon, I'll have to pay you along with the rest of the whores. In fact, if you take requests, a bit more effort on your downstroke, luv—"

I threw a punch that should have sent my fist all the way through his head. His neck bent at the last second while the back of his body surged up. Too late, I realized the trap. My fist ended up flying past his head while the rest of me was catapulted off him.

Before I could regroup, he leapt on top of me. In the next instant, he was holding me down, and I felt the distinct burn of silver stabbing me between the ribs.

Damn him! He'd managed to goad me into recklessly acting without thinking again. If my legs hadn't been pinned by his, I might have kicked myself for being so stupid.

"Don't move," Ian said in a conversational tone. "I don't want to kill you, but I will if you force me."

"Where did you get that knife?" I hadn't been so distracted before that I'd forgotten to frisk him.

"From my jacket."

"Liar. I felt you for weapons when I was on top of you."

"Was that what you were doing?" His lips twitched. "Thought you were feeling around for something more interesting."

At my contemptuous look, he shrugged and said, "You didn't

feel the knife before because it was only a small silver ball a few moments ago."

My eyes widened. "You're admitting to a Law Guardian that you used *magic* to transform a silver ball into a knife?"

"Did I forget that using magic is a death sentence for vampires?" Ian used his free hand to mime clutching a strand of pearls. "And so is striking a Law Guardian. Dear me, I've condemned myself twice! Please, have mercy!"

"Now you're begging?" I let out a soft snort. "Don't bother. I'm still going to punish you for what you've done."

He laughed. "I have a knife in your heart and you're still threatening me? I don't know whether to keep laughing at you for your delusion or applaud you for your optimism."

"If you'd listen instead, you could learn how to prevent Dagon from taking possession of your soul in two years."

Nothing in his expression changed, though suddenly, I felt as if I were staring at a different person. A hard, dangerous one that I'd vastly underestimated. Then Ian flashed another carefree smile at me—and shoved that silver knife deeper.

I gasped when it pierced my heart. Ian tutted as if I was a child who'd merely stubbed my toe. "I warned you not to test me. Now, tell me what you know about my deal with Dagon."

Silver twisting through the heart was one of the few ways to kill a vampire. It felt as if hot lava was being poured into me. Ian hadn't twisted the blade, but the majority of my physical strength left me. Despite that, I kept my reply steady.

"I know I'm your only chance of escaping the deal you made with Dagon. If he's dead, he can't collect your soul."

Ian let out a scoff. "If Dagon could be killed, I'd have done it myself decades ago."

"*I* can kill him," I replied, and though it might be a long shot, it was still the truth.

He rolled his eyes. "Hate to be rude—actually, that's not true, I love being rude—but I'm far less powerful than Dagon and I bested you inside of five minutes."

"You didn't best me. I stopped beating on you when I realized you *liked* it."

"Most enjoyable part of our time together," he agreed. "But now I'm bored, so let me simplify things. I'm going to bash your brains in. Try to stop me, and I'll twist this knife. Cooperate, and by the time your head heals, I'll be gone and you can go back to scaring young vampires into obeying the ridiculous restrictions you call laws."

Bashing my brains in would indeed work to incapacitate me. It was the same thing I'd been intending to do with him. His fist clenched. Before it could connect, I released an ability only one other person in the world knew I had.

Power flashed out, filling the basement in a blink. Ian's expression showed the beginnings of disbelief before it, his fist, and everything else suddenly froze. Even the countless dust particles in the air now hung in suspended animation instead of floating in lazy, aimless circles.

I was the only one unaffected as time itself paused within the confines of the basement. That was the upside. The downside was the power that kept boomeranging back into me, hitting my body with invisible, painful waves before arcing out to fill the room again. Between that and the silver in my heart, my nerve endings felt like they were being hit with a blow torch. I couldn't maintain this for long, so I had to make it count.

With Ian frozen, I used his hand to pull the knife free from my heart. Then I uncurled his fingers from its hilt and tucked the blade into my back pocket. Finally, I shoved him off me.

"That's better," I muttered once I felt my heart heal. Then I flipped Ian over and got to my feet. When I unfroze him from this moment, I wanted my face to be the first thing he saw.

It was tricky unfreezing a person from time without dropping my hold over the entire room. That's why I started slow and only released Ian's head. His eyes widened when he realized he was now in a completely different position than he'd been before, then narrowed when he tried to move the rest of his body and couldn't. When he glanced around and saw the whole basement trapped in a state of suspended animation, they widened again.

"Bugger me blind," he said softly. "Aren't you full of surprises?"

He had no idea. "As I said, I'm your only hope of keeping your soul. Dagon might be able to freeze time, but I have that ability, too. That means his power won't work on me, and I can also use my power to free anyone he's caught in his time web."

I left out the part where Dagon's abilities were far more advanced than mine. I could freeze time in small spaces, but I couldn't hold it for very long. Dagon could freeze time for days, and I'd heard he had once done it to an entire town.

Ian didn't have to know that. All he had to know was that he needed me. I could imagine the wheels in his mind turning as he processed that. Once again, he didn't let his real emotions show. They were hidden behind his half smile. The most real emotion I'd gotten out of him was his eyes widening. And his erection, I supposed.

"If I release the rest of you, will you listen, or attempt to fight me again?" I continued.

"Listen," he said, with a new, impish smile, as if he found the prospect amusing.

"As I was saying, we have something in common, Ian . . . what is your last name?" I hadn't been able to discover it, and I normally had extensive dossiers on the people I hunted.

"No need for formalities. They're only for people impressed by the superficial and that's neither of us."

He was right, which surprised me. I hadn't expected us to have anything in common except a hatred for Dagon.

"Then as I was saying, you want Dagon dead because that's the only way out of your deal with him. I want Dagon dead for reasons that don't concern you. I propose a temporary alliance so both of us can achieve our goal, but let me be clear: You would have to follow my lead and my rules. Do you agree?"

His impish smile never slipped. "Before I answer, tell me, how *did* you get this amazing ability? I searched for decades looking for someone of our kind with a hint of it, yet found nothing."

You don't want to know how I can do this, I thought grimly. *And if you ever find out, I'll have to kill you.*

"That's not important. What is important is that I can use it to counter Dagon's time-freezing on both of us, and that means we can kill him. Do we have an agreement or not?"

"Of course," Ian replied, as if there was never any doubt.

His tone was sincere and his bright turquoise gaze never wavered, but all my instincts told me he was lying. Even if I didn't have those, everything I'd learned about Ian said he'd never give another person this much control over him. He must be intending to double-cross me the first chance he got.

Well, I had plans I wasn't telling him about, too.

"Good," I said, and released the power, which felt like it had been frying my every nerve ending. At once, heat blew from the vents again, dust particles swirled, and that oppressive pain left me.

Ian stood up and stretched as if relieving a kink. The motion almost concealed him taking in a deep breath, but I noticed because I'd been expecting him to do that.

I hid my smile. *No, you don't smell sulfur or anything else that would indicate another demon's presence. I really am the one who stopped time the same way that Dagon can.*

When he turned back to me, his cocky half smile had returned. "Now that we have an accord, where do you want to begin?"

"By leaving," I said promptly.

Ian swept out both arms, drawing the jacket back to fully display his naked body. "Fine by me, but most people prefer that I wear trousers out in public."

I found my gaze drawn downward, then quickly diverted it back to his face. He was smirking, which was the same as saying, *Ha! Made you look.*

It was nothing to look at a naked man. To do so and then glance away guiltily? What was the matter with me?

Maybe it was my circumstances. The brands Ian carried were my ticket to trapping Dagon—a feat that had eluded me for millennia. Now that it was within my grasp, I was feeling emotions I hadn't allowed myself to feel for a long time. That must be it. In any event, I needed to get them back under control.

That's why I crossed my arms and gave Ian a deliberate look from the top of his head down to his toes. Then, I met his eyes so that he could see he had no effect on me this time.

"By all means, get dressed, but only after you take a shower. I don't need to tell you what you smell like."

"Over two dozen whores?" he supplied.

"Exactly, so use plenty of soap."

He winked. "Looking for an excuse to watch? Just ask, and I might let you."

I was about to tell him I'd rather watch paint dry. Then, I caught myself. Clever. I'd been about to insist that Ian shower as far away from me as possible, giving him an excellent opportunity to escape or to conjure up more magic against me.

"In fact, I *would* like to watch," I said, arching my brow. "Unless you're going to claim that you're suddenly shy?"

His gaze narrowed. Icy fingers skittered up my spine. In all my years, I'd never felt that unless I was in the presence of someone truly dangerous. Everything on paper said that Ian shouldn't be, yet right then, I knew I could never drop my guard around him. If I did, I might not live long enough to regret it.

Then Ian smiled. It was so flirtatious and relaxed, I almost believed I'd imagined his hidden dangerousness. Almost.

"Shyness is a virtue, and you'll be glad to know I have none of those."

With that, he swept me a bow that managed to look elegant despite his being clothed only in a circus ringleader jacket. We might both be pretending that this was a real agreement instead of a race to see who could use the other person first, but I knew better. For now, though, I'd keep up the pretense.

And since I was currently pretending that I wanted to watch Ian shower . . . "After you," I said, and followed him up the stairs.

*I*an went to one of the second-level bedrooms as if he were very familiar with it. He probably was. Judging from what I'd seen, he'd been at this brothel for at least two days. That mock carnival in the basement certainly hadn't been set up in a mere afternoon.

He stripped off his jacket as soon as he crossed the threshold. I made sure to keep a close watch on his hands as I followed him into the bathroom. I couldn't allow him to magically fabricate another weapon. There were plenty of things in this room that a highly skilled practitioner could use.

Ian's dossier revealed that he had spent time in the company of witches and mages, but it posited that he'd done so for excitement and socializing. Wrong and wrong. Most practitioners would've needed to recite an incantation in order to get the power to transmute one type of object into another. Another way would be to draw several specific magical symbols to create the necessary power. Ian had changed a silver pebble into a knife without a single word or scribble, and he'd done it while I was beating his skull half in.

If that wasn't impressive enough, tactile magic was one of the highest forms of the craft. That's why I couldn't take my eyes off his hands. He'd need to use at least one of them to conjure up more of that kind of magic. Right now, he wasn't doing anything threatening. He stepped beneath the shower spray and closed his eyes as that first blast of water hit him. Then, he washed his hair, his movements brisk and efficient. When he picked up the body wash, however, he slowed down, working the liquid into a rich lather before running his hands over his body.

Did he think I'd never seen a man make a show out of washing himself before? I had, and even the most seductive of them had always been a little too obvious, a little too sleazy. Women were much better at this form of manipulation, but if he wanted to give me something to look at, let him.

After a few minutes, I had to give Ian credit—he was good. He didn't attempt to meet my eyes to gauge the effect of his actions. He also didn't go right for his groin as most men did. Instead, he acted as if I wasn't even there while he started with his arms, washing each with smooth, sweeping strokes that emphasized the muscled elegance of his limbs. Then he moved on to his chest, soaping it with a languid thoroughness that highlighted every ripple, hollow, and chiseled inch.

He gave the same unhurried attention to his lower body, his hands running down the tautness of his abdomen before sweeping over the hard globes of his ass. Those hands lingered over the thicker muscles in his thighs before moving down to his well-defined calves. Even his feet weren't neglected.

Somehow, the never-ending sweep of his hands started to feel hypnotic. If I were a few thousand years younger, I might even start to imagine how each muscle, hollow, and sinew would feel if *I* were the one touching him. Or notice how his muscles appeared even more defined when the water washed away another swath of suds, or how his skin glistened beneath the bright lights in the shower stall.

Or fixate on how the thick appendage between his legs was growing as if also longing to feel the touch of those slow, skilled hands.

When I realized I was staring, I gave myself a hard mental shake. Again, I'd underestimated him. Ian was obviously as skilled at using his body as he was at using magic. That, or I wasn't as immune to his decadent beauty as I'd assumed. Whether it was my newfound compromised emotional state or my extended bout of abstinence, I didn't know. Either way, I had to keep my focus on *both* his hands. Not just the one currently slicking suds over the impressive appendage between his legs.

"I say, you're looking in all the wrong places now."

His voice held the silkiness of honey along with the lure of wine, but deadly potions could also taste sweet. My careful watch on his other hand revealed his true intentions. He wasn't trying to seduce me. Like a magician, he was drawing my gaze one way while the real trick was about to take place somewhere else.

I gave a pointed look at his left hand, which was creeping behind his back. "Keep *both* your hands where I can see them."

His smile changed into a scowl. "You're no fun at all."

He wasn't even trying to deny that he'd been about to fling a spell at me. I'd take that roundabout honesty as progress.

"Law Guardians aren't supposed to be fun," I noted dryly. "We're supposed to be good at our jobs, and despite a few slip-ups already with you, I am. Even if I couldn't stop time, there's still no spell you could fling at me that I haven't defeated a thousand times before."

He smiled again. For the first time, it seemed genuine. "I take that as a challenge. Let's make it interesting, shall we? If I use a spell on you that you're unable to defeat, you'll drop your requirement that I follow your lead on our quest to kill Dagon. Instead, you'll follow mine."

He hadn't been following my lead as it was, but damned if I'd let him off the hook. Plus, his arrogance could be useful. Good to know I wasn't the only one letting emotion cloud my judgment.

"How long are you giving yourself to attempt this supposedly unstoppable spell?"

"Two weeks."

Perfect. If all went well, I would be done with him by the time he tried it. "Fine, if you agree to stop trying to escape or trick me until this grand attempt. And *when* you fail to hit me with a spell that I can't defeat, you'll follow my lead plus give me three unquestioning acts of obedience."

"Done," he said at once.

He seemed so confident. He even smiled with the kind of anticipation I'd seen only on gladiators right before they struck a killing blow. Was it possible I'd made another mistake? He'd already surprised me several times today.

But no. He couldn't best me in this.

"Done," I said after a slight pause.

His smile turned sly. "How shall we seal this new accord? A blood oath?"

As if I'd assume his shedding a few drops of blood would suddenly make him honest. "Something else. Hold out your hand."

He arched a brow but extended a still soapy hand. I closed my fingers around his, not surprised that his flesh felt far warmer than a vampire's normal temperature. His time in the shower had heated his skin, and now, that water would provide me with what I needed to ensure an oath he couldn't break.

Water was one of the main natural elements of the world. That made it powerful, if one knew how to extract that power. I did since I had a special talent with water. I hadn't wanted to use more of my hidden abilities today, but if I didn't, I'd soon be fighting off attacks from my duplicitous ally in addition to the ones that would be coming from Dagon.

A ripple of energy flashed through the room when I began to speak in an ancient language, the first one I'd learned. That energy settled on our joined hands. Ian hissed when he felt it.

"What are you doing? And why are you speaking Sumerian?"

I wasn't about to answer either of those questions. In truth, I hadn't expected him to recognize the long-dead language. Not that it mattered. These words weren't significant.

Ian tried to pull his hand away. The spell I was creating trapped him. It wrapped around me, too, feeling inside us for the promises we'd both just made. When it found them, it tightened our hands together. Then I felt its energy crest before it slid beneath my skin to dissolve inside my bones.

Once it did, I opened my eyes. "Now neither of us has a choice about keeping our latest promise. The spell found them, and if one of us were to renege on them, it would rot our bones faster than either of us could heal."

$\mathcal{I}$ an's eyes were lit up with emerald, and the muscle ticking in his jaw showed how displeased he was by this turn of events. But when he spoke, his voice was light, and instead of trying to pull his hand away, his fingers now caressed mine.

"A Law Guardian who practices forbidden magic. How irresistibly hypocritical of you."

I wasn't about to tell him I'd learned this spell well before the vampire council had outlawed magic. Or that more than a few Law Guardians were versed in at least mid-level magic. Otherwise, how were we supposed to go after rogue practitioners when even an amateur would be able to take us down?

"Now we each have something on the other," I replied.

His lips curled. "No one would believe me and you know it."

True, but . . . "You know a bigger secret about me. Even if you weren't believed by the vampire council, it would still present problems if word of my stopping time reached the wrong ears."

His smile only grew. "Subtlety doesn't suit you. Just tell me you'll kill me if I reveal your secrets."

"Fine. I'll kill you and it *will* hurt," I said bluntly.

He laughed and chucked me under the chin. "As I said before, that's the spirit."

Ian seemed as entertained by my threat to kill him as he'd been when he thought I was about to go down on him. He might be morally bankrupt, chronically dishonest, and inexplicably dangerous, but he was also . . . fun. That, or my spirits were lifted by the knowledge that, if all went as planned, Ian was going to bring many people their long-awaited justice.

Before I could get to that . . . "There's one more thing we need to do before we leave," I said, taking Ian's silver knife and a small pouch from my back pocket.

Ian eyed the pouch with more interest than the knife. "What's in that?"

"Salts." I put the stopper in the sink before I dumped the tri-colored salts into it. Then I cut my wrist with the knife, willing my blood out from the wound.

I had the amount I needed before the cut healed. Vampires might not have beating hearts, but we did control the flow of blood in our bodies. As my final ingredient, I laid the knife on top of the now-bloody salts.

Ian leaned against the shower wall. "Salt, blood, and silver. If you had ink and the proper tools, I'd think you were about to attempt a demon-repelling warding tattoo."

"How do you know about those?" I asked without looking up. The spell I'd cast meant I didn't need to keep a constant watch on him now.

"I pissed Dagon off decades ago, yet he didn't find me until *I* summoned him this past month. Think my avoiding him was nothing more than luck?"

Now I did glance up. "You warded yourself against Dagon using a locator spell to find you?"

An auburn brow arched. "Him and every other demon that might try that. Demons can be loyal sods. If you wrong one of them, many of the rest are all too happy to deliver you up to the offended party."

I thought I was done being surprised by him. Wrong again. "How do you know so much about demons? Vampires and demons are normally hostile toward each other, but only another demon could have taught you a warding symbol that powerful. Why would one?"

His grin was instant. "I'm that good."

Oh, I could just imagine. I could even see it for myself, if I wanted to look up one of the many sex videos he'd posted online. Thankfully, I had more important things to do.

"If that's the case, why didn't you ward yourself again after Dagon branded you?"

"Tried." Ian's grin remained despite his tone turning flat. "Three times. One moment, the artist would be starting to ink the necessary wards over the brands. The next, I'd be covered in the artist's butchered remains while Dagon danced around me. Didn't matter that I'd started each attempt inside a private residence. Also didn't matter that each time, it had been daylight. The salt walls I'd built around myself also did nothing. Each time, I suddenly found myself in a new place, covered in gore, with Dagon laughing his demonic arse off."

Against any other demon, his precautions would have been enough. Movies portrayed vampires as being unable to walk in the sun. That wasn't true. Vampires also didn't need to be invited in to enter a private residence. But those things were true for demons, and salt burned them like acid, so a salt wall should have been impenetrable to Dagon.

Dagon's ability to stop time meant that he had a way around all that. "Dagon probably felt the weakening in his tie to you after the first few lines of the warding tattoo," I said. "It would only take him moments to use the link to teleport to your location, stop time around you and the tattooists, then retreat out of the sun. With all of you trapped, Dagon could summon a non-demon mercenary, send him inside the home to knock down the salt walls, bring you and the tattoo artists out, then have all of you brought to whatever dark, safe place he wanted."

"Where he killed the artists and decorated me with their corpses." Ian gave a pointed look at the ingredients in the sink before looking back at me. "Still want to attempt that tattoo?"

He was warning me about the danger. How unexpectedly sweet. But I had no intention of giving Dagon enough time to find Ian.

"I have a way around that," I said, then spoke a single word in Sumerian. The knife melted into a silvery puddle over the salts. Both Ian's brows went up.

"If you can do that, why didn't you melt that knife when I had it in your heart?"

I let out a soft scoff. "And get silver poisoning from it getting into my bloodstream?"

"That's better than instant death if I'd have twisted it."

I left that alone. "Hold very still," I said, closing my eyes. "This will sting."

Three softly spoken words later, the melted silver, blood, salt, and magic had all fused together. Eight words after that, and I didn't need to open my eyes to know that the entire mixture was now floating in the air. Thirteen more words, and Ian let out a shout that hurt my eardrums as that magic-infused mixture slammed into his groin, instantly covering the smoky-dark patterns of Dagon's brand.

When I opened my eyes, Ian was staring at his groin with disbelief. Dagon's brands were now covered with an intricate pattern of red, black and silver. Those colors slowly faded as the silver, blood and salt settled in past the skin level. Within moments, the smoky brands faded, until there was no visible proof of the claim that Dagon still held on Ian's soul.

Ian looked around the bathroom as if expecting Dagon to suddenly appear. I was braced, too, but I'd cut the locator aspect of his tie in those brands too quickly. By the time Dagon would have felt it being altered, his connection to Ian would be gone. Without that, he had no way to find Ian, unless he'd already known where he was.

But why would he? Ian had been moving around a lot and Dagon had no reason to keep tabs on him. Not when Ian had been marked with the demon's own version of a supernatural GPS.

Still, a few tense minutes passed in silence. When those minutes continued to trickle by without a sudden blast of power indicating that Dagon had arrived, Ian finally met my gaze. Before his features slid back into their usual devil-may-care expression, I caught something new that pierced me.

Hope.

A long time ago, someone else had given me hope after I'd thought myself incapable of feeling it. That's why I knew how precious it was. It was also why I'd devoted my life to being a Law Guardian. I wanted to bring that same hope to all who suffered when the powerful took advantage of the vulnerable.

Sometimes, however, the law wasn't enough. Dagon was a demon, so our laws didn't apply to him. That wasn't going to stop me. Dagon thought he'd gotten away with wrecking my life and countless other people's lives long ago. He hadn't. He'd just delayed his reckoning. Bringing Dagon to the justice he so richly deserved could cost me my position and my life, but those were prices I was willing to pay. Too much blood had been unavenged for too long, mine included.

That's why I couldn't allow myself to feel anything for Ian, even if I could relate to him on this. He'd only use my feelings against me. It had certainly happened before.

Ian wasn't just fighting for his life. He was also fighting for his soul. Our goals might be aligned now, but the moment they weren't, Ian would turn on me and the spell I'd cast would only protect me up to a point. After that, we'd probably fight to the death, and I had no intention of letting that death be mine.

Right now, we weren't in a death match, so I smiled at him. As I did, I realized it was my first genuine smile in a long time. "See? Dagon *can't* find you any longer."

Ian smiled back, emerald green lighting his turquoise gaze. "That means that somewhere out there, Dagon is going insane with rage."

Dagon might not be able to track Ian through his now invisible brands, but I was still in a hurry to get out of here. Ian was right—Dagon would be beyond furious. While I relished the thought, I also recognized the danger. This bordello wasn't too far from where Ian had made his deal with Dagon, in Minsk, Belarus. Dagon could do what I had done: start searching the more prominent whorehouses in Belarus until he found one that Ian had been to, then follow his trail from there. It had taken me two weeks because I'd had to drive from Minsk to Poland. Dagon could teleport, so his search might only take him a day.

That's why I wanted to be away from here by nightfall. When I saw Dagon again, it would be on *my* terms, not his.

"Come," I told Ian. It was past time we left.

He snorted. "Keep speaking to me as if I'm a dog and I'll either hump your leg or bite you."

I suppressed my urge to tell him exactly what I'd do if he tried either. In all fairness, I *had* been acting highhanded. If we were going to work together, I needed to treat him with the same respect I was demanding for myself.

"I'm sorry," I said, stumbling over the word. When was the last time I'd apologized? I couldn't remember, so obviously, it had been too long. "It's, ah, habit. The only times I deal with vampires like you are when I arrest them or judge them. Law Guardians have to be unbending in those moments or it implies the law itself is vulnerable, which can't happen."

"Of course not," Ian agreed, though his eye roll showed how little he cared about the law. Then he gave me a surprisingly serious look. "You've probably had to be twice as hard because you're a woman. Can't let the council claim your gender makes you too soft for the job, can you?"

How right he was. Sexism was alive and well in vampire society. I was older and more qualified than most of the council members, but my decisions were still challenged with far more regularity than similar ones made by male Guardians. Equally irritating was how perpetrators always attempted to run or fight when they saw me, yet many surrendered when confronted with weaker, younger male Guardians.

I cleared my throat and attempted a more conciliatory tone. "Now that you've reminded me of my manners, you do agree that we're not safe here and we have to leave, right?"

He gave me a quick grin. "You're the one blocking the door, little Guardian."

TWENTY MINUTES LATER, we were on the road. We would have left sooner, except we had to mesmerize all the prostitutes into forgetting that either of us had been there. Dagon had a lot of abilities, but he couldn't break through vampirically altered memories. Now, this bordello was one less trail the demon could follow.

Ian had been quiet during our car ride to Warsaw, occupying himself with his mobile phone. I welcomed the silence. It gave me time to muse over the unexpected parts of today. Ian would be harder to manage than I'd anticipated. While that required adjustments, it shouldn't require a new plan. His desire for self-preservation was strong, and that's what I'd been counting on. With that foundation in place, I could work around the other issues—

"What the bloody hell are we doing at an airport?"

Ian's sharp question cut through my musings. I pulled into the parking lot, which was more than half empty. This was a private airfield, so we didn't have any of the inconveniences common with a bustling commercial airport.

"Flying," I replied, which should have been obvious. "I chartered a plane days ago in anticipation of finding you."

"You chartered a plane?" he repeated. "Tell me you're joking."

What was his problem? "You're not afraid to fly, are you?"

"It's boats I'm afraid of, but that's off topic. What's *on* topic is the fact that you chartered a plane with what I'll assume is a reputable company out of an easily found private airport in a major city of the country I was last seen in. Why don't you draw Dagon a map of where we're going, too?"

I tempered my tone so I didn't snarl at him. "I'm using false names. Dagon won't know it's us."

Ian's face showed all the aggravation I was smothering. "You might do a bang-up job of upholding the law, but you clearly have a lot to learn about being on the run. You don't use regular airports or charter companies because aliases aren't enough. Dagon might not have pictures of you, but he does of me. One glance will confirm I'm the John Doe on your flight manifest. You also can't mesmerize everyone into forgetting we were here; there are too many people, plus there are security cameras."

I was still rankled by his tone, but he had valid points. It would be foolish to ignore them. "You suggest driving?"

"No, that's too slow and it won't get us far enough away."

"Then what?" This time, I didn't tamp down my irritation. "I don't own a private plane and unless your dossier lacks another important detail, neither do you."

He gave me a jaded look. "I'm sure my dossier lacks quite a bit, but as it happens, I know someone with his own plane and he's not far from here."

"Wouldn't one of your friend's planes coming here also be an obvious trail that Dagon could follow?"

"It would, except this vampire is *not* my friend," Ian said, and started dialing.

I saw the country code before Ian tipped his mobile and the rest of the numbers moved out of view. Forty. Romania.

Contrary to popular belief, Romania wasn't a hotspot for vampires because it was home to one of the world's most powerful. If that's who Ian was calling, he was correct. *No one* would believe this particular vampire would come to Ian's aid.

"Ian," I heard an accented voice say on the line. With that single word, my suspicions were confirmed. "I'm surprised to hear from you," Vlad the Impaler continued.

"Believe me, Tepesh, I'd rather shag myself with a sandpaper dildo than speak to you."

My eyes bulged. Ian saw it and waved as if unconcerned that he'd insulted someone who'd been feared for his mass slaughters even before he became a vampire.

"But I have to travel under the radar in a hurry," Ian went on. "I need to borrow your plane. Should only take a few days. How fast can you get it to Poland?"

Silence on the other line. I tensed, half expecting Ian's mobile to burst into flames. When Vlad got angry, things usually ended up on fire. Ian should be glad that he was nowhere near Vlad, who was only called by his other, more famous name of Dracula by those who wished to die.

"Where in Poland?" Vlad finally replied.

Each word sounded bitten off from anger, but I was shocked that he appeared to be agreeing. I'd expected Vlad to tell Ian exactly how he was going to kill him.

"Look for the remains of a large movie theater complex inside of Klomino. Should be enough space in front of it for the plane to land and take off. Klomino's mostly abandoned, but still, come after dark so there's less chance of a bystander taking video showing the call numbers on the plane."

"I'll have them painted over." Vlad's tone remained sharp. "The plane will be there by midnight." Then he hung up.

Ian began to whistle as he ripped the memory card out of his mobile. Then he got out of the car, dropped the memory card and his mobile on the ground, and stomped on them. When he lifted his foot, only crushed pieces remained.

I got out, too, and went around to his side of the vehicle. "How did you do that?" I asked in disbelief.

He glanced down. "Boot plus force."

"Not that." I dismissed his shattered mobile with a swipe of my hand. "How did you get Vlad Dracul to do your bidding?"

"Bidding?" Ian gave me a knowing smile. "Most times, you sound exactly like a modern woman, yet every once in a while, you slip and prove there's nothing modern about you."

"You're avoiding my question," I said, although he was right about the slip.

"Vlad owes me," Ian replied in a tone that was now darker than obsidian.

Once again, I felt icy tingles race up my spine. Who was the real Ian? The carefree rogue who amused me despite myself? Or the dangerous man who set off all my inner alarm bells?

"Why would Vlad the Impaler owe you?"

He gave me a slanted look. "Thought you'd know since you turned up with information that only Dagon, Vlad, and Vlad's wife knew about."

Leila had indeed been the one to tell me that Dagon had tricked Ian into bartering his soul to the demon. That's why I'd searched for Ian as soon as I'd finished my other business. I hadn't cared enough to ask Leila how Dagon had tricked Ian. All I'd cared about was finding a vampire that Dagon had branded so I could use him to draw the demon out. Now, I wished I'd gotten the entire tale. Judging from Ian's shuttered expression, I wouldn't be hearing it from him.

Ian took my silence as proof of my ignorance and shrugged. "Doesn't matter. What matters is that while Vlad and I detest each other—and that's describing my feelings for him in the mildest possible way—he doesn't shirk from paying a debt. Now, we have a way out of here that can't be traced."

"Excuse me."

We both turned. A young man with the name of the aviation facility emblazoned on his shirt had come out of the building and was walking toward us.

"May I assist you with something?" the man continued.

We'd been arguing in the facility's parking lot long enough to attract notice. Whether this young man was security or merely an attentive concierge, it was still time to go.

Ian gave him a brilliant smile. "That your mobile?" he asked, nodding at the square-shaped bulge in the man's pocket.

The man's demeanor changed from polite to wary. "Why?"

"Give it to me," Ian said, an emerald glow spilling out of his eyes.

The man handed over his mobile, helpless to do otherwise under the power in Ian's gaze. Ian took the phone and held it in his teeth while he used both hands to pull down his pants. He wasn't wearing anything beneath them and my brows went up.

"What are you doing?"

Ian only winked at me. Then, pants around his ankles, he took the mobile from his teeth, held it behind him with one hand, and took a selfie of his bare ass.

"Is this juvenile behavior necessary?" I asked stiffly.

"Absolutely." Ian held the phone with his teeth again while he readjusted his clothes. Once done, he checked the picture and smiled. "Perfection." Then he handed his mobile back to the now openmouthed attendant. "When a big blond sod named Dagon comes looking for me, show him this and tell him I said to kiss it."

We waited near the remaining wall of the former movie theater in Klomino. Ian had been right; the entire town looked as if it had been abandoned decades ago. The last time I'd been in this area had been after World War II. Then, the Soviet army had turned it into a military base. Now, the only signs of life were the few faint heartbeats coming from the rubble around the former theater. They probably wouldn't have mobile phones. Even if they did, they might not bother to come out in this weather. It was bitterly cold. Homeless humans seeking temporary refuge, no doubt.

We'd left the car several miles away and walked to Klomino. We drew less notice this way, but I hadn't dressed warmly since I hadn't intended to be outside for long. My coat was more to give myself a place to put my weapons than to protect against the cold. Being a vampire meant I wouldn't get hypothermia, but it did nothing to insulate me from the freezing temperatures.

Another gust of wind sliced into me, bringing with it the scent of snow. It would be a white Christmas in a few hours. I hoped to be far away by the time the first snowflakes fell.

I glanced over at Ian. He didn't seem bothered by the cold and his coat was as thin as mine. Then again, he was from England and I came from the warmer climate of the Middle East. Some things not even the passage of time could dilute. My dislike of cold was one of those.

I checked my mobile again. Quarter to midnight.

"I hope Vlad didn't pick tonight to go back on his word," I murmured, more to myself than to Ian.

He cast an unconcerned glance at the sky. "He won't." Then he looked back at me. "I've run through many possibilities, but I can't place the origin of your accent."

"My accent?" I had mastered so many languages over the centuries, I thought I'd long gotten rid of any telltale hallmarks from my original one.

"It's very slight," he assured me. "Yet every so often, it peeks out, just like when you occasionally use words that haven't been popular since America sewed its first flag."

"Vampires might not be modern humans, but we should keep striving to sound like them," I said, repeating one of Tenoch's most frequent admonitions. Then I paused. Why had I shared that?

He nodded. "Too right. We'd whip heads around if we spouted *thee's* and *thou's* everywhere. Some old vamps refuse to modernize. Outs them to humans faster than flashing fang."

Tenoch had felt the same way. That's why my sire had been so adamant about my embracing the new, whether that was speech, clothing styles, mannerisms, or technological advancements.

"You didn't answer my question," Ian went on, a gleam appearing in his eyes. "Where did you get your accent? Ancient Sumer, perhaps? You do speak Sumerian better than anyone I've ever heard."

"When have you heard it?" I asked to turn this line of questioning around. "It's long been a dead language."

His brow rose. "Yes, and most of Sumer's culture's been lost to history, too, so no one would know an authentic accent even if they heard it. I happened to learn Sumerian when a demon I was mates with taught it to me. How did you learn it?"

Nothing changed in my expression although inwardly, I flinched. How did I end up on the defensive end of a conversation about demons and my original homeland? I had to redirect the conversation. Fast.

"Some spells are more effective in their original language. When you're a Law Guardian tasked with fighting various forms of magic, it behooves you to learn those languages. Why would you bother to learn one no one speaks anymore?" I let out a slight scoff. "Although I'm not surprised a demon taught it to you. Demons have been around longer than humans and vampires both, and they love to prove their imagined superiority over lowly walking corpses, as most demons see vampires."

Ian appeared to mull that over. "Plausible." Then he threw a cheery grin at me. "But you're still hiding something. Rest assured, I *will* find out what it is."

The roar of an approaching plane kept me from responding, which was good. Otherwise, I might have threatened to kill him again. That would have only made things worse. Ian tended to take a death threat as a challenge, a joke, or an aphrodisiac.

After it landed, the sleek plane used all of the empty parking lot to come to a stop. Then it waited, exterior running lights off so it didn't stand out like a beacon in the dark. We ran over to the plane, reaching it right as the door opened.

"Cheers," Ian said, vaulting into the open doorway. Then he stopped so suddenly that I plowed into his back when I jumped in after him. I pushed Ian aside so I wasn't hanging half out of the doorway anymore. With him no longer blocking me, I saw the plane contained more than the two vampire pilots.

A third vampire reclined on the leather sofa in the plane's sumptuous interior. His long black hair matched the stygian shade of his eyes and his skin was the same golden bronze as my own. I should have felt him before I saw him, except he was one of the few vampires in the world with enough power to tamp his aura down until he felt like a mere human.

Now that he'd succeeded in surprising us, Mencheres released his hold and an invisible shockwave filled the plane. It felt like thousands of stings erupted across my skin as his aura rolled over me. At the same time, the air suddenly felt heavy, as if it had morphed into the ocean and we were plunging toward the crushing pressure of the bottom.

I had to fight the urge to take a step backward. I would show no weakness, even if Mencheres was one of the few people that I considered to be a friend. I was old enough to remember Mencheres before he had fangs, let alone a pyramid built in his honor.

"Bugger," Ian swore. "What are *you* doing here?"

Ian's sire smiled at him. "Happy Christmas, Ian." Then Mencheres's dark gaze landed on me. "Veritas," he said, drawing out all three syllables of my name. "Please enlighten me as to what you *think* you're doing with one of my favorite offspring."

I exchanged a glance with Ian. In that single look, I knew Ian didn't want me to reveal our true mission. I agreed. Mencheres was what they called old school when it came to the long-standing practice of vampires staying away from demons. That's why he really wouldn't support our attempt to kill one. The one thing demons could be counted on for was how they avenged the death of their own. No sensible Master vampire of any line would involve his people in that quagmire. A smart one like Mencheres would also take active steps to stop someone he cared about from doing it, too.

That's why I'd rather stare down the entire ruling council than the vampire opposite me. For one, Mencheres might be the only vampire with enough power to actually stop us, if he knew what we intended. For another, I didn't want to involve him in something that would likely get at least one of us killed.

"Mencheres. How lovely to see you," I said in my most innocent tone.

"Don't patronize me," he replied irritably. That put me on alert. Mencheres could level this area with a thought, so he rarely bothered to let himself get to the point of annoyance. "Vlad already told me Ian was in serious trouble."

"Diiiiick," Ian breathed. "Leave it to Vlad to both honor his debt and get revenge at the same time."

"Have you placed Ian under arrest for something?" Mencheres asked me, ignoring that.

"No," I said, relieved to tell the truth about that, at least.

Mencheres's gaze narrowed. "Then why would you, a Law Guardian, be spending time with him? Ian's contempt for the law is outweighed only by his abhorrence for celibacy."

Ian mimed hefting a glass in salute. "True, that."

I cast about for a quick excuse. "I'm, ah"—what was the modern term?—"slumming it. I do that sometimes to relax."

"Lies," Mencheres said sharply. "You haven't relaxed since Caesar was stabbed by Brutus. You also almost never take vampires as lovers, so—"

"Oh?" Ian interrupted, interest sparking in his gaze.

"So since you're not arresting Ian or 'slumming it' with him," Mencheres continued. "What are you doing, Veritas?"

I couldn't think up a convincing excuse, so I decided to go with brazenness. I straightened to my full height. "Ian is Master of his own line, and he can tell you himself that he's with me of his own free will. The rest isn't your concern."

Mencheres stared at me until it felt as if his gaze was boring into me. I didn't flinch. We might be nearly equal in strength, but even with all his great power, he couldn't kill me. Not permanently.

Ian tapped on the plane's open door in obvious impatience. "Can we continue this pissing contest in the air?"

Mencheres took that destructive gaze from me and settled it on Ian. "Why? What sort of trouble are you in a hurry to escape from?"

The words *this time* weren't spoken, but they hung in the air. From the way Ian stiffened, he sensed them, too.

"As the lady said, I'm here of my own will, so it's not your concern. Happy Christmas, Mencheres. Grand to see you, but you have a wife to return to and we have our own places to be."

Mencheres released more of his power. The entire plane began to shake from the force of his aura. I had to resist the urge to wrap my arms around myself. It felt as if my guts might spill right out of me. All Ian did in response to this tremendous display was yawn. Since vampires didn't need to breathe, it was as blatant as a stiff middle finger.

"Have it your way," Mencheres finally said in a dark tone. "I will get the truth from Vlad."

"No you won't," Ian said instantly. "If that wanker was going to sell me out, he already would have."

Mencheres drew all his power back in. My stomach dropped and my coat fluttered as if buffeted by a strong breeze. Then the former pharaoh's gaze softened as he stared at Ian.

"Why, after everything we've been through, will you not simply trust me enough to confide in me?"

For a second, pain darkened Ian's gaze and his cocky demeanor cracked. Just as quickly, those flashes vanished and he smiled, bright and confident as the rising run.

"Don't fret. I've got things well in hand."

Mencheres said nothing. The silence turned into a weight that should have dented the floor. I didn't glance at my mobile, but I was keenly aware of the minutes ticking by. We needed to leave. Soon, this plane would attract the wrong kind of notice.

"Have it your way," Mencheres said again.

A flick of his hand later, the door closed by itself. Then the pilots turned the plane around and began to taxi down the lot. Within moments, we were in the air, the faint lights of the city growing dimmer beneath us.

I sat down in one of the cream-colored seats. Now that the standoff was over and Poland was disappearing behind us, I was relieved enough to realize I was hungry. I hadn't fed since yesterday morning. Maybe I'd be lucky and Vlad's plane would be stocked with a few blood bags.

Mencheres leaned back on his couch. His posture was still relaxed, but when I met his gaze, I knew that was a lie. His eyes resembled black diamonds as he stared at me.

"We share the same sire and we have known each other for thousands of years. That is why I want you to mark me well now, Veritas. Ian is reckless and impulsive, but you are not. You plan everything down to the last detail, so factor this into the plans you refuse to share with me: I will hold you responsible if Ian dies in whatever scheme you're involving him in."

"Mencheres," Ian began.

"Do not interrupt," he said harshly. "You are correct; I cannot command you any longer, but neither can you command me. If I choose to avenge you if she is careless with your life, that is *my* concern, not yours."

He'd thrown our earlier, defiant words right back at us. My teeth ground. Mencheres's threat might not be Ian's concern, but it was now mine. He didn't bluff. His normal course of action was to telekinetically rip the head off anyone who pissed him off. That sort of decisiveness made threats unnecessary.

Mencheres had taken the time to threaten me. I took that seriously, even if he couldn't kill me as easily as he could the rest of the world. Instead of being comforted by his sire's vow of vengeance, Ian appeared exasperated.

"Know what you are, Mencheres? You're a bloody helicopter mom."

I stifled my burst of laughter, turning it into a wheeze that fooled no one. Mencheres gave me a sour look, but now I couldn't stop picturing him as one of those overprotective parents who constantly hovered over their children.

Mencheres gave me another "this isn't funny" look before returning his attention to Ian. "You are not so strong that you are immune to death. I care for all the vampires I have sired, but there are few I love as if they were my own children. You are one of those few and something is very wrong with you. I could sense it even before Vlad warned me tonight."

Ian came and slung an arm around my shoulder. I stiffened but allowed it, willing to see where he was going.

"See this lovely hellion?" he asked. "She's so powerful I can barely keep my cock from standing at constant attention around her. More to the point, she's extremely invested in keeping me alive. Take assurance from that, even if you can't take assurance from my own determination *not* to get killed."

Mencheres looked back and forth between us. I schooled my

features to show nothing except confidence. Ian took another approach. He looked me up and down with leisurely appreciation, then pulled me even closer.

"And soon, this little vixen will want to keep me alive for many more reasons than that," he all but purred.

I was willing to appear friendly, but I would *not* be treated as if I were a predetermined conquest. Ian claimed to enjoy pain? Let's see how much he enjoyed this.

I threw an elbow into his side that broke all the ribs it came into contact with. While he let out a loud "oof!" I removed his arm from my shoulder with enough force to break that, too.

"If your cock comes anywhere near me, I will rip it off," I said in my most pleasant voice. "However, I am very invested in keeping Ian alive, Mencheres," I added, pivoting back to him. "Regardless, your threat is noted. Now, continue your conversation by yourselves. I'm keeping my own company for the rest of the flight."

Then I moved to the section of the plane that was the farthest away from them. I could feel someone's gaze on me the entire time, but I didn't turn around to see if it was Ian or Mencheres.

Mencheres didn't stay long. When the plane flew over Romania, he left. He could have had the pilots land first. Instead, he used his power to form an invisible barrier over the door so we didn't suffer a catastrophic loss of cabin pressure when he opened it. Then he jumped out, closed the plane door and resealed it with his power, and flew away.

Mencheres wasn't normally this showy with his abilities. His dramatic mode of exit was another warning. I'd known he was fond of Ian, but I hadn't expected *this*. Mencheres was making it clear that he held Ian's life in the highest possible regard—and I had better do so, too.

That was a problem. I'd meant it when I told Mencheres I was invested in keeping Ian alive, but that investment had an expiration date. Once Ian succeeded in bringing Dagon to my trap, my focus would shift to bringing the demon to his long overdue justice. Not to preserving Ian's life. Now, I had to kill Dagon while making sure *both* Ian and I survived? How?

"Thank God he's finally gone," Ian said, sauntering over to my side of the plane.

I considered ignoring him. I'd told him I was keeping my own company, after all. Then, I decided to ask what I'd been wondering about this past hour.

"Why are you refusing to tell Mencheres about Dagon?"

His lips tightened before he covered that with a careless smile. "Because he'd ruin our fun."

"His power would be very useful," I pointed out.

"Think he'd agree to use me as bait to draw a *demon* out?" Ian rolled his eyes. "Naïve doesn't suit you."

"It doesn't," I agreed, my tone hardening. "So stop pretending Mencheres wouldn't agree to *anything* if he knew your soul was on the line. I didn't know that two hours ago, but now, it's obvious. So why are you refusing to tell him about Dagon even though his involvement would increase your chances of survival?"

"I don't owe you a reason," Ian said, spinning around.

I caught him before he made it down the aisle. "Yes, you do. Mencheres all but said he'd murder me if you died, so if I survive and you don't, I'll have to battle one of my oldest allies to the death. I refuse to do that without at least knowing *why*."

Ian's jaw clenched and emerald blazed from his eyes. At the same time, I felt his muscles coiling beneath my hands, as if he were trying to hold back something wild inside him. If we weren't several thousand feet in the air, I'd think he was about to attack me. But if we fought under these circumstances, we'd bring the plane down, and that would cause bigger problems for both of us.

"Mencheres saved me," Ian finally said.

I didn't let go of him. "All vampires save the humans they sire. That can't be all there is."

Now his hands landed on my shoulders as well. "Ever been lost? I don't mean unaware of where you are. I mean lost in every sense of the word. Hundreds of years ago, I fled a brutal New South Wales penal colony for the even harsher Australian outback. I was dying of thirst, half blind from the sun and wracked with pain from fighting off the local wildlife. It didn't take long to hope to die by croc or venomous snake so it would be quick instead of more agony, but none of that was the worst part." His voice thickened. "The worst part was knowing no one cared enough to save you. That's what you remember forever. Not the physical pain or the never-ending fear, but the despair of being utterly alone and knowing you'll die that way. Ever been lost like that?"

Memories rocketed to the surface, so strong and fast, my throat closed and my eyes stung with the instant surge of tears. It took all of my willpower not to allow these tears to fall as something long buried inside me began to scream.

Tenoch! You saved me, and I failed you when you needed me the most. I'm so sorry, my beloved sire. I'm sorry, I'm sorry, I'm sorry . . .

I had to look away from Ian or I'd lose the remainder of my control. I couldn't bear to see the echo of my own pain reflected in the naked emotion of Ian's gaze. He might be loath to reveal his real feelings, but when he did, he let them burst forth in all their scalding intensity.

"Yes." I could barely force the word out for fear of my voice breaking. "I've been lost like that before." *Many times.*

He released me so abruptly, I took a step back to steady myself. "Then you know why I refuse to hurt Mencheres by telling him the truth. If Dagon kills me, Mencheres will grieve, but if he knew my soul was lost, too . . ." His lips twisted. "Not that I'd given him any cause to hope for that stained, shriveled husk even before my deal with Dagon, but Mencheres has ever seen the best in me, and I can say that about no one else in this world."

Tenoch had always seen the best in me, too. He'd also never given up on me, not even when he'd given up on himself. If I could have saved him from one more moment of pain, I would have done so. Gladly. That's why I had only one response.

"I won't tell Mencheres about your deal with Dagon."

"Ever," Ian stressed, tilting my chin so I'd meet his gaze.

I looked into his vivid turquoise eyes and repeated the vow. "Ever."

He smiled then. The lines from his former pain wiped from his expression as if they had never been there. "Grand. Now, since I'm supposed to be following your lead—and don't think *that* won't change soon—let's hear your doubtlessly boring plan to murder Dagon."

I forced the pain he'd brought to the surface back down until it was contained by the cell that had long housed it.

"Well," I said, my voice as light as his even though both of us were faking it, "I was going to start by parading you in front of other mages, witches, and demon-kin with a near reckless disregard of the danger so word of it could reach Dagon."

Ian laughed, throwing his head back until I could see the vibrations in the pale expanse of his throat. When he stopped and met my gaze, he had a devilish curl to his lips and his gaze was lit up with more interest than I'd ever seen.

"*Now* you're talking."

*S*everal days later, we were in Horseshoe, Ontario, on the Canadian side of Niagara Falls. I had a great view of those falls through the floor-to-ceiling windows in our hotel suite. I was surprised to see how crowded it was since it was winter. Perhaps the additional people were tourists who'd chosen to celebrate New Year's Eve here. A few more might have braved the temperatures from the recent freeze to see the formations that coated the rocks and trees around the falls in dazzling layers of ice.

Either way, it would serve to our advantage. We could get lost in the crowds, if need be. Furthermore, with the incredible energy these falls produced, it would be easy to tap into my connection with water to fuel a spell. As a last resort, the falls themselves could provide protection. A continuous mist rose from them, and I had several demon-repelling salt bombs that could be widely dispersed through it.

Ian came out of the suite's second bedroom. He wore black leather pants that hung low on his hips and a silver dress shirt. When Ian came closer, I saw his shirt was so sheer, it revealed far more than it concealed. Ian's flawless skin gleamed beneath the fabric, catching the eye and holding it. That must be why he'd chosen such a wholly inappropriate garment. His only nod to the near-zero temperatures were boots and a thick coat slung over his arm.

He laughed when he saw me. "You're wearing that ridiculous uniform? Thought you left the other one in my room as a joke."

I cast a look at my long-sleeved, high-necked black unitard. "There's a reason we have to wear these tonight."

"Let me guess: We're cosplaying as Storm and Cyclops?"

I was about to explain the need for the rubberized unitards, then I paused. Let him deal with the consequences of not following my lead, as he'd repeatedly failed to do.

"Have it your way," I said, encasing my high heels in thick rubber boots that gripped my calves.

Ian's pitying gaze swept over me. "If this is how you dress when you socialize, I'm starting to understand why you're still single."

I arched a brow. "How do you know I'm single?"

He sauntered over. "We've been together for days, yet you've not once called someone to check in. Furthermore, you certainly *smell* single. If celibate were a fragrance, consider yourself doused in it."

I ignored that. "Before we leave, I'm going to use glamour to change my appearance. Needless to say, I don't want to be recognized."

"Lest every vampire run for their lives when they realize a Law Guardian caught them indulging in magic?" he supplied.

"Exactly." With that, I sprinkled some finely sifted powder over my head and spoke in a language Ian shouldn't know.

He regarded me with amusement. "Been a while since I heard Icelandic. Superb pronunciation, by the way."

Dammit! Did I need to speak Klingon to finally stump him? I ground my teeth but finished the spell. I could tell from the look on his face when it set in. A slow whistle escaped him.

"Bugger. Me."

My golden bronze skin stayed the same, but my hair was now longer, thicker, and so light blonde it could have been mistaken for platinum. Gold and blue lowlights wove through it, giving the tricolored mass a dyed look even though it was natural. My dark blue-green eyes had also lightened to silver and I'd grown until I was just under his six-two frame in my heels.

My body had filled out, too. Gone was the litheness that had led him to wonder if I was half his weight. Now, my breasts were round and generous, as were my hips, and my arms and legs were well fleshed with muscle. Even my scent had changed. After Ian's gaze had done a thorough mapping of my body, it kept returning to my face, where features that had been moderately pretty before were now on the startling side of beautiful.

I ignored his fixation and wound my hair into a knot on top of my head. Then I affixed a rubber hood over it and tucked it into my neckline so I was fully covered. The last touch was tight rubber gloves that went to my elbows.

Ian finally stopped staring. "If your aim was to take the edge off this spectacular appearance, you failed. Everyone will still want to shag you, even if they laugh at your ridiculous onesie first. You should have glamoured a less dazzling appearance if you didn't want to stand out so."

"This is my usual look when I visit these places," I said, which was the truth.

"'Least it will keep me from being called a cradle robber," Ian said cheerfully. "You might be lovely, but you do look more like a prom queen than one of my usual dates in your normal appearance."

"I'm so glad I can protect your reputation," I said with false sweetness. "More importantly, with this appearance, I can be recognized by my former friends, if any of them are here. Allies will be useful if we need to engineer a quick escape."

"You have friends in magical places?" His smile turned sly. "Why, little Guardian, do you indeed go 'slumming' at times?"

"When you're as old as I am, you end up doing a little of everything at some point," was my evasive reply.

His chuckle was a low rumble of amusement and sensuality. "I'd say I could imagine, but I'd rather you show me."

I gave him a pointed look. "Not in this lifetime."

He let out a dramatic sigh. "Another sexual hoarder. Can't escape them these days, it seems. Ah, well, we have places to be and a demon to mercilessly taunt, so let's get to it, shall we?"

I hid my smile as I gave his barely clad chest and thin leather pants a last look. "Yes, let's."

"What the bloody hell did you say?"

The sound from the falls was loud, but I didn't think that was why Ian was pretending he hadn't heard me. He just didn't like what I'd said. That's why I relished repeating it.

"We have to jump into the river so we can go over the falls."

He glanced at the churning waters, where thick ice chunks regularly crashed into each other. "Like hell we do."

"The place we're going to is spelled to prevent just anyone from coming in," I said, fighting back my grin. "I don't know the new magical version of a password, but I remember the old one. It requires going over Bridal Veil Falls while wearing the right symbol." Then I couldn't resist adding, "I told you to put on the unitard. Next time, follow my lead."

He stared at the icy, frothing water before he gave me a truly evil glare. "Enjoy your victory now. I know I'll enjoy mine when I repay you for this."

"Ooh, I'm shaking in my warm, waterproof boots," I mocked, my grin finally breaking free.

He kept glaring as he stripped off his coat, shirt, and boots, placing them by a nearby tree. Then he gave the river a resigned glance. "My knobs will turn into ice cubes."

"Probably," I agreed, and took a small rouge pot from inside my boot. The substance inside wasn't rouge, so it didn't leave a visible trail as I traced the necessary pattern first over my face, then over Ian's. When I was done, I threw the pot aside and gave a final glance around.

No one was watching us. The few remaining tourists out at this hour were near the head of the falls, where multicolored lights shone on the roaring waters, giving the falls an ethereal look as they endlessly spilled over the ledge.

"Keep hold of my hand," I told Ian as I held it out. My grip was strong but so were these waters. Plus, there were many rocks hidden beneath the surface, and all this was *before* the treacherous drop over the falls.

His fingers tightened on mine as he took it. Then he surprised me by grinning. "Can't say I prefer the cold, but I *have* thought of doing this before. Here's to crossing one more item off my bucket list!"

With that, he yanked me into the freezing depths of the fast-moving water. I stifled a gasp as it hit the bare skin on my face. Extreme cold didn't feel freezing—it *burned*. I instantly felt guilty as I imagined how much pain Ian must be in. I should have insisted he go back to the hotel to put on the rubber unitard—

Ian's roar when his head broke the surface caused more guilt to slam into me. That turned into amazement when I realized he was laughing. "Lucifer's flaming farts, now *this* hurts!" he cried, attempting to spin me in a circle. The water was too strong. He only succeeded in dunking us both.

"You can't be enjoying this," I sputtered when we broke the surface again.

"Right you are!" he sang out, the words choppy because currents kept slamming water into his face. "Know . . . how many . . . props it takes to . . . duplicate this?"

"Don't want to," I managed before the current choked off my reply. We were picking up speed as the precipice neared. Bridal Veil might be the smallest part of Niagara Falls, but it was still a very significant waterfall.

"Brace!" I shouted, gripping his hands with all my strength when the horizon of water abruptly disappeared.

I thought I heard him laugh again as we went over the falls, but I couldn't be sure. The roar of water deafened me.

Chapter 10

$\mathcal{I}$ coughed out the water that had flooded my lungs, hearing Ian do the same. The alcove behind the falls fit us both, but I was surprised to see there was no longer a cave beyond it, too. At some point since I'd last been here, the cave must have been demolished. Good thing the place we were going wasn't in there.

I realized I was still holding Ian's hand and finally let go. He immediately began rubbing his arms and torso. "T-tell me it's w-warm where we'll be," he said through chattering teeth. Looked like he was over the thrill of the icy pain.

"It should be," I said, feeling guilty again.

I went over to the farthest corner of the alcove. Good, the large, flat rock that marked the entry was still there. I rested my face against the smoothest part, making sure the invisible symbol on my forehead touched the rock. After a second, the stone dissolved and an entryway appeared.

"This way," I said.

Ian sprang up and followed me through the new door. "What would happen if anyone tried to go through without this mark?"

"If they didn't have the other magical pass code, the wall would rematerialize and bash them in the face."

He let out a snort. "Effective."

It was, which is what had made this place a favorite sort of speakeasy for the magically inclined. Having to access it by going over the falls was inconvenient, but there were other ways to get in. If I had bothered to keep in touch with my old friends from this place, we could have found out those ways and climbed down the cliffs to this entrance without needing to go over the falls and get soaked.

I began to strip off my hood, rubber boots and the rest of my wet suit as we walked deeper into the narrow passageway. Beneath it, I wore a form-fitting black velvet dress that redirected Ian's attention in a flash when he saw it.

"We'll start off by looking for Rufus," I said as I shook my hair out from its bun. "He's an old friend of mine . . ."

My voice trailed off as the passageway ended in a large, open space. The last time I'd been here, countless orbs had floated around the room, illuminating everything with their beautiful, silvery glow. It had also been filled with people, music, laughter and magic. Now, it was as silent and empty as an abandoned tomb. I walked further into the room, the remnants of old magic touching me like cobwebs. That was all that remained of the place I'd known. Everything else was gone.

"I don't understand," I whispered.

Ian looked around, then inhaled deeply. "Barely a hint of scent anywhere. This place hasn't seen action in a decade, at least. How long did you say it's been since you were here?"

"Not that long," I began, then paused. Uh, I guess it *had* been a while.

"Ten years ago? Twenty?" When I stayed silent, his stare grew pointed. "More?"

"A little over ninety years," I said, feeling sheepishness wash over me.

"Ninety?" he repeated in disbelief. "Why in blazes did you pick this place, then?"

"It was the most recent magic club I'd been to," I admitted.

His brows nearly flew into his hairline. "*Ninety years?* Blimey, no wonder you're so uptight! Every senior citizen in the world has cut loose more recently than you."

I stiffened. "I don't appreciate the sarcasm—"

"And I don't appreciate my balls freezing to my bishop," he interrupted. "Yet here we are, and since we're being honest, you've got something stuck in your teeth."

"What?" I didn't remember eating any real food . . .

"Right between the two front ones," he said, pulling out a compact cosmetic mirror from his pocket. He must be more vain than I'd realized, bringing that with him. I'd brought weapons.

"See for yourself," he said, holding the compact open.

I glanced at the mirror—and the dark cavern vanished while an endless array of mirrors shot up to surround me. I tried to run and more popped up, blocking my path. Incensed, I punched the nearest one. The shiny, reflective surface didn't even crack. Instead, more mirrors appeared, until I began to feel dizzy from the endless copies of myself.

"Damn you, Ian!" I shouted, punching another mirror. Once again, it did nothing except make my fist sore.

I couldn't see him, but the laughter that rumbled into my ears was unmistakably his. "I can't believe you fell for 'you have something in your teeth.' Really, little Guardian, that has to be as old as you are."

I stopped my attempts to beat my way out of this. They only served to increase the mirrors and my own sense of disorientation. "Impressive spell," I said in a tone that belied the rage coursing through me. "Where did you learn it?"

Another laugh, sounding closer this time. "From a witch who caught me and several other vampires in it. None of us could get free until the spell expired. Necromancers couldn't break it when we used it on them later. Even Mencheres hadn't heard of it. That's how I reckoned it should work against you."

He'd actually shown me a spell I'd never seen before. I'd be impressed if I wasn't so furious. "Don't congratulate yourself yet. I'm not done trying to get out of this."

It sounded as if he'd settled himself into a more comfortable position. "By all means, do your best, but the spell expires in three hours. If you can't find a way out by then, I win."

I could buy more time by using my abilities to freeze it, but I wouldn't use that power unless I had to. Until then, I had other tricks to try.

By the end of the first hour, I was cursing Ian in every language I knew, although I made sure to do it in my head since vocalizing the curses only amused him. When I was well into the second hour, I'd stopped being angry. Instead, I was testing the limits of the spell with a growing sense of excitement.

So far, I'd been unable to beat it. Blasting all my supernatural power at the mirrors did nothing to break them. I finally resorted to freezing time in an attempt to move around the mirrors while everything was still. It didn't work. Punching and kicking the mirrors only served to multiply them. So did stabbing them with one of the silver knives I'd hidden in my boots. In fact, the mirrors were so impervious to harm, I finally came to the conclusion that they couldn't be real.

If they were, I should have been able to at least cause a hairline crack in one. The fact that I hadn't meant I probably wasn't doing any of the things I *thought* I was doing. For all I knew, I was still standing in the same spot I'd been when I first looked into the mirror Ian had spelled to become a trap.

If so, I shouldn't be focused on trying to destroy the mirrors or get away from them. I shouldn't pay attention to them at all. Instead, I needed to focus on myself. I closed my eyes, taking in deep breaths in an attempt to center myself.

It sounded like Ian shifted from his seated position. "Breathing? Think you can meditate your way out of this?"

I ignored the amusement in his tone to focus on the more important issue: He'd noticed what I was doing. He hadn't commented on any specifics of my actions before. That only strengthened my suspicion that I hadn't been doing any of it. Ian would have been unable to resist mocking me for trying to beat my way through the mirrors, let alone my other efforts.

I continued to focus on my breathing, until through force of will, I couldn't hear Ian anymore despite the fact that he was still talking. After several minutes, I became aware of something I'd been oblivious to since this ordeal had started.

The feel of cold, hard stone beneath me.

I must be on the ground. Sprawled out, judging from the chilliness against my arms, legs, and torso. I must have been like this the whole time, considering how cold my limbs felt. Oh, what a clever spell! If I could, I'd congratulate the person who'd created it. Like quicksand, the more I'd struggled to escape it, the deeper I'd sunk into it. This spell could be useful in my attempt to bring Dagon down while trying to ensure that *both* Ian and I survived.

And if I could breathe, then I could move. If I could move, I could reach my silver knife *for real* this time. No matter how ancient or powerful, all spells ceased in one of three ways: when they were finished, when they were beaten, or when the bespelled person died.

I just needed to intensify my focus first. I concentrated on my breathing until nothing else existed and nothing else mattered. Then, when I was hovering between that perfect state of complete self-awareness and complete oblivion, I reached down and pulled my silver knife from my boot.

"Sonofabitch."

Ian's muttered curse broke through my concentration, but it was confirmation that I'd succeeded in actually getting the knife this time. I trusted his reaction more than I did the feel of smooth silver in my hand. I'd been fooled by my senses before with this spell.

It took another few minutes before I could will myself back to where I was able to move the knife again. This time, I brought it to my chest—and instantly felt an unseen force seize my hand.

"What the bloody hell do you think you're doing?"

Ian sounded as if he was snarling the words into my ear, but when I opened my eyes, I saw nothing except mirrors. I couldn't see his hand on mine, and now, I could no longer feel it, but I knew he was still gripping my wrist.

What was I doing? I was making sure that I *could* do what was necessary to end this spell. This spell might be useful in our trap for Dagon, but the demon was far more powerful than I. If I'd figured out a way out of this, he would, too. It had taken me the better part of three hours; I didn't dare to hope it would take Dagon that long. He wasn't just more powerful than me; he was also eons older. For all I knew, he'd been the creator of this spell, for all magic had its origin in demons.

Besides, if I did what was necessary to defeat this spell in front of Ian, he would figure out what I was. I couldn't let that happen, since I didn't want to kill Ian. Surprisingly, that wasn't out of fear for what Mencheres would do. No, it was Ian's devotion to his sire that had changed my mind. The kind of loyalty that looked hell in the eye and told it to do its worst because nothing would make you endanger the person you loved . . . That was rare. Well deserving of protection. The bruise to my ego was a small price to pay.

Better to have Ian think he'd used a spell on me I couldn't defeat. Let him revel in his supposed win. It might be best to let Ian take the lead on choosing the hotspots, anyway. Had it really been *ninety years* since I'd gone out for some fun? How embarrassing.

And if I did strongly disagree about Ian's methods, I could wait until I was out of his eyesight, then extract myself from this spell. Ian would never even know I'd done it.

Decision made, I opened my eyes, seeing only never-ending reflections of myself in the countless mirrors. "You win."

"Come again?" Ian said, sounding surprised.

"You win," I repeated. "I can't break the spell and my time is almost up, isn't it?"

"Five more minutes." He still sounded much closer. "Why do I have the distinct impression that you haven't truly given up? I don't know what you intended before, but you damn near stabbed yourself in the heart, so I'm not letting go of your wrist."

I couldn't tell if I smiled for real or if the spell only tricked me into believing it. "And you saved me. My hero."

"My arse," he responded at once. "Somehow, you're playing me. I can feel it."

He had good instincts. It's probably what had kept him alive when one of the underworld's most powerful demons had been after him for decades. But there was a time-tested truism on my side: Men always wanted to believe they'd won a match of wits against a woman, even if their instincts told them otherwise.

"How many different ways do you want to hear me say you won?" I asked in a faux exasperated tone. "Very well, I concede, I surrender, I hand over my sword, I wave the white flag—"

"Enough." His voice changed. Suspicion gave way to the steel of resolve. "As I've told you before, I can wait to find out what you're hiding from me, but make no mistake—I *will* find out. What's more"—now silkiness replaced that steel—"you'll tell me willingly, little Guardian."

It had to be the spell that caused me to feel as if his words danced along my nerve endings. Yes, that's what it was, I told myself firmly. The spell.

"If I had a secret as big as you're implying," I replied, "I'd never share it with you."

He laughed, low, sensual, and oh so enticingly confident. "Now that is a wager you *will* lose. Count on it."

The entrance to our hotel had been swept clean, but the rest of Times Square was still coated with streamers, confetti and other remnants from celebrations the night before. Seeing it, I wasn't sorry we'd spent New Year's Eve over the border in Canada. Not that I had anything against confetti or streamers; it was the crushing crowds I wasn't fond of. Times Square on New Year's Eve was the epitome of that.

When we exited the hotel, the bellhop offered to hail a cab for us. Ian turned to me. "Up for a walk instead?"

"Sure." My ice-blue dress might be formal, but it didn't restrict my stride, and since I was a vampire, I couldn't get blisters despite today's foot-contorting high heels.

Ian offered me his arm, which I took after a brief arch of my brow. "Careful, someone might mistake you for a gentleman."

He flashed a grin at me. "Anyone who'd make such a mistake deserves what they get."

His smile made his looks even more distracting, and that was quite an accomplishment. Once again, we'd gotten a suite with two bedrooms, so we'd had privacy while readying ourselves for tonight. When Ian had come out of his room with his auburn hair slicked back so his impossibly beautiful features were highlighted for maximum effect, wearing a tuxedo that draped his tall, muscled form as if the tailor who'd fit him for it had been in love . . . I'd had to look away before I did something ridiculous. Like proposition him on the spot.

I don't know why I was having such a strong reaction to him. A week ago, I'd seen him naked and felt less affected. But I hadn't really seen Ian as a man then. I'd seen him as a necessary burden that might end up stabbing me in the back. Now, I knew Ian was dangerously smart, complicated, loyal, powerful, lethal, sexy . . . and arrogant. Proudly so.

He took every second and third glance from the normally jaded New Yorkers as his due. He even flashed pitying looks at the people who abruptly turned and began to follow him, glancing at me before raising a brow at them as if to say, "Sorry, I'm hers tonight, and yes, that *is* your loss."

After several instances of this, I was getting irritated. These people could clearly see my arm folded in his. Did I need to take more drastic measures to show that he was *not* available for their pleasure? Perhaps I'd feed from the next person who spun around and began to follow him like an animal catching an irresistible scent . . .

"Gods," I muttered out loud. What was wrong with me?

Ian glanced at me. "Something amiss?"

"No," I said while thinking *yes!*

Nearly all vampires were possessive over their personal food sources, their offspring and their lovers, yet Ian was none of those to me. I'd never turned a human into a vampire, so I couldn't speak for offspring, but I'd never experienced that trademark surge of territoriality with any of my former lovers. Or the humans I'd put under my protection. For the past four thousand years, I'd been glad to find myself above such pettiness. So why was I now fantasizing about biting every male and female who had done nothing more than make their interest in Ian known?

Lack of control, I decided in a grab for an excuse. I was in the very unfamiliar position of being spellbound into following Ian's lead tonight. I must be trying to distract myself from that by inventing a possessiveness I didn't really feel.

Yes. That had to be it.

"Which act would you prefer for tonight?"

His questions broke through my musings. I was all too glad for the interruption. "What do you mean?"

He shrugged. "There's the new lovers act, the friends-who-fuck act, the swingers act, the gold-digger and sugar-daddy act, the fighting couple act—"

"What about a platonic friendship act?" I interrupted.

He looked at me as if I'd finally spoken a language he couldn't understand. "Is that a joke?"

"Hardly. You might be attractive, but not *everyone* wants to have sex with you." As soon as I said it, I cringed. Did that sound as overly defensive as I felt?

"No, some people also want to kill me," he said at once. "Some want me to turn them into a vampire, some want my money, some want me for my rare artifacts, some for my fighting skills, and one wants to dangle me out as bait for a demon she's trying to kill. See? *No one* is with me simply to be with me."

Guilt pricked me, followed by a rush of empathy. I knew what it was like to be considered an object first and a person last. In fact, I couldn't remember the last time someone had been with me just to be with me, either. Wait . . . yes, I could. Tenoch.

Loneliness and a far deeper wave of guilt swelled, followed as always by pain. How could I have not known what Tenoch was trying to tell me the last time we were together? How could I have been so blind as to miss that he'd been saying good-bye?

As much as I wanted to, I could do nothing for Tenoch. But I could do something for the man next to me, if Ian allowed himself to accept it.

"I might be with you for ulterior reasons now, but it's well established that it's been a while since I've gone out for fun," I said in a carefully nonchalant tone. "And whatever else you are, you are fun, Ian. So, assuming we're both still alive when this is over, would you accompany me for an evening out?"

He looked at me in amazement. Then he began to laugh. "Offering me a pity date? *Now* I've heard everything."

"It's not pity and it's not a date," I said, a testier note creeping into my tone when he continued to laugh as if I'd told the funniest joke ever. "Since you've never gone out with someone just as a friend, and I'm in clear need of an update on places to have a good time, I thought . . . oh, never mind, if you can't stop laughing at me!"

"My apologies," he said, still chuckling. "It's only that I can't decide which is funnier—my being pitied for an assumed lack of companionship, or the look on people's faces if they saw you, a venerated Law Guardian, out with an infamous, law-scorning rakehell like me."

He was right that I'd hear no less than a decade's worth of snide remarks from some of the more sexist council members, not to mention a few from my fellow Law Guardians, too. But that didn't matter. "Long ago, I decided I wouldn't let other people's disapproval dictate my actions, so as the saying goes, I can handle it if you can."

His laughter stopped and something flashed over his face, too quick for me pinpoint what it was before it was gone. "If you hadn't played a part in the execution of my friend's child, I think I would very much like you, Veritas."

She's still alive.

I couldn't say that out loud without endangering her, and I wouldn't do that despite the surprisingly strong urge I had to redeem myself in Ian's eyes. On that awful day, I'd been close enough to the "little girl" to know she wasn't the real human/vampire/ghoul hybrid who'd been sentenced to death. She was a demon-branded shape-shifter disguised to look like her. Thankfully, the council members and other Law Guardians hadn't noticed. They couldn't sense demons the way I could. When I realized the switch had been made, I knew I didn't have to freeze time to save her, which was what I'd intended.

I told Ian none of that. All I said was, "You'll never forgive me for her death, will you?" As if there were any doubt. His calling me by my name instead of his usual moniker of "little Guardian" had been enough to tell me how serious he was.

"No, I won't," he said in a low, steady tone.

I met his eyes and held them. "Good. Some things should remain unforgiveable." I'd never forgive Dagon for what he'd done. Every once in a while, I still woke up screaming from the memories. Unlike the popular saying, time did *not* heal all wounds.

In truth, I was grateful for Ian's reminder of how he saw me—as another merciless player in the execution of a child whose only crime was frightening the bigoted because she'd been born different. Now, I could stop with these ridiculous thoughts and feelings about Ian. They were a waste of time and more importantly, a waste of energy. Nothing mattered except bringing Dagon down. Tonight was one more step toward accomplishing that.

"Pick whatever act you want," I said, and stared straight ahead for the rest of the walk.

*C*entral Park was bathed in a blanket of white. Lights from the surrounding buildings reflected off the snow and made it appear to glimmer. New York was the city that never slept, but at midnight at the famous park located in the heart of the city, things appeared to be winding down.

I'd been to New York City many times for business, but I couldn't remember the last time I'd strolled through Central Park. A few decades? Longer? Many things appeared new, such as the Alice in Wonderland sculpture and the ice-skating rink. I had seen Belvedere Castle before, but back then, it had been in a state of disrepair. Now, the faux castle looked fully renovated. It was also the location of exhibit rooms, an observation deck and the local weather station, according to a sign we passed.

Ian took us around the main entrance of the castle to the back side of it. There, on the rocky foundation that faced a small pond, he stopped and gave me a serious look.

"I've been asking your preference on things because I don't want the spell to force you into acting against your will. But I don't trust you not to return here in your official capacity later. That's why I'm claiming one of my acts of obedience. By the spell that binds us, Veritas, I command that you will never prosecute anyone for their magical actions tonight, and you will also never tell other Guardians, Enforcers, the council, or other law-worshipping vampires about this place."

I felt the spell responding to his words, tightening around me until they were part of me. At the same time, it was all I could do not to whoop in relief. *This* is what he was spending one of his acts of unquestionable obedience on? When he said "I command" I'd almost whipped out my silver knife in fear that it would be something I couldn't tolerate. But I never would have told anyone about this place. I only prosecuted people for magic when that magic harmed others.

Not that the council or anyone else knew that about me. If they did, I wouldn't be a Law Guardian. "Done," I said at once.

My breezy tone caused his gaze to narrow, as if he just realized he might have wasted one of his commands. I smiled innocently while on the inside, I was chuckling. *One down, two to go.* If the rest were anything like this, I wouldn't need to bother with the effort to get out of this spell.

A gust of frigid wind caused me to tighten my coat. The wind had been picking up, but we must have been near the place, or Ian wouldn't have forced an unnecessary vow out of me.

"I'm going to glamour myself now," I said, taking a pouch from my coat. Then I sprinkled the contents over my head while saying a few words he shouldn't be able to translate.

Both auburn brows rose. "The fictional Elvish from *The Lord of the Rings*? What sort of spell uses a fictional language?"

Dammit, dammit, dammit! "When did you have time to learn every language ever spoken?" I demanded. "From what I know about you, you should have been too busy fucking everyone near you to bother with that kind of extensive linguistic study!"

His laughter rolled over me. "Know the best thing about being dismissed as an insatiable whore? People don't mind their tongues around you. I've learned more information eavesdropping while I was mid-orgy than I have from spying on G7 summits, but that's off topic. What's on topic is that thus far, none of the spells you've uttered have made any sense. They seem to be only a collection of random words."

I stopped before I took an instinctive step backward. *Oh, no. If he tried to command the truth out of me . . .*

He caught my flinch and moved closer. "Know what I think?" he asked in that deceptively smooth tone. "They're not real spells at all. They're camouflage to mask how powerful you are."

Dammit times a hundred! But I couldn't let him see that he'd scored a hit. That's why I straightened my spine.

"How flattering, but if you live to be my age, you'll realize only certain words have power. The rest have only been added by the uninitiated in order to make the spell sound better."

"Bollocks," he said in that same silky tone. "I yanked the guts out of a thousand-year-old necromancer to read his entrails for information recently. He never once flinched, know why?" Now he was only centimeters away. "He was trapped inside the mirror spell. It froze him in place as if time itself had stopped. But when I used that same spell on you, you were grabbing weapons without an ounce of pain as motivation. Explain *that*."

I couldn't let him force the truth out of me. I couldn't. I braced, ready to freeze him in a time trap if he even *started* to say the words "I command you."

As if he sensed the power coiling inside me, his mouth curled and he stepped back. "No need for dramatics. I won't use one of my commands to force you to tell me. Besides, I think I already know your secret."

"Do you?" I asked, fighting a sense of dread.

He raked me with a gaze. "Time will tell, won't it?" Then, he waved almost diffidently in the direction of the pond: "Your glamour's in place, so it's time to pay the troll."

"The troll?" I repeated, turning around, but all I saw was the clear, flat surface of the pond.

Another careless wave. "You can't see him until the bridge becomes visible. He's under it, of course."

"Oh, of course," I said sardonically, but I was glad to have the subject change. "And where is the bridge?"

"Right in front of us, but it won't appear until we cast in an acceptable, bespelled offering."

With that, he withdrew something from his jacket. When he opened his hand, I saw a diamond-studded gold locket suspended from a long, thick gold chain. An antique, judging from the old-fashioned clasps that modern jewelry didn't have.

"Expensive," I noted.

He gave me a humorless grin. "Anything less and we risk becoming a snack. Enraged mafiosos are more merciful than a troll who thinks he's been disrespected."

I didn't know what this creature was, but it couldn't be a troll. To my knowledge, those creatures didn't exist. Or did they? It felt like I'd been wrong about so much lately . . .

"Take my hand," Ian said, bringing my attention back to him. "We have to throw it in together for the offering to be considered from both of us."

I laced my fingers in his and waited for his nod. When it came, we threw the necklace into the pond. The surface rippled from the impact, then rippled in a stronger way after the jewelry sank out of sight.

"He must've liked that one," Ian said, watching the pond. "The bigger the ripple, the more he's pleased by the gift."

By the time he was done speaking, moonlight illuminated a bridge that hadn't been there before. It looked far older than the manufactured aged appearance of Belvedere Castle. It also appeared to be made entirely of stone. But the most impressive sight was at the end of the bridge.

The castle that materialized was twice the size of Belvedere. It hovered over the water, covering almost the entire pond. Unlike the bridge, it didn't appear to be made of stone. In fact, I couldn't determine what the multicolored walls, turrets, and balconies were made of. If I had to guess, I'd say they appeared to be impossibly large opals.

"Beautiful," I breathed.

Ian's mouth quirked. "Not upset that a magical abode has been under the council's noses this entire time?"

Please. I'd long suspected that something magical resided in Central Park. How else could you explain such a large tract of the most expensive real estate in the world remaining undeveloped? "No," was all I said.

"Then come." Ian extended his arm with a hint of a grin. "I've decided our act tonight will be the fighting couple. Shouldn't present too much of a challenge, should it?"

I felt a wry smile tug at my mouth. "I think we'll manage."

We were almost at the end of the bridge, when a strong gust whipped my hair around. My hair clip fell out and was immediately snatched up by the breeze. It landed in the pond. A second later, the surface heaved as if a car had plunged into it instead of a small piece of hair jewelry. Ian pulled me closer, his other hand disappearing into his coat pocket.

"What's rattled him?" he muttered.

A shadow suddenly covered us despite it being dark out. When I tried to turn around to see what had cast it, Ian's tight grip stopped me. Then a noise like thunder crashed over us.

"Arr-eee-ell?"

My whole body tensed. I recognized what that rumble was saying. Ian didn't, but he took it as a threat. He shoved me toward the doors and withdrew the three-pronged end of a small yet lethal-looking trident from his coat. The weapon's middle blade was silver but the outer two appeared to be made of some kind of bone . . .

"Don't!" I shouted when I tasted the magic emanating from the creature. I caught Ian's arm mid-thrust. The deadly bone tips of the trident missed the creature, but before Ian could regroup, I threw myself between it and him. Ian lowered the three-pronged weapon and grabbed me.

"Are you out of your mind? That thing will *eat* you!"

No, he wouldn't. I'd recognized the taste of the glamour surrounding the fearsome creature. That glamour could only come from one source—me, and I had only gifted it to one creature.

"Nechtan?" I asked with a surge of joy.

Bulbous-looking lips pulled back in a smile revealing rows of huge teeth that one would expect from a troll. "Arr-eee-ell!" he repeated, then hopped up and down in joy.

If he'd been as large as he appeared, his treating the bridge like a trampoline would have shaken many of the stones loose. But they didn't as much as quiver, because the creature looming over us was no bigger than a child in his true form. Glamour was highly effective in fooling the senses, but it couldn't fool rocks.

Ian's grip on me didn't loosen, but he did lower the trident all the way down. "What. The. Hell?" he enunciated, staring back and forth between me and Nechtan.

I wasn't ready to explain. I was too busy flinging myself at my old friend to hug him. That caused Ian to curse in three different languages, but I didn't care. I'd long feared that Nechtan was dead. Now, here he was. Alive, whole . . . and making a damn good profit with his fearsome troll-under-the-bridge act.

"I never thought to see you again!" Nechtan's normally rumbling voice sounded even more ragged from emotion. "I felt your magic when the comb hit the water, but I still could hardly believe—"

"Shhh," I interrupted. Nechtan was speaking in an ancient Celtic dialect, but with Ian's linguistic skills, he probably understood it. "Speak carefully, my friend."

Nechtan looked behind me at Ian, baring his teeth in a snarl. "Is this man your enemy?"

"No," I said quickly. Small true size or no, Nechtan was deadly when he wanted to be. "He is an ally tonight."

Nechtan read the subtext between my words and a knowing expression fell over his features. Then he began to press kisses onto my hands. "I thought you were dead, Ar—my friend," he corrected himself. "Please, take all the gold in this pond as the smallest token of my gratitude for how you saved me."

He'd always been so kind. "Nechtan, there is no need—"

"No need?" Ian interrupted, striding over. He kept the trident tip lowered, but his grip on it didn't loosen. "Refusing a fae's gift is a deadly insult. How do you not know that?"

Fae? I pressed my lips together to stop my smile. Is that what Ian and everyone else thought Nechtan was? He'd taken his ruse to the next level by pretending to be from a race of creatures that didn't exist.

"I see," I said in as serious a voice as I could manage. "In that case, your generosity is appreciated, Nechtan." I didn't say thank you. If I remembered correctly, fae lore also said to never say thank you to a fae. Besides, I'd return Nechtan's gold later, when Ian wasn't around.

"Saved your life, did she?" Ian asked Nechtan in a casual tone. "Sounds like a story worth hearing."

Of course he'd understood what Nechtan had been saying. "Another time," I said. "We have business now, remember?"

Ian smirked as if he knew why I was suddenly in such a hurry. "Right you are." To Nechtan, he said, "About this gold, mate. Will we need a crate to carry it, or a truck?"

"Truck," Nechtan responded promptly.

I was about to object again, but Ian said, "Splendid, I'll make the arrangements," and walked toward the doors while pulling out his cell phone. This gave me a few moments with Nechtan without Ian's full attention on us.

I bent down even though Nechtan's glamour made it appear as if his ears were meters above me. "I'm a vampire Law Guardian now," I whispered as softly as I could. "I go by the name Veritas. But if you ever need me, contact me in the old way."

"A Law Guardian?" Nechtan wheezed and his huge body began to shake. Soon, he was laughing so hard, he was crying.

I glanced at Ian, but he seemed absorbed in his call with someone named Ted who apparently had a truck. "I know," I said, flashing a rueful grin at Nechtan when I looked back at him. "Life leads us down strange paths sometimes."

"All set," Ian announced, returning to our section of the bridge. "Finished on your end, poppet?"

My teeth ground. "Little Guardian" was one thing, but "poppet"? He'd only called me that when we first met and he thought I'd been another of his whores. "Sure, sugar nuts," I said with the barest level of civility.

His brows rose, but then he shrugged. "Getting into character for our act, I see."

Nechtan noticed my irritation. "He disrespects you?" he asked, the faintest pinprick of red appearing in his eyes.

Only one type of creature in the world had eyes that glowed red, and it wasn't the mythical fae.

I immediately started to cough, which was enough to get Nechtan's attention back on me.

Nechtan must have realized what he'd almost done, so he jumped over the side of the bridge and began to sink beneath the water. "We will speak later. For now, farewell . . . Veritas."

"Farewell, my friend," I said, waiting until he disappeared beneath the pond's dark surface. When he was completely out of sight, I turned to Ian, fixing a bright smile on my face.

"Looks like you'll be getting your necklace back soon."

"Yes," he drawled, a smile edging his mouth. "Seems as though tonight's our lucky night."

I didn't like the look in his eyes. I also didn't want to give him more time to muse over what had just taken place. On top of all that, I was more than a little rattled by the weapon he'd chosen to bring. The silver prong in the middle of the small trident was self-explanatory, but where in the world had Ian gotten the two demon bones on either side of it?

Oh wait. I think I knew.

Ian would have to keep his extremely rare, deadly weapon hidden. We might not encounter any demons inside, but if we did, none of them would take kindly to seeing a weapon capable of killing them, especially since the necessary component was bone from the body of another demon.

"Put your trident tip away, Ian," I said, my fake smile still in place. "We're supposed to be here to party, remember?"

As soon as we crossed the castle's threshold, I felt a wave of magic move over me, then quickly disappear. I was wondering what it was for, when Ian pulled out his mobile and grunted.

"Just as I thought. Battery's dead now."

Ah, more security measures. Mustn't let pictures or cell-phone video incriminate anyone. The lack of functioning mobiles also aided our cause. Now Dagon couldn't get a call from a friend and show up to surprise us.

Once inside, orbs provided all the light, either hanging in the air or streaking around while forming into various animals, birds, and fantastical creatures. When we entered the huge foyer, the cluster of orbs in front of us swirled to form a dragon. It opened its mouth to release more brightly lit orbs in a mime of breathing fire, then the beautiful creation burst apart and the orbs streaked off to form something new.

There were also fountains around the entire room. Each contained a water nymph, which stayed in the center of the fountain like a living, aquatic statue. The nymphs changed their appearance whenever someone passed by, forming into watery versions of beautiful men, women, marine life, or combinations of all three. The nymphs' artistry was stunning, but water nymphs were as dangerous as they were dazzling.

If a human made the mistake of touching one, that person would drown. Water nymphs body-jumped with a single touch. Vampires and ghouls could survive days of vomiting up streams of water until they finally expelled the nymph, but no human could.

Still, the nymphs called to the part of me that had a unique connection with water. If I concentrated, I could feel the energy coming from them as they shaped the water into whatever they willed it to be. That energy beckoned me, inviting me to participate in their artistry.

I must have stared at them too long because Ian took my arm to get my attention. I glanced away to find him frowning at me. "You know not to touch one, right?"

"Yes." But I didn't think their positioning in various parts of the castle's foyer was an accident. Someone with little to no magical experience would easily be enthralled by the wondrous nymphs. They must be another example of the castle's security. The invisibility spell and Nechtan's magical bridge toll might be to keep out innocent humans, but the former was meant to trap people like me. Most Law Guardians, Enforcers, and Enforcer trainees wouldn't know not to touch a water nymph. Doing so would out us more thoroughly than a blaring alarm.

I normally took issue with magic that harmed people, but water nymphs didn't kill out of malice. They couldn't *stop* the transference when they were touched. Punishing them would be as senseless as punishing a Venus flytrap for eating an insect.

I looked back to see that the nymph I'd been staring at had formed into an exact replica of me. I smiled, then let loose a tendril of my power to gently ripple the water around the nymph. It was as close as I could come to showing my appreciation. Ian didn't notice that I'd moved the water with my power. He was too busy tugging on my arm.

"Come on, luv. Most of the action takes place in the next rooms."

First "poppet," now "luv." I ground my teeth before I forced myself to relax. He could be calling me these names because Veritas or "little Guardian" would draw all the wrong attention. I didn't need to worry about calling him by *his* name. We wanted people to know who he was. That was the entire point of coming here tonight.

"Action sounds good." Even though I'd tried to relax, my voice still came out crisper than I intended. Then again, our act did call for quarreling.

Ian led me past the fountain room to a different one, which could double as an erotic version of Eden. Vines, branches, and flowers covered the walls and ceiling and made up the furniture, too. Many of the people lounging here had decided to copy the garden theme by wearing only leaves and petals as clothing. So much for Ian saying tonight was black-tie formal.

Moans drew my attention upward. Long, thick clusters of white and lavender wisteria hung from the high ceiling. A few of the wider clusters had arms, legs, and other body parts protruding from them. Some mage or witch must have bespelled the wisteria bunches so that whoever was inside them could float. People had taken advantage of that perk and were making love with a fervor that made me hope none of them were human. If they strayed too far from the gravity-defying clusters, they'd harm themselves from the fall.

"Keep going," Ian said, though his brow flicked suggestively as we passed another wisteria cluster with at least three people writhing inside it. "Unless you're slowing down because you want us to join them?"

I glared at him as I quickened my pace. "No."

He gave me a speculative look as we continued through the room. "What *do* you do for erotic recreation? Mencheres said you almost never shag vampires, which for the life of me I can't understand. Ghouls are vigorous lovers, yes, but they don't have fangs, so you're missing half the fun. Humans are tasty and enjoyable, but they tire so easily, plus someone with your strength would likely break one during orgasm—"

"Would you shut up?" I snapped. He'd hit too close to home with that last remark.

He pulled me back when I attempted to stride ahead of him. "What, then?" he went on as if I hadn't spoken. "A combination of ghouls, the occasional vampire, and battery-operated devices?"

Once again, he was closer to the truth than I was comfortable with. That's why my tone was even sharper. "Wouldn't *you* like to know?"

His turquoise eyes began to fill with emerald. Then he began to propel me toward the nearest wall. "Perhaps I would."

I didn't know what had caused his abrupt change in behavior, but I dug my heels in to stop his progress. Faster than a blink, he picked me up. I debated punching a dent into his head for his impertinence, then decided to see where he was going with this. He might only be acting out the "fighting" part of our ruse, though I had a feeling this was more serious.

"If I'm wrong about my other guesses, what then?" he murmured, moving so close the full length of our bodies touched. Then he leaned down until his forehead rested against mine. "Demons? They are, as the saying goes, a hell of a ride."

I wasn't a fan of being swept off my feet and backed against a wall. If anyone else had manhandled me this way, I'd be slamming my head against theirs hard enough to split their skull. But for reasons that had nothing to do with maintaining our ruse, I didn't smash Ian's head, stomp on his feet hard enough to break them, punch a hole through his ribs or do anything else violent. Instead, filled with an urge I couldn't explain, I trailed my fingers down Ian's chest with taunting flicks.

"Why do you care who or what I have sex with? You're not tempting enough for it to ever be you, so how is the rest of it your concern?"

As soon as I said it, I regretted it. It was a blatant dare—and Ian loved dares. His eyes lit with emerald flames and his arms hardened around me. I squirmed, but not nearly as much as I could have if I truly wanted to get away. Instead, my efforts only pressed me against him in more suggestive ways.

His nostrils flared. Oh yes, he knew the difference between what

I was doing now and what I did when I was serious about breaking someone's hold. It's not as if our first fight had left Ian any doubt as to how I acted when I really wanted to get free.

Soon, only scant bits of air separated the most intimate parts of our bodies. Another centimeter would have those parts touching. I found myself taking in a breath just to inhale his scent. He glanced down as if wanting me to know that he was thinking about closing that space between us, but he didn't. Instead, his eyes glowed a brighter shade of green as his mouth slid down until it touched my ear.

"What if I told you I had every intention of changing your mind about taking me for a lover?"

The breath from his words felt like feathers brushing my skin. His hands were on my arms, lightly kneading the pressure points in the softer areas of my flesh. I wouldn't have considered arms to be an erogenous zone, yet each touch elicited shivers of pleasure that traveled far beyond my limbs.

I should tell him to get away from me. Right now. But what came out was a breathy, "Aren't you supposed to be fighting with me instead of trying to seduce me?"

His low laugh tickled my ear in all the right places. "Who says I can't do both?"

I didn't trust my body's reaction to that. It didn't help that his light touches and the brushes of his mouth were heightening an ever-growing need. Soon, it was all I could do to keep my hands at my sides instead of sliding them up his back to pull him closer.

"Quit playing."

I'd intended my tone to be sharp, but once again, it failed. What came out was almost a purr instead. Gods, had it been so long since I'd indulged in a little pleasure that I was about to surrender to the most dangerous supplier of it?

"If you want me to stop, then stop me," he murmured before I felt the brush of his fangs on my throat. If my heart had still been capable of beating, it would have started to race. I could not be in a more treacherous situation. So why did a reckless part of me want to tilt my head back to give him better access?

"Say no," he went on. "Or shove me away, and I'll stop." Then his tone turned darkly promising. "But if you do neither, I absolutely won't stop."

His lips brushed against my skin with each word. I shivered and his breath hit me in a sharp exhale as he felt it. His scent changed, deepening into a more luxuriant mix of caramel and cognac. I found myself breathing it in until my chest swelled against his. A lower, rougher sound escaped him and he closed the last space between us. All my nerve endings jumped when his hips pressed against mine. When he gave a slow twist that rubbed me right in my most sensitive spot, I moaned.

He gripped me tighter and his mouth sealed over my neck. I gasped when I felt the silkiness of his tongue, then pushed him back with a surge of panic when I felt the pressure of fangs.

"No!"

He stopped and I felt crushing relief when his head lifted. Every warning bell I had began to ring as the sensual haze I'd been in dissipated. Had I lost my mind? The obvious answer was yes.

Ian stared at me, not moving closer, but not moving farther away. I gathered my shattered control to give him as firm a look as I could manage. "I think we've acted out enough of the 'couples' part of our roles tonight."

His lips curled. "Acting? How strange. I feel as though the last few minutes are the first I've seen of the real you."

I refused to look away, but oh, I wanted to. His knowing stare felt as intimate as that slow, deep rub against my loins. He was right—I'd let far too much of my guard down. A little more of the skillful touch of his hands and mouth, and I might have revealed my secret without even intending to.

I wasn't too arrogant to admit when I'd been beaten, and Ian had blasted through my self-control with laughable ease. For reasons that had nothing to do with sanity or self-preservation, I was ridiculously attracted to him. He now knew that beyond all doubt. I had to make sure he lost interest in seducing me. If I couldn't trust my self-control, I had to trust his. Ian had few weaknesses, but there was one way I could wound him where he'd never touch me again.

"The real me is the same person who stood by as your best friend's child was murdered, remember?"

Each word sounded as cold as the council's order had been when they'd handed it down. The only reason I hadn't killed the ones who'd voted for her death right then was because I needed their trust so I could help her and others like her later. But Ian didn't know that. His face hardened with all the rage I'd felt when my protests to the council had fallen on deaf ears. Then his grip tightened until it was painful.

I tried to wrest free for real this time. Incredibly, he matched me for strength. Then he blocked the knee I aimed at his groin by using his legs as a vise around mine.

"Let me go," I demanded.

"No."

Now he leaned forward with brute force instead of sensual insistence. He even pressed my head against the wall with his so I couldn't rear back and head-butt him into unconsciousness. All I could do was bite him, but that would be disastrous since he would absolutely bite me back.

"Not freezing time to stop me?" he asked in a low, furious whisper. "You can't, can you? This place has too many trueborn witches and warlocks who are immune to that trick. If they saw what you can do, they'd reveal your powers to everyone else. Can't get to your weapons with your arms pinned down, either, so now you have no choice except to answer what I ask you."

I'd pushed him too far. He'd said he wouldn't use the spell to force my secret out of me, but that person was no longer reflected in his gaze. The one I'd taunted with the supposed death of his friend's child was, and he had no mercy.

"Ian, don't—" I began.

"I command you by the spell that binds us to tell me if you're a demon possessing the body you're in," he interrupted.

At once, the spell activated. Agony scalded me, growing every second that I didn't answer. Lava pumping into me wouldn't hurt this much. My legs gave out and I slumped as, true to my warning, my bones also rotted faster than I could heal. Only Ian's tight grip kept me from spilling onto the floor.

"No." Anguish made my voice ragged as the answer was torn from me. "This body is mine and no one else's."

The truth of that instantly doused the pain. Even still, it took a few moments to find my strength despite my bones beginning to heal. *Thank all the gods above and below the earth that Ian hadn't guessed the right question to ask.*

"How?" he answered in a hard tone. "Your power is far beyond what a normal vampire should have. Only time I saw anything like it is when an ancient demon simultaneously possessed several of my mates."

A demon strong enough to manage multiple possessions at the same time *was* impressive, but that wasn't my secret.

"You have only one command left," I said, still trying to steady my legs. "And we have a long road ahead. Do you truly want to waste it on this?"

From the way he stared at me, I might have once again pushed him too far. I tensed, ready to do something drastic if the words "I command" started to leave his lips. But instead, he moved away so abruptly that I was glad I was still leaning against the wall. Otherwise, I would have fallen.

"I don't," he said, his light tone at odds with the unsettling darkness in his gaze. "Now, let's make a scene so word of our visit gets back to Dagon."

$\mathcal{I}$ soon realized why Ian wanted us in black-tie attire. Most of the castle's rooms catered to either whimsical or erotic forms of entertainment, but there was one room where the fun was all business.

The high-stakes gaming room.

Vampires, witches, mages, and warlocks played magical versions of craps, roulette, blackjack, poker, and more. A few heads lifted when Ian and I entered, but most of the players didn't look up. I agreed with their unbroken concentration. From the fortune in magic-infused vouchers floating above the tables, it would be foolish to take attention from the game just to check out new people walking in.

Several glamorous-looking men and women passed around trays of drinks and hors d'oeuvres, while others handled the castle's version of magical gambling chips. We had barely entered the room when a tuxedoed attendant approached us and bowed.

"May I assist you in exchanging your currency for vouchers, Madame and Monsieur? As a reminder, the minimum buy-in for vouchers is two hundred thousand dollars."

My eyes bulged. I came from a time when entire countries didn't contain such wealth, but Ian was unfazed.

"We'll start with this," Ian said, withdrawing a hefty pouch from his pocket. Then he dumped its contents into the attendant's white-gloved hand. My eyes widened at the diamonds, rubies, and emeralds that spilled out. Soon, the attendant had to use both his hands to hold all the bounty.

That got more attention directed at us. Ian flashed a wolfish grin at the people giving his pile of jewels hungry looks. "Plenty more where that came from, if any of you have the stones to beat me and win it."

Men. Everything circled back to their genitals.

"Ian!" The smoky feminine voice jerked my attention to the right. A beautiful bejeweled woman with inky black hair and sienna skin made her way toward Ian. Three men followed after her, their expressions the opposite of her happy one.

"Ananya." Ian kissed both her cheeks and then her lips when she pressed them against his as he was about to pull away.

I ground my teeth. This woman was lucky I was only *pretending* to be with Ian tonight. If I hadn't been pretending, I would have bloodied her mouth for plastering it against his. And *he'd* be walking with a permanent limp for returning her kiss.

Looked like I was capable of extreme vampire possessiveness after all. And they said you couldn't teach an old dog new tricks . . .

"Ananya, you're as lovely as ever," Ian told her when he finally pulled his mouth away from hers.

Dark, doelike eyes glanced my way before Ananya returned her attention to Ian. "As are you, darling, and I see your taste is still faultless. Your latest acquisition is simply stunning."

Acquisition? I crossed my arms behind my back so it wouldn't be obvious that I'd just clenched my fists. Worse, Ian chuckled in a knowing way. "I collect only the best. And you? Who are these fine new lads you have in tow?"

She flicked her fingers and they came forward. "Meet Hans, Steven, and Amir. Boys, meet Ian. And your pet's name is . . . ?"

That was it. I walked away without a backward glance. Let Ian continue to cozy up to his former lover without me. I'd busy myself with exploring the rest of the room.

Unlike the other rooms in the castle, these walls were dark, as were the floors and ceiling. Rich, luxuriant drapes hung over alcoves where muffled moans indicated that transactions of a more personal nature were taking place. The air was heavy with the scent of cigar smoke, different perfumes, greed, despair, exultation, and sex. Not a combination I wanted to savor, so after one exploratory breath, I stopped trying to see if I recognized scents from people I used to know when I was a regular visitor to places like this.

My wandering took me to the farthest corner of the room. A velvet curtain blocked what looked to be another room beyond it. Murmured voices indicated that this room was occupied, too. I was about to peek inside when a pale hand landed on my arm.

"That game's not for you, sweeting."

Ian's latest nickname made me bristle more than his attempt to tell me what to do. "Why not?" I asked with all the annoyance I felt. *Fighting couple, present and accounted for.*

"Because I didn't take you for someone who liked to chase the dragon," he drawled. "Was I mistaken?"

I recognized the slang referring to drug use, but there were no heartbeats in the room beyond. Ian could only mean one thing. "Vampires are drinking drugged blood in there?"

Ian's hand tightened as many heads turned. Guess my abhorrence to Red Dragon, which was what the drugged blood was commonly referred to, had caused my voice to carry.

"Remember my first command," Ian said low. "You're not here as anything except a partygoer."

My anger grew. This time, it wasn't caused by his highhandedness. Unlike humans, vampires couldn't become inebriated by the right mix of synthetics, plants, or chemicals. There was only one substance strong enough to intoxicate us, and while most vampires had no idea what it was, I did. Ian was right—I couldn't let my role as Law Guardian affect my response, and that had nothing to do with Ian's magical command.

"On the contrary," I said in a voice so loud, it carried to everyone in this room and the curtained-off one beyond. "Not only do I love Red Dragon, I can drink every vampire here under the table, and I bet every voucher you have to prove it."

Ian wanted a scene that was bound to get back to Dagon? I was about to give him one.

Ian's eyes glittered with angry sparks. "Assumes all my money is hers to spend," he called out in a falsely jovial tone. "Spoken like every woman and man I've ever dated."

Laughter and grunts of commiseration met his response, which covered his far lower hiss of "Are you mad?" at me.

"I know what I'm doing," I snapped in an equally low tone. "For once in your life, trust someone other than yourself. Please," I added, using that word for the first time with him.

The hardness in his gaze didn't vanish when the attendant returned with a large tray full of different-colored vouchers. Then, with a harsh twist of his lips, Ian took the tray the attendant handed him and held it over his head.

"All right, mates, everything on this tray says the lovely lady can make good on her boast."

Several vampires immediately cashed out of their current games. Soon, Ian was surrounded with people taking him up on his extravagant bet. It came as no surprise that almost all of those bets were against me. All I did was smile.

Let the games begin.

When I started drinking, twenty-eight competitors sat at the table with me. An hour later, there were thirteen. An hour after that, there were six. Now there were only two, and one of those listed so heavily in his chair, his friends stood on either side of him to make sure he stayed upright.

I was leaning on my arms because I'd decided that sitting up straight was overrated after my last shot. Dozens and dozens of crystal glasses were stacked to form a mini castle in front of me. The attendants had been creative with how they'd arranged the empty glasses after I'd finished each shot.

"S'posta be on ur ass b'now," Andrew, the heavily listing vampire, slurred. Then he wagged a finger at me. "'Ow oldru?"

I was fluent in drunk talk so I knew what he was asking. "Rude to ask a lady her age," I said, making sure to slur my words enough to avoid suspicion. "'N' quit stalling. Your turn."

Andrew gave the full shot glass in front of him a baleful look. "'Ate you," he told it, then brought it up. He missed his mouth and the tainted blood sloshed onto his cheek. He frowned as it spilled onto his formerly immaculate tuxedo, then accepted the new glass that an attendant quickly poured for him.

I watched with pity but no real concern. Vampires were incapable of drinking themselves to death. Granted, Andrew would have a terrible hangover tomorrow, but I hoped that would cause him to think twice about drinking Red Dragon again.

Ian wasn't watching Andrew or my other remaining competitor. He was watching me, as he had been this entire time. Worse, I didn't think his attention had to do with concern over losing the lavish bet he'd placed on me. I met his gaze before quickly glancing away. His stare was too knowing, as if he were somehow compiling my secrets one by one.

I didn't see Ian leave his position on the other side of the table. I felt him as he came nearer. His aura cascaded over me, distinctive even in this crowd and growing stronger as he approached. He stopped when he was behind my chair. Then I felt the glide of his hands across my shoulders.

His power made my skin vibrate with pleasurable tingles. I fought a moan as I leaned back, unable to keep myself from moving closer. Wasn't my fault, I decided. It was all the Red Dragon I'd consumed. That's why it felt as if every stroke of his hands was a spell I was falling deeper into.

His fingers slipped beneath the thin straps of my ice-blue dress as he kneaded my shoulders until the tension melted out of them. Then he stroked the back of my neck until it was all I could do to stop myself from rubbing against him like a cat. This might have looked like a simple back rub, but it felt far more intimate. In a different, more private setting, it could even be considered foreplay.

Shayla, the vampire who'd appointed herself the moderator of this contest, gave Andrew a dispassionate look. "Only one minute left for you to finish that shot or you forfeit."

The crisp pronouncement splashed my nerves like a bucket of icy water. I shook Ian off, glad when his hands left me and he backed away. Now, I could think again. Andrew gave the moderator a hostile glance. Or tried to. I'd seen sleepy puppies appear more threatening. "'S coming," he muttered, then sloshed the glass's contents into his mouth.

The crowd around the table started to clap. That stopped when Andrew's eyes rolled back and he fell facefirst into his castle of overturned shot glasses. His friends immediately pulled him up and tried to shake him awake, but it was no use. Andrew was, as they say, down for the count.

"Time," Shayla announced moments later, nodding to the waiting attendants. "Take him away."

Lyndsay, my sole remaining opponent, gave the vouchers swirling several inches above the table a hopeful look. Then she gave the shot glass in front of her a grimly determined one. She missed grabbing it on her first try but picked it up on her second. Then she downed the tainted blood in one gulp.

Cheers sounded, but I was more aghast than impressed. Gods, the amount of Red Dragon Lyndsay would've needed to drink over the years to build up her tolerance to this! I hoped she had no idea where it came from. I hoped none of them did. If they knew and still swilled it regularly . . . well, there was a reason the tainted blood was illegal.

"Your turn," Lyndsay said, slamming her shot glass down.

I picked mine up, careful not to make my movements too precise. This liquor was affecting me, but not nearly as much as it would have if I were a normal vampire. I even took a deep breath before swallowing, as if trying to summon up the fortitude. Then I poured the contents into my mouth, held it there for a moment as if fighting not to spit it out, and finally swallowed.

More applause broke out. Lyndsay grabbed her head as if the noise was agony. Then she spewed a stream of red vomit right into the swirling vouchers she'd tried so hard to win. She kept heaving, her body apparently trying to expel most of the Red Dragon she'd consumed. At once, attendants snatched the vouchers out of the air and began shaking the splatter off of them.

"Winner," Shayla announced, pointing at me. The rest of the room roared their disappointment or their victory, depending on how they'd placed their bets. "And the name of our victor is . . . ?"

"Ian's Little Poppet," I declared, shooting him an arch look. As if winning this contest hadn't been enough to get tongues wagging, now there was no chance Dagon wouldn't figure out that Ian had been here tonight.

Ian's lips curled as he came back over to my chair. "Think it's time to take Ian's Little Poppet to bed so she can truly celebrate her victory," he said, to a round of ribald applause this time. He picked me up, ignoring my protest that I could walk, and nodded at the moderator. "If you'll cash us out?"

Shayla flicked her fingers. At once, the vouchers above the table compacted themselves into a squarish shape and then rushed over to her side. Then she indicated the velvet curtain that cordoned off the room beyond this one. "Follow me."

Ian carried me into the room, the vouchers between us and Shayla. Once we were inside, it was so dark I couldn't have seen anything if not for my vampire vision. Still, the effects of all my imbibing must have been catching up with me. I could barely make out the low couches and wide pillows that made up most of the furniture. Shayla led us past that to a door that was made of thick wood in-stead of more velvet hangings. It led to a small, enclosed area with .three more doors. Shayla chose the one on the right and the bright-ness of the light that spilled out made me close my eyes and wince.

I might not be puking or passed-out drunk like my former com-petitors, but I was nowhere near sober. That light hurt. So did my head. Also, either this room was rotating or my brain was doing its own spins. Maybe it hadn't been a bad idea for Ian to carry me, even though I couldn't remember the last time anyone had done that. Still, his arms felt strong and secure and his body was warm and solid and he smelled really, really good . . .

"Stop that," Ian said, lightly tugging my hair. Only then did I realize I'd ripped his collar open to nuzzle his neck.

Instead of being embarrassed, I found myself giggling. "Sorry. Want to eat you," I said with complete sincerity.

"Of course you do. Everybody does," he replied while his grip on my hair held me away from his throat. "But not here. Shayla, if we could hurry this along?"

"Certainly," she said. A light seemed to go off in my aching head. That's right, I had something very important to do.

"Want more Red Dragon," I told her, miming drinking another shot in case she didn't understand. "Now."

Ian sighed. "Ignore her. She's had more than enough."

"Haven't," I said firmly, elbowing him. Why was he trying to stop me? Didn't he know what I was doing? Oh, right, he didn't because I hadn't told him. Whatever.

"Red Dragon," I repeated. "To go," I added, giving Ian another hard elbow when he opened his mouth to argue. "Uncut."

Shayla had been regarding me with boredom until that last word. "Uncut?" she drew out, her eyes narrowing.

I nodded, ignoring how Ian stiffened. "Easier to take." Then I gestured at the vouchers floating between us and her. "All of that for a whole uncut bottle."

"I don't think—" Ian began.

"Tonight," I stressed, marshalling my reeling senses as I watched her eyes flick from me to the compacted bundle of vouchers. "Please," I added to Ian, hoping he understood the subtext. Once more, I needed him to trust me, even if that went against everything he was and everything appearances showed.

He shifted until he was only holding me with one arm. Then he let go of my hair to give Shayla a resigned look. "Give it to her. There'll be no living with her otherwise."

Shayla gave the vouchers another glance. I strained my senses to their inebriated limit. A haze flickered around her, invisible to everyone else. When it turned green, I had my answer. Then she smiled coolly and that haze vanished.

"Very well, but tonight is impossible. I would need time to put together such a specialized order."

"Bollocks," I said cheerily, using one of Ian's terms for calling bullshit. "You've got it here. Drinks were fresher and tasted stronger later in the game."

They must have run out of their original stock of Red Dragon since they hadn't been prepared for a mass drinking event. To keep supplying the contest, they'd had to make more on the spot, but there must not have been enough human blood on hand to dilute the mixture the same way.

"Do you consider yourself a connoisseur?" Shayla asked with false pleasantness.

I hiccupped and it wasn't even fake. "Isn't it obvious?"

"I grow bored," Ian said tersely. I was about to protest until I saw that he was looking at Shayla, not me. "Aside from switching out the potency—which is damn near cheating—she's consumed enough Red Dragon to know the difference between fresh brew and old stock. Give her what she wants, or we'll take our winnings elsewhere and find someone who can."

Shayla drew herself up indignantly. "We are the sole supplier in the state."

Ian snorted. "Second time this week I've heard that."

"Then that other person *lied*," Shayla began furiously.

"Getting bored, too," I interrupted, sagging in Ian's arms.

Ian settled me more comfortably against him. "I know, luv, we're leaving. Shayla, this offer is going once, going twice . . ."

"Sold," she said, glancing at the vouchers again before looking back at us. "Wait here."

"Need to go outside," I said, running my hand down my front as if the thin material of my blue dress was stifling. "Too hot. Need air. Starting to feel . . . sick."

Ian gave me a jaded look. "You're going to paint the walls red in the next five minutes, aren't you?"

I burped and visibly swallowed what came up. "Maybe."

"Yes, go outside." Shayla yanked the door open. "We'll bring the bottle to the weather center's observation deck."

I made sure to grab Shayla and give her a sloppy hug before Ian hauled me back. "Thanks!"

"My pleasure," she said in her most obvious lie yet. "See you soon."

Ian carried me out of the many rooms of the castle, getting back-slaps from some of the people he passed. I didn't know what the hell they were congratulating him for. I was the one who'd won the contest. Once outside, I took in a grateful breath of cold air as

Ian carried me to the end of the bridge. I hadn't been faking about feeling hot and sick. Everything I'd consumed felt like it was hitting me all at once.

As soon as Ian set foot on the ground, the castle and the stone bridge disappeared. Ian walked a little ways away and then set me down near the rocky base of Belvedere castle. Then he waited to see if my legs could hold me before he stepped back.

"I know you aren't truly intending to consume more Red Dragon, so what are you intending with this latest ruse?"

I met his turquoise gaze and gave him a lopsided smile. "Going to paint the walls red, just like you said."

*I*an's gaze hardened until it resembled pale blue-green diamonds. "So the spell *isn't* making you obey my command?"

"Spell works," I said, hiking up my dress as I started to climb the rocky ledge around Belvedere Castle. "Not acting as a Guardian. About to break a lotta laws instead."

He vaulted up after me with one leap, reminding me that I could fly, too. How had I forgotten that? I must be much drunker than I realized. "How so?" he demanded.

"F'eeing a p'isner." Okay, I slurred that too much. I tried again. "Freeing a prisoner. The Red Dragon source. You should help. With your demon brands, could be you held as source one day if you"—loud hiccup—"survive Dagon."

He stared in shock, then hauled me close. "What did you say?"

"Who's drunk, you 'r me?" I asked, exasperated. "Don't you know what your blood is now that Dagon's brands are on you? Eh, maybe you don't. Not like vampires drink themselves when they're hungry—"

"Stop." If his grip on me was any tighter, my bones would crack. But from the wildness in his gaze, he was holding himself back. "You're saying you know the other effect of demon brands?"

"Red Dragon. In your veins. Making you a source," I confirmed. "C'mon, you *must* know. Your friend was a demon-branded shapeshifter—"

"What friend?" he asked instantly.

"Herrrr." Was the ground tilting, or was I swaying? "S'pose it could've been a he," I amended. "Couldn't tell. He or she had shape-shifted to look like Cat's little girl at the execution—"

"Lucifer's bloody bones!" Ian shouted, shaking me until my head felt like it would fall off. "You knew the council had been tricked? You knew they didn't really murder my friend's child? This whole time, *you knew?*"

"You knew she was alive, too?" Somehow, that struck me as funny. "Heh, I thought I had to pretend she was dead to protect her, and here you were pretending she was dead for the same reason. I'd laugh if I didn't think it might come out as vomit."

"*That's* why you insisted Cat be given the executioner's sword!" Even though he was no longer shaking me, it still felt like my brain was sloshing around inside my skull. "Thought you only did that as a gesture of remorse, but if the executioner had tasted a drop of her blood, he'd have known he'd just beheaded a shape-shifter and not Cat's little girl! You made him give up the sword so he'd never get that chance. All this time, in different ways, you've been protecting her!"

"We should probably stop talking about this," I said, staring at the ground. See? It wasn't heaving. It was just my imagination.

"Stop?" Ian repeated. "Veritas, *look* at me."

I refused, so he tilted my head up and forced me to meet his gaze. "It's Ian's Little Poppet now, remember?" I said snippily.

His eyes were blazing with green. "Oh, it is indeed, and more than you realize."

I stared at him, a different sort of dizziness overtaking me. The intensity in his gaze invited me to fall into it as if I were a human under his thrall. Oddly, the thought didn't rankle me. Instead, I found myself fantasizing about surrendering to him. Another wave of dizziness hit me and I swayed. He had me in his arms at once. I found myself smiling. He'd caught me before I fell. And I'd let him. When was the last time I'd trusted anyone to do that?

Then, I felt a set of pings, like sensors going off inside me, and turned toward the weather station at Belvedere's Castle. "Shayla's going there," I mumbled, pointing.

He cast a doubtful look in that direction. "She hasn't left the castle. I've been keeping an eye on the bridge."

"Under us," I said, pointing at the ground.

"A tunnel?" He looked intrigued. "Why do you think that?"

"Put a tracking spell on her when I hugged her." Even drunk, I sounded smug. "Knew she'd go right to her source to fill that bottle. Her aura turned green. She wanted that money."

A gleam appeared in his eyes. "You don't say?"

I didn't like feeling as if I'd let another important secret slip. Damned Red Dragon. Why did people willingly drink that stuff? Made you talk too much. And made you tired, gods, so tired. I could sleep on this rock, if I didn't have to kill a bunch of people first. Eh, I'd deal with what I said to Ian later. Right now, had to free the captive.

I pushed at him. "Gotta rescue the prisoner—"

"No, you need to sit down before you fall down," Ian interrupted. "Stay here. I'll sort this myself."

Outrage had me sputtering. "I can kill 'em all!"

"Of course." Was he stifling a laugh? "You're beauty, you're grace, you'll shoot them in the face."

I smiled. "That's pretty."

"So are you, my lethal one, but you still need to stay here. Shayla might send one of her attendants to check on us. If we're both gone, it will look suspicious."

That made sense, but . . . "You could get hurt."

He laughed. "You're a sweet drunk, aren't you?"

"Not sweet," I said, glaring. "Unkillable."

"Indeed?" he drawled. "Should've plied you with liquor instead of wasting two commands on you, but to your point, these brands make me almost unkillable, too."

I poked him where I could feel the hard lines of the weapon in his coat. "That demon bone in your eyes can kill you."

He gave me a jaunty smile. "Yes, but when people see a vampire, they reach for silver, not demon bone . . ."

"What?" I demanded when his voice trailed off. His smile faded, too, and when he crouched down—when had he lowered me onto the ground? I didn't remember that—he looked serious.

"What?" I repeated, but from the jolt thrumming through my veins, I knew. I'd let slip too many clues and he'd figured it out. If not all of it, enough of it. Maybe I'd always known he would piece it together. That's why I didn't stop him when he lifted my hand and brought it to his lips. A courtly gesture, but there was nothing chivalrous in his gaze. It burned with the intensity of a predator making a kill.

His warm lips touched my skin. Then his fangs slowly pierced my flesh. The bite was shallow. Just enough to draw twin pearls of blood that stood out like rubies against the golden topaz of my skin. Then his long, slow lick erased them and I felt him shudder as he swallowed.

I closed my eyes. *Now you know I'm not only a vampire. Oh, it's been so long since I shared this secret with anyone . . .*

My eyes snapped open when that internal ping went off again. Shayla must be crossing beneath me once more. Since she was going in the opposite direction, she must have completed her task. We needed to move.

"Whatever you want to say, it can wait," I said, suddenly feeling a lot more sober. "Have to storm the castle."

He glanced where the bridge was despite it still being hidden from our view. "Best wait until later, where there are fewer people to stop us."

"Not that castle." I pointed over his shoulder. "Belvedere."

"You should've stayed back," Ian muttered for the second time. "I've done this before, and let me assure you, Red Dragon sources are guarded more securely than Fort Knox. Besides, you're so drunk, you can barely walk."

"Can still fight," I told him. It would've sounded more badass if I hadn't ended my boast with a loud burp, but oh well. "Quit complaining and let's do this."

Then I jumped up and kicked the boulder in front of me with both feet. The tunnel was behind it; I could feel it. But while the boulder smashed as if hit by a wrecking ball, it didn't break through the magic-infused shell around the tunnel.

An alarm began to blare, and it wasn't just the painful ringing in my head after that exertion. Ian pushed me back before I could react. Then he swiftly executed a series of hand movements. The shell in front of us shattered beneath his spell, revealing the tunnel behind it.

"Niiiice." He really was superb with tactile magic.

He threw a grin at me as he ran inside the tunnel. "You should see what else I can do with my hands."

I left that alone and stumbled after him, cursing when my legs wouldn't move in smooth, coordinated strides like his.

"Don't bother," he said, whirling around to stop me in mid-stagger. "We need someone to stay here and stop anyone who comes down the other end of that tunnel. You can still do magic?"

"'Course," I said, affronted.

"Then you stay."

I wanted to argue, but we did need to prevent getting boxed in. Plus, my body might not be cooperating, but my magic would still work. Hopefully. I nodded and sat down right where I'd been standing. "Go on. Yell if you need help."

"I won't," he said and disappeared down the next bend.

Almost at once, I heard what sounded like explosions, then the sharp sound of screams. The tunnel shuddered as the screams abruptly cut off and a rolling cloud of dust filled the air. Another quickly silenced round of screams rang out, then another blast that made the walls tremble. Finally, a shockwave of magic rolled down the tunnel. It diminished with distance, but when it reached me, it was still strong enough to sting.

What kind of supernatural firepower had Ian walked into? "Ian!" I yelled, staggering to my feet. "I'm coming!"

"Stay there!" I heard him shout, and was shocked at how maniacally cheerful he sounded. "I've got this!"

Ian had done all that? I had to admit, I wanted to see the specifics for myself. But then I heard running footsteps coming from the other end of the tunnel and remembered what I was supposed to be doing. Right, the blocking spell.

I started formulating it, frustrated when something that should have come easily now felt as if it took all of my concentration. Damn that Red Dragon! It was kicking my ass worse than any opponent had in recent memory. When the group of guards came into view, the blocking spell still wasn't ready.

If I were acting in my official capacity, I would identify myself as a Law Guardian, arrest them, then take them before the council for holding someone hostage in order to produce an illegal substance. But Ian's spell-sealed command meant I could do none of that. In my intoxicated state, I wasn't even sorry.

"You," I said, pointing at the first two vampires while quickly working up a much simpler spell. "Meld."

They shot toward each other as if pulled by a magnetic superconductor. Then their bodies melded together until they were one double-sized torso, two heads and eight limbs.

"Meld, meld, meld," I said, pointing at the next three.

They smashed into the flesh mass with the same force. Soon, all the limbs going in different directions made the flesh mass continually fall over, right itself, and fall over again.

"What do you remind me of?" I wondered, cocking my head. "Vampire centipede? No, wait, vampire slinky!"

The last two vampire guards were now backing away. I wagged my finger at them. "Ah-ah-ah. Meld, meld."

They screamed as they joined the pile. Their cries and the other guards' howling made me wince. "Oh, stop. This'll wear off in a few hours. You should hear what's going on at the other end of the tunnel. *That* sounded permanent."

The hulking, howling mass of vampires might be making my head pound, but it served to scare off the next group of guards who ran down the tunnel. I gave an approving nod as they ran the other way after seeing what had become of their friends. But one more guard came down the tunnel and didn't stop when he saw the writhing, rolling vampire mass. Instead, he threaded his way around it to stand opposite me.

I didn't have time for this. I still had to finish my blocking spell, which was taking for*ever.* "Your friends who ran were smart," I told him. "Be like them and leave."

He bared his fangs at me. "You don't scare me, witch. I know spells, too." And he began to recite the beginning of a lethal curse.

Couldn't have him do *that* while in the vampire slinky, or was it centipede? Whatever. "My killing spell's faster," I said, flicking my hand in an old, tactile spell. "Splat."

He blew apart, but only in sections instead of goo like he should have. I frowned. My strength must be waning. Hopefully, it was because I was channeling enough of it to fuel the blocking spell. That was the far more important one . . . and when had I fallen? Last I'd checked, I'd been sitting, but now I was lying on the tunnel floor and my skull hurt as if a team of miners were drilling for gold. Worse, I could feel more people coming from the opposite end of the tunnel. From the swell of magic preceding them, they were trueborn witches.

I had to get this blocking spell done *now.* I cast about for an additional energy source. Couldn't do it from the trueborns or practitioners in the castle. Magic bonded to its owner. But there was something near . . . yes, the pond! How did I not think of drawing energy from water before now? Being drunk sucked.

I was pulling everything I could from the nearby pond when Ian came into view. He was covered in blood and dirt and his tuxedo was ripped in several places, but what really puzzled me was the bundle in his arms. It was the size of a burlap bag and smelled like demon and the shot glasses of Red Dragon I'd drunk.

"What's that?"

He gave a brief, admiring look at the carnage beyond me before answering. "The source. Weren't exaggerating about painting the walls, were you? And what is *that*?"

"Vampire slinky," I said dismissively. "Or centipede. What do you mean, the source? It was a *baby?*" Horror filled me and I nearly vomited all the Red Dragon I'd consumed.

"Not a baby," he said with a grunt. "Not human, either. Looks like a winged dog demon." Then he shifted so he had one arm free to haul me up. "Can you walk?"

I stood but immediately sagged. My strength had been spent between the spells and drinking myself stupid. Ian caught me before I hit the ground, then hoisted me over his shoulder.

"Faster this way, anyway," he muttered.

He ran out of the tunnel right as I finally finished the blocking spell. It sealed the tunnel off so no one could enter or leave it. It also formed a seal over the hidden bridge and the magical castle. Now no one could leave any of those places for at least an hour. We should be long gone by then, unless . . .

I hoped I hadn't underestimated the supernatural juice I'd put into the spell. If so, it might only keep everyone trapped for minutes. I was so drunk, I couldn't tell how much I'd put into it. I actually thought I might pass out, and that was *with* being repeatedly bounced on Ian's shoulders as he ran over the uneven ground. He made good time, though. Within moments, the Fifth-Avenue entrance of Central Park was in view.

Then Ian stopped so abruptly, I was catapulted over his shoulders. I didn't hit the ground, though. I was caught midair in what felt like a giant, sticky spider web.

"What fresh hell is this?" I demanded.

"My thoughts exactly," a cool voice answered in Mandarin.

I froze. I knew that voice, could pick it out from thousands. "Xun Guan. What are *you* doing here?"

*I*an didn't wait for a response. He held up his hand, ignoring my scream of "Stop!" and flung a spell at Xun Guan.

I threw a protective spell at the same time. She flew backward from the impact of Ian's spell, and for a few horrified seconds, I didn't know if he'd succeeded in killing her. Then Xun Guan sat up, her waist-length black hair falling out of her normally impeccable bun. A large, rapidly healing hole was in her chest. I could smell the burning scent of silver, but my protection spell must have protected her heart.

"You," she said to Ian with icy fury. "For the crime of using magic to attack a Law Guardian, I sentence you to death."

"No!" I shouted. "It's not what you think. He's with me!"

She tilted her head and gave me a look that normally heralded someone's instant decapitation. "And you are?"

Right, she had never seen me in this appearance before. "Veritas," I said, straining against the invisible web that held me, but unable to move. "It's Veritas, Xun Guan."

Winged black brows went up. Then the smallest of frowns touched her mouth. "The Veritas I know would never allow herself to be caught in so obvious a trap."

"That's true, but I'm really, really drunk." Then I caught one of Ian's hands sliding behind his back. He was about to use tactile magic to hurl another spell at her. "Don't," I said. "She's a friend, Ian."

"She set a magical trap that nearly caught all of us," he replied in a silky tone. "And she just threatened to kill me."

"She didn't know you were my partner in tonight's secret raid," I said in the strongest tone I could muster. "We just shut down a major Red Dragon supplier and killed its source," I lied. "That's why I'm drunk. I had to sample lots of the product in order to get to the right people."

To Ian's credit, not a hint of disbelief showed in his features at my string of lies. Instead, he gave a jaunty bow to Xun Guan. "Always happy to do my civic duty."

"And this?" Xun Guan said, gesturing to the bloody, blanket-clad bundle. "What is this? It reeks of Red Dragon."

Ian must have dropped the source right before he flung that spell at Xun Guan. I didn't know what sort of creature was in that blanket—winged dog demon, Ian had called it?—but if Xun Guan saw anything she deemed threatening, she would kill it. Or she would bring it to the council and the creature's fate would be the same. Either way, I couldn't allow that.

"Someone had a baby there, probably to use its blood to mix with the source's," I said quickly. "It smells like Red Dragon because the source bled all over it when he died."

While speaking, I pushed through my inebriated senses to direct a single command toward that swaddled bundle as Xun Guan approached it. *Baby,* I thought fiercely when she was almost close enough to pick it up. *Turn into a human baby!*

An ear-splitting shriek sounded when Xun Guan reached down and picked up the bundle. Then I almost whooped in relief when she drew back the bloody blanket and revealed pale human skin and two tiny, babyish fists waving in fury.

Xun Guan winced as the baby kept screaming. "One of you, take this," she said, with a jerk of her head. That's when I realized she wasn't alone. Two Enforcers came out from behind the trees about twenty meters away. Neither looked anxious to take the squalling baby, but they didn't dare refuse her.

"I'll take it," I said at once. "There's a baby drop at the fire station not far from here. I'll leave the child there."

"Until then, do I have permission to stop it from screaming?" the dark-haired male asked Xun Guan.

She let out a short laugh. "You could try, but you would fail. Babies' wills are too focused to be affected by our mind control. Humans are only susceptible when they're older." Then her dark brown gaze swung my way. "Prove to me you're Veritas beneath that glamour. What birthday gift did you last give me?"

Even though I was still reeling, I didn't need time to think. "A jade bracelet from the first Imperial dynasty."

Ian whistled through his teeth. "You two must be *special* friends to warrant a gift like that."

Xun Guan stabbed a finger at him even though she didn't take her eyes off me. "Unless you don't want to live long enough to appeal your death sentence before the council, be silent."

"Xun Guan, I told you, he was with me—"

"He shouldn't have been," she said curtly. "Only Enforcers or Guardians are allowed on raids of this level."

"Think you can take me somewhere against my will?" Ian's smile was an open dare. "Try it and I'll kill you."

Xun Guan drew her sword and the ancient, elegant steel caught the moonlight. Then she tilted it and a pale line appeared across Ian's throat. As was her custom, she'd marked the spot she intended to sever.

"Xun Guan, no!" I said, a crazy thought occurring to me. "Ian had every right to be here as my backup!"

Xun Guan didn't relax her stance. "What law protects him as you claim?"

I gulped in a breath of air. I'd need it to help get out this monstrosity of a lie. "The law giving spouses permission to go anywhere their husband or wife is."

"What?" Ian said with all the disbelief Xun Guan showed.

"No," Xun Guan breathed. "He cannot be your husband."

I tried to laugh but it came out as a high-pitched giggle. "We were going to wait to tell everyone, but saving his life takes priority over spoiling the surprise—"

"The surprise?" Ian repeated, his tone bordering on shrill.

I laughed again and it was worse. Cackling witches would envy what had come out of my mouth. "Don't mind him, he's still getting used to matrimony. But as my husband, he's allowed to go anywhere I go. That's why he was my backup tonight. I taught him that spell in case I got into trouble, which he had every reason to believe when you caught me in that web and failed to identify yourself as a Law Guardian."

Finally, Ian got over his horror enough to understand where I was going with this. He still looked rattled, but he stopped arguing. Xun Guan didn't.

"I know who he is," she said flatly. "I find it hard to believe you would lower yourself to marry one such as he."

Anger flashed in Ian's gaze. Then it vanished and he smiled with luxuriant sensuality. "You'd be amazed at what I can get people to do."

"Your wiles are wasted on me," Xun Guan said coldly.

"Obviously," he continued in the same purr. "You're too hot for Veritas. While I'd normally find that arousing, I don't share what's mine. So . . ." he flicked his fingers in a clear translation of *back off*.

Xun Guan gave him another withering look before returning her gaze to me. "I understand why you wouldn't tell the council, but why would you keep news of your matrimony from me?"

I heard the slight waver in her voice at that last word and felt awful. I hated lying to her. Xun Guan was precious to me, but that was the point. I couldn't risk her life if they fought. I also couldn't risk Ian being brought before the council. He'd say something worthy of death within five minutes. Lying was the best way out of this, and while it hurt her, it also saved her. And him. That mattered more than anyone's temporary discomfort.

"I knew you wouldn't approve," I said softly.

She blinked and it could have been a trick of the moonlight, but I thought I saw a tear. Then her lovely expression hardened. "Prove to me he's your husband."

"You want to interrogate the marriage ceremony witnesses?" If so, who could I get to say they were there . . . ?

"No, repeat your vows," Xun Guan stated. "Now."

"Xun Guan." My voice was sharp from the dread erupting in me. "You ask too much. You know how I cherish my privacy."

"He doesn't," she said, using her sword to point in Ian's direction. "I've seen one of his many Internet videos. You ask me to ignore a magical attempt on my life *and* you bringing a civilian to a high-level raid. I cannot do that without proof. If he is what you say he is, why hesitate to repeat your vows?"

Ian's gaze swung toward me. The horror it contained made my body turn to ice. He was going to refuse. Then Xun Guan was going to raise her sword and Ian would conjure up a killing spell and I couldn't get between them because I was stuck in this damn web! Panic swelled until I vibrated from it. I had to stop him before he blasted apart our only attempt to resolve this without someone dying.

Freeze, I thought urgently, trying to will the necessary power out of myself. *For the love of all the gods, freeze!*

Chapter 20

*M*y power spilled out. Not in its usual flash, but like a fog rolling in, from how drunk and depleted I was. For a few moments, I watched as Ian's mouth opened to protest and Xun Guan's sword started rising. Then, they slowed until they both froze where they were. I wasn't sure I'd summoned enough power to encapsulate more than the two of them until I saw the brunet Enforcer freeze in mid ball-scratch and the other Enforcer's head stay half angled so she could get a better look at Ian's ass.

The only one that wasn't frozen was the creature in the bloody blankets. Tiny arms continued to beat at the air while its wails made my head feel like it would split open. It proved Ian was right, though. Only demons and other demon-kin were immune to this type of magic.

I freed Ian from his stasis and started talking fast. "I can't hold this for long, so be reasonable. I don't like the thought of marrying you, but we have to do this. Would you rather die?"

"Yes," he said at once.

Okay, I hadn't been expecting that intractable of a response. "But it's not like the marriage will be *real*."

"Repeating vows in front of witnesses makes it real." He began to pace in front of where I was stuck. He also kept giving Xun Guan's frozen form several dangerous looks. "Why don't we just leave? She certainly can't stop us now."

As if I hadn't thought of that. "Sure. Pull me out of this web and let's get going."

He tried and began cursing when his first touch caused the same impossibly sticky strands to latch onto his hand and not let go. Soon, he was using every magic trick he knew in an attempt to free himself, and his hand still remained stuck.

"Not as easy as you thought, is it?" I said sarcastically. "This spell can only be revoked by the same person who cast it, and I know because I taught it to her."

He gave me a fraught look. "But vampires can never divorce. Worse, our laws say you can kill anyone I shag!"

"Oh, *now* you care about the laws?"

"I care about my freedom." Instantly. "It's all I have left."

I seized on that. "That's right, one of us will probably die before this thing with Dagon is over, so you're not sacrificing your freedom if that turns out to be me!"

"And if it's me, I'd die a married man." He shuddered. "I'd rather take my chances in a fight with her."

The outline around my small time-bubble began to waver. Soon, it would drop. I might only have seconds left. "And if she kills you, you'll go straight to hell, or have you forgotten Dagon's claim on your soul?"

He gave Xun Guan another withering look. "She can't kill me *because* of Dagon's brands on me."

"She's a two-thousand-year-old Law Guardian who knows about demon brands. When her sword won't do the trick, she'll stab your eyes out with the demon bone she always carries on her."

"Not if I kill her first," he replied darkly.

"You can't," I said, anguish gripping me at the thought.

A harsh smile curled his lips. "So I was right about you two. Seems you broke your 'no vampires' rule for her."

Appealing to his reason and residual sense of mercy wasn't working. I had to make a play for his selfishness instead. "Let's say you do kill her. You'd also have to kill the Enforcers, too, since they'd never let her death go unavenged. Then you'd have Guardians, Enforcers, and the council screaming for your blood *plus* a pissed-off demon on your tail. Even if I didn't leave you to them for murdering my friend—and I *would*—how long do you think we'd last with that kind of heat on us? Is being *technically* married to me worth losing your soul and forfeiting your long-awaited revenge against Dagon?"

At last, I could tell I'd hit a nerve, but that stubbornness didn't leave his expression. "Well?" I pressed.

He gave me a hostile look. "I'm thinking."

"The spell's going to drop," I warned him.

Another glare. "And I said I'm *still thinking.*"

I was shaking all over trying to keep this area frozen. All the strain made nausea rocket up in my throat. "Even if we both survive, I won't enforce my claim on you," I said desperately. "In fact, the first thing I'll do is drop you back at that bordello in Poland *and* order you a new carnival orgy, promise!" Then I threw up, spraying a stream of crimson all over him as I lost my fight against the nausea.

"See?" I managed when I finished puking. "Vow sealed with a blood oath."

He looked down at himself in disgust. "This is everything I knew marriage would be."

"I'll take that as a yes," I muttered, and gratefully let the spell drop.

Xun Guan appeared startled to suddenly find Ian behind her instead of in front of her. Then her eyes widened when she saw the bloody vomit coating him. "What? How?" she sputtered.

"He saw me getting sick and rushed over to help," I supplied. Then I let out a small, shaky laugh. "And got caught in your web for his trouble, as you can see."

Her deep brown eyes narrowed as she looked at where Ian had been standing before and where he was now. "No one can move that fast," she said, almost to herself.

"Except me," he replied, an edge in his tone. "Now, if you'd be so good as to release us."

Her gaze met mine. "Not before you prove your claim."

Ian ripped his shirt open with the hand that wasn't glued to Xun Guan's magical trap. I wasn't sure where he was going with that, or why he ripped his jacket off next. Then I saw him grab his three-pronged weapon, the falling fabric concealing what he did from Xun Guan's gaze, and sucked in an appalled breath.

He'd tricked me! He intended to fight her all along!

Ian threw the trident head to the ground and the breath exploded out of me as if I'd been hit by a battering ram. "Not going to repeat my vows while covered in Red Dragon vomit," he said, using his jacket to wipe the last of the smears from his bare chest. Then he used the clean side of it to wipe my face, too.

"Beautiful as always," he said with a hard little smile when he was finished. Then he gave a disparaging glance at Xun Guan. "She'll need her hands free, or have you forgotten what a repetition of the ceremony entails?"

Xun Guan looked at me as she said the necessary words to draw the power out of the web. When it faded, I dropped out of the air and landed in Ian's arms. He held me for a second, glancing over at the nearby gates as if contemplating running for it with me slung over his shoulder. Then, with another twisting smile, he set me on my feet and picked up the weapon he'd so recently flung to the ground.

I knew how much he didn't want to do this, which is why I was surprised when he didn't hesitate before slicing his palm open with the sharp silver prong of the trident tip.

"By my blood, I declare that you are my wife," he said, then held out his bloody hand and the weapon to me.

I was the one who trembled when I accepted the weapon. I'd never in all the long years of my life expected to do this with any-one, let alone him. Even though it was farce, it still felt more mo-mentous than I could handle.

"By my blood," I said as I sliced a line into my palm and then grasped his hand so the vow was made while our blood mingled together. "I declare that you are . . . my husband."

A soft sound escaped Xun Guan and she closed her eyes. The

two Enforcers didn't. They shifted and flicked their gaze around as if trying to alleviate their boredom. Their apathy didn't matter. We'd made the vow in front of witnesses. That was all it took for a vampire marriage to be valid—and forever.

"You were telling the truth," Xun Guan whispered. "He really is your husband."

Ian grunted. "Took me by surprise, too, luv."

Her eyes snapped open. "Do not speak so familiar to me. I might no longer demand your life, but you are *not* my equal."

"Oh, on that we agree," Ian said with a gleam in his eyes.

After the price I'd paid to keep them from fighting, I wasn't about to let them start because of this. I quickly changed the subject. "You never mentioned why you were here with a trap at the ready tonight, Xun Guan."

She finally took her gaze off Ian. "A friend at the police station told me several people had reported seeing a troll dragging piles of gold through Central Park." Her mouth curled down. "That sounded unusual enough to investigate."

Inwardly, I groaned. Nechtan. His gift to me had turned out to cost far more than it was worth. Why hadn't he dropped his glamour before trekking back and forth through the park? Didn't he realize there would be onlookers even at this late hour?

"What were you doing in New York to begin with?" I pressed. "I thought you were in Frankfurt."

She glanced away. "I was mentoring some Enforcers here—"

"But it was your idea for us to leave Frankfurt and come here," the female Enforcer interrupted before a laserlike look from Xun Guan shut her up.

Ian began to laugh. "You were following Veritas, weren't you? How very stalkerish. Were you being modern and tracking her through credit cards and cell-phone signals? Or did you go old school and use a locator spell?"

"Don't be ridiculous," I began, then stopped as a half-sheepish, half-angry expression crossed Xun Guan's face. "You really were following me?" I breathed, shocked. "Why?"

"I was worried about you," she said in a defensive tone. "You have been behaving erratically for months. Then you took a leave from your role as Guardian. You have never done that before!"

I hadn't, but I hadn't wanted anything to distract me from finding Ian and taking out Dagon, even a job I'd devoted most of my life to. "Everyone's entitled to a vacation."

"This was no vacation." Her angry swipe encompassed Ian. "You bound yourself in marriage! That is an act of *lunacy*—"

"We agree again," Ian muttered.

"—and you know it!" Xun Guan continued, her eyes shooting angry darts at Ian before returning to me. "He is a law-scorning whore! *How* could you marry him?"

I was about to respond but Ian got right up in Xun Guan's face. "Did we shag at some point and I forgot about it? Is that why you detest me so? Or is because you're realizing your unrequited love for *my wife* will now forever stay unrequited?"

Her eyes went from cocoa to bright green. "How dare—"

"Enough," I said sharply. "He dares because you've insulted him several times. That insults me, too, and I will not have it. Your opinion is noted, Xun Guan. Now, keep it to yourself."

The glamoured demon dog began to scream louder, reminding me that we needed to get out of there. My blocking spell must be holding on the castle and the tunnel, but it would drop soon. I wouldn't mind if the remaining Red Dragon dealers came across Xun Guan, but I didn't want innocent vampires, witches, and mages to come face-to-face with a Law Guardian and two Enforcers tonight.

"This child needs to be returned to the humans," I said, picking up the swaddled bundle. "And as you can see, there is no troll and no gold, so the calls were a prank, the Red Dragon den has been dealt with, and I'm tired. If there's nothing else?"

"There is more," Xun Guan said with another pointed glance at Ian. "But it will wait."

"Enchanting to meet you," he drawled. "The four of us should have dinner soon."

"Four of us?" she repeated. "There are five here."

"Not them," he said, dismissing the two Enforcers. "I meant you, me, Veritas, and your raging case of jealousy."

"Ian!" I snapped, seeing Xun Guan bristle. Gods, would this night not end without bloodshed between them?

He patted my arm. "Don't fret, I'm finished with her for the moment. Now, let's get this child settled so we can start properly celebrating our most recent wedding night."

I felt Xun Guan's eyes on me as we walked out of Central Park, but that wasn't what unnerved me. It was the dangerous thrill I felt while I wondered if Ian had said that last part because he was still acting out his role . . . or if he was serious.

My thrill only lasted until my nausea came back, which happened in less than one block. There, I retched what looked like a murder scene on the sidewalk. After that, Ian had to carry both me and the little demon as he flew us back to the hotel. Walking would have been easier on my stomach than those aerial dips and whirls, but we didn't want anyone seeing where we were staying. An astute vampire tailing us might have been able to hear us, however. Between the demon's screaming and my retching, I could understand why Ian kept cursing under his breath. What was less clear was why he hadn't just abandoned us both outside the park.

By the time we finally made it back to our hotel suite, all three of us were splattered with vomit. Ian took us directly to the shower, turned it on, and set me and the tiny demon on the shower floor beneath the cleansing spray. I expected him to leave, but he unzipped my dress, helped me out of it, and hunkered down on the floor next to me.

"What're you doing?" I mumbled.

"Cleaning myself up while making sure you don't pass out and choke on your own vomit," he replied, handing me several washcloths. "Tell me if you need help."

"No innuendo about what parts you'd prefer to wash?" I said in a weak attempt at humor.

He gave me a sardonic smile. "Between a shotgun wedding, that thing's constant squalling, and being repeatedly soaked by your vomit, I'm temporarily out of innuendo."

I shouldn't have had anything left in me to still be drunk, but I must have been, because I did something I hadn't done in almost six hundred years: I started to cry. "I'm sorry. I really am. I feel so bad about all this . . ."

Surprise number ten thousand—Ian obviously couldn't stand a woman's tears. He was up in a flash, awkwardly dabbing at my face with a washcloth while patting my shoulder with his other hand. "Now, now, stop that. It's not so bad, I suppose. I've been covered in blood and vomit countless times before, and I should probably get used to demon shrieks, considering the place I'll end up at."

"We'll free you from Dagon," I said, "but if we don't, I'll put in a good word for you with one of the guys down below." Then I blew my nose into the washcloth before handing it back to Ian. Too late, I realized how gross that was and snatched it back. "Uh, sorry. I wasn't thinking . . ."

"Clearly not," he said with a snort. "Know someone in the bowels of the underworld, do you? Anything else you'd like to reveal before you sober up?"

"Gods, no," I moaned, dropping my head onto my knees. I should just pass out before I said something else I'd regret.

A sharp poke on my ankle snapped my head back up again. The baby glared at me, tiny hand poised to poke me again if I kept ignoring it. Right, I had to drop its glamour and see what sort of demon we were dealing with.

"Reveal," I said, so exhausted I resorted to spoken magic.

At once, its chubby pink skin turned into feathers so short, fluffy and soft, they resembled fur. Then its nose and mouth elongated into a snout. Its eyes also changed and its arms and legs stretched into something that resembled paws. It didn't have a tail, but it had two wings that began to tentatively wiggle when I reached out and patted its head.

"Oh, that's what you are," I said with relief. To Ian, I said, "Don't worry, he's harmless."

"Looks like a small Samoyed with a lion's mane and wings," he replied, eyeing the creature.

"He's a Simargl," I said. "Simargls have all the loyalty of a dog combined with the best qualities of a demon—"

"Would that be greed? Or narcissism?" he interjected.

"—combined with the sweet innocence of a child," I went on, glaring at him. "Receiving one is a great honor."

"Receiving?" he said, with a snort. "Is that what the kids are calling it these days?"

He was so crass. "Simargls are created, not reproduced."

He rolled his eyes. "Didn't know you hadn't had *that* talk yet. Well, little Guardian, when one dog demon really likes another dog demon, they give each other a special hug and—"

"Enough!" I said, splashing him.

He only grinned. "At least you've stopped crying."

He was right. Now I was irritated. It felt so much better than the exhaustion, worry, guilt, and nausea that had gripped me. Since I was mostly clean now, I picked up one of the cloths and began to wash all the various stains from the Simargl. He flinched under my touch, then relaxed when he saw I wasn't going to hurt him. Poor thing. He hadn't tried to run even when he expected pain. Now I wished I'd killed *all* the vampires who were helping to hold him prisoner. I hadn't been exaggerating when I said that Simargls were treasured because of how rare they were. To see one so misused made me furious.

The Simargl moved his head to allow me to better access his ears when I cleaned behind them. Sweet creature was trying to please me even though I'd given him no reason to trust me. He must consider me his new owner since Simargls normally only changed hands when they were given a new protector. I kept washing until the Simargl's fur looked more silvery than ashlike, resisting the urge to turn the Simargl over so Ian could see how wrong his "special hug" comment had been. Simargls had no genitalia. The only reason I could tell that this one identified as male was because of his ears. He'd groomed them to be pointy instead of more rounded, something male-identifying Simargls tended to do.

Ian cocked his head. "You treat it like it's fragile, when it must be tough, else it wouldn't have survived."

I gave him a level look. "Just because he can endure hardship doesn't mean he shouldn't experience mercy."

"I suppose that's true," he said, holding my gaze. "It's also why I didn't murder your friend tonight."

The whiplash change in subject left me feeling dizzy, or maybe that was the remaining intoxicants in my system. "What?"

"You're regretting what I've discovered about you, but you shouldn't," he said, stretching his legs out. "If you hadn't been so blind drunk, you never would have revealed your role in Katie's rescue."

"Is that her name?" The council hadn't bothered telling me when they'd handed down her death sentence.

"It is now." Ian's voice softened. "Those sods only gave her a number when they spliced her genes to add ghoul DNA to her half-vampire makeup, but one of the soldiers they captured changed 'K80' to 'Katie' so she'd have a real name. Cat and Bones kept it when they finally found her."

I had to look away because of the sudden stab through my heart. "Yes, names are important," I whispered. "Especially after you've been treated like a thing instead of a person." For a long time, I hadn't been considered worthy of a name, either. That was another thing I owed Dagon for. Then, needing to stop those memories before they wrecked me in my weakened state, I added, "But what does this have to do with you and Xun Guan?"

Something hard settled over his features. "There are few people I truly care about in this world. You already know Mencheres is one of them. Bones is another, and Katie is his wife's child. If I'd believed you'd assisted in Katie's execution, I would have murdered Xun Guan in front of you and considered it payback. Then I would have used my last command to ensure that you continued to help me."

The temperature of the water hadn't changed, but I suddenly felt much, much colder. The Simargl felt the new, icy lethalness coming from Ian, too. He huddled behind me, making barely audible whimpering noises. Then, just like that, Ian's expression cleared and that frigid tension shattered.

"But you helped Katie. Could've cost you your job and even your life if you were caught, yet you did it, and you didn't even know her. Weren't friends with her parents, either. In truth, I can't understand why you did it. Cat and Bones might not realize the debt they owe you, but I do, and I couldn't repay that debt by murdering someone you care for." He paused to let out a self-deprecating laugh. "Even if it meant becoming the living embodiment of my worst nightmares—a married man."

I was touched by the deep sense of honor behind his actions. Once again, he'd chosen to sacrifice himself rather than take the easy way out. Ian might be extremely selective in whom he gave his loyalty to, but once he gave it, he upheld it with everything he had.

"Mencheres and Bones are very lucky to have you as their friend," I said with the utmost sincerity. Then, because I knew he'd hate to be continually praised for his good deed, I moved on. "And once again, let me state that I renounce all my rights as your wife. Seriously, you'll celebrate our victory over Dagon with a new carnival orgy on my dime, promise."

"So you say," he replied with the barest smile.

"I promised with a blood vow. And when vampires make a blood vow, they don't break it."

His scoff was instant. "Vampires break blood vows all the time."

"I don't," I said firmly.

"No, you don't." His tone was soft, but the new intensity in it made me shiver. "Someone like you wouldn't give your word unless you intended to keep it."

Then he reached out, tracing a finger over the curve of my jaw before catching a drop of water that clung to my lower lip. I don't know why it hadn't occurred to me before that he was half naked and I was clad only in my bra and panties. Yes, I was drunk, but I should've been aware of *that*. Especially with how the water clung to his bare upper body as if loathe to abandon the deeply rippled muscles.

Maybe I hadn't noticed before because I'd felt safe. I could hardly remember the last time someone had made me feel that way, and I couldn't blame it on the Red Dragon I'd consumed. I'd been drunk before and had never spilled any of the secrets I'd told Ian tonight. No, for reasons that defied logic, I must trust Ian on a level that I hadn't trusted anyone since Tenoch. It made no sense, yet I couldn't deny it. Not with so many of my secrets laid bare before him. But now, that sense of safety changed, turning into something else. Something far stronger and not at all safe, considering the ferocity of what I was feeling.

"You shouldn't touch me like that," I whispered.

"Why?" His voice was as low as mine, but the look in his eyes wasn't gentle. It was full of the same dark wildness that seethed inside me. "Afraid I'll take advantage of you in your inebriated state?"

"No," I said, moving closer to him. "If you keep touching me like that, I'll lose control and take advantage of *you*."

His deep, sensual laugh felt like it brushed my most sensitive nerve endings, leaving them aching for more. When he leaned closer, I met him halfway, and when I slid my hands over his chest, I felt how much he wanted me in the sudden clenching of his muscles and the changing of his eyes to purest emerald.

That's why I was shocked when he grasped my hands and set me back. "No. You've already done many things you'll regret when you sober up tomorrow. I won't let this be one of them."

"You're rejecting me?" I asked with complete disbelief.

A harsh laugh escaped him. "Yes, and if my cock could talk, it would be screaming its disagreement. But while you've been more honest with me drunk than you've ever been sober, I don't know if this is real. And if it isn't, then I don't want it."

He was serious. I felt it in the finality of the way he set me back. How admirable of him, dammit. I leaned against the shower wall and let out a frustrated sigh. "Your unbreakable sense of honor is your biggest damn secret, isn't it?"

He laughed more naturally this time. "Never tell anyone. My reputation would be ruined." Then he touched my face with affection instead of enticement. "And your biggest secret is that you're demon-branded, like I am."

Maybe it was my exhaustion. Maybe everything I'd drunk hit me with its final, best shot. Either way, I did what I should have done before I revealed too many of my secrets.

I passed out.

Chapter 22

*N*ip. Nip, nip, nip!

"Stop it," I muttered, swiping at whatever was nipping me. A frightened squeak made me open my eyes and sit up. Immediately, I wished I hadn't. Even that small movement made my head clench as if it were being compressed by a vise.

Through barely open lids, I saw the Simargl dart under the covers. I didn't remember getting tucked into bed, let alone the Simargl getting tucked in with me, but here we both were. Now, I'd terrified the poor thing.

"I'm sorry," I said, wincing because each word made that pitiless hammering in my head even louder. But the Simargl was still shivering beneath the covers and I hated that I'd scared him. "I'm not mad at you," I continued, trying to croon as I petted the blankets over him. "It's okay. You can come on out."

Slowly, his head peaked out. I smiled encouragingly even though it felt like my face split from the effort. It had been nearly a thousand years since I'd last had a hangover. It was every bit as horrible as I'd remembered. Worse, even. Had I longed for death to stop the pain like I did now?

Finally, the Simargl came all the way out from beneath the blankets. Once he did, he looked beseechingly at the door.

"What?" I asked in confusion. "You don't need to go out to pee; you don't have those parts."

The Simargl's look-at-the-door, look-at-me gestures grew more frantic. Something had him agitated. I didn't know what it was, but it obviously involved the other side of the door.

I got up, then instantly grabbed my head because it felt like it was about to explode. I only managed not to throw up because the thought of how much that would hurt scared me pukeless. Worse, the sun was up. All that light streaming through the windows made me recoil as if the rays posed a real danger, like all the old vampire myths claimed. By the gods, had the sun always been that horribly, hideously *bright*?

A knock on the door felt like it boomed through to the back of my skull. "Room service," a male voice called out.

Had Ian ordered breakfast? If so, then sensing the hotel attendant must be what had rattled the Simargl. He didn't like strangers, judging by how he cringed away from the door.

"Coming," I mumbled, deciding I could use a sip from the attendant's neck, anyway. Maybe some fresh, clean blood would help with the relentless pounding in my head. I was almost at the door when the Simargl threw his paws around my leg and used all his strength to try and stop me.

"What?" I began, then looked at the door with new understanding. I didn't sense anything threatening on the other side, but everything the Simargl was doing warned *Danger!*

"Be right there," I called out, changing tactics as I gestured for the Simargl to hide under the bed. Once he did, I started looking for my weapons. "Just have to get my robe—"

The door burst off its hinges and nearly hit me as it flew across the room. Then a grinning attendant pushed a meal cart into the bedroom. Before he'd finished crossing the threshold, vampires started to come out from beneath it, so that the small cart reminded me of the clown car back at the Polish whorehouse.

They weren't just vampires, I realized when my defensive spell bounced off the first ones it hit. They were also trueborn witches, aka demon-kin, and that made them very dangerous. My freezing spell wouldn't work on them. Neither would most of my magic, and I was hardly up to fighting form when it came to conjuring something more powerful. That's why I threw myself at them and began to brawl the old-fashioned way.

The other bedroom door burst open. Ian, clad in only a pair of black jeans, joined the fray. After a few moments of catching his movements out of the corner of my eye, I realized he must have been holding back in our first fight. He'd been formidable but not unbeatable then. Now, he looked like a grim reaper with terrible anger-management issues. Soon, I was only getting the stragglers because Ian tore into the brunt of the attackers with such effective, gleeful viciousness; it left body parts flying and much of the hotel room demolished.

"Love a good slaughter in the morning!" he shouted before his next aerial assault drove five of them through the wall and into the next hotel room. It left me facing four, and I managed to take care of two of them before the bed flipped over, revealing the cringing, whimpering Simargl.

"There you are!" the ivory-skinned, Nordic-looking vampire exclaimed. "Boss's tracking spell on your blood wasn't wrong after all."

I dove in front of him, snatching up the Simargl and holding him between my back and the window.

"Come closer and I'll carve out your heart," I warned, holding my very bloody silver knife in front of me for emphasis.

Nordic vamp and his swarthier, brunet buddy exchanged a glance before they looked at the food cart behind them. It was vibrating and magic tasted heavy in the air around it. That meant it probably contained a portal. How else could a dozen or so vampire-witches use it to get in this room?

"Why don't you stop fighting?" Nordic vamp suddenly said. "All we want is the source. Give it to us, and we'll let you live."

His inky-haired companion grunted. "That's not what the boss ordered."

The blond gave him a look that said, *I'm lying, stupid!* Then he smiled at me as if I hadn't noticed the subtext. "Come on, you don't want to die for a furry-winged version of heroin, do you? And believe me, your other friend is coming with us one way or the other. I've seen his picture on the demon boards. He's got a bounty on his head that'd make leveling this hotel worth it to get him."

I gave a quick, calculated look around, wincing when I heard more walls break in the next room. Ian and I could probably win this fight, but at the cost of how many innocent lives? We couldn't let this brawl spill out to the rest of the hotel floor. Dagon had put a bounty out on Ian. These mercenaries wouldn't worry over collateral human damage to collect it.

The wall nearest me suddenly burst open and Ian tumbled into the room. He had two vampires by the neck when a vicious twist narrowed that number down to one. Then, in an impressively athletic move, he punted the head he'd twisted off while simultaneously breaking the back of the vampire in his arms.

"Goooooooal!" he cried out when that head sailed right between the two vampires opposite me. Then he ripped the arms off the vampire he still held and began stabbing him with the rapidly withering limbs.

Some people were cold and ruthless fighters. Others were reckless yet talented. Ian combined all those traits with a joy that made watching him feel like taking in a blood-soaked ballet. "I could watch you fight all day long," I said with complete sincerity, but more vampires were starting to come out from the food cart. I was right; the damned thing was a portal.

This had to end before anyone got hurt who didn't deserve to. I had never wanted to do this next thing in front of Ian, especially with an additional audience, but I had to. If I didn't, I'd be just like these mercenaries—fine with sacrificing the lives of innocent people to suit my own purposes. I set the Simargl down and used my knife to slice open my hand, running it over the Simargl's gray head. Then I sliced it again and ran my blood over Ian's arm.

"Stop fighting them," I told Ian as more vampires came from the portal in the food cart. "Go with them instead. Remember what I told you last night because I *will* see you again soon."

Then I stabbed the silver blade into my heart and twisted it.

"No!" I heard Ian scream before agony stole his voice away. I felt Ian clutching me, then the new, horrible pain of fire erupting all over me. Ian let me go when the fire intensified, which was a good thing, because I exploded.

I didn't feel anything after that.

*D*ying is terrifying the first dozen or so times you do it. It flat out takes a while to get used to being a disembodied form flying toward the cusp of eternity. And don't get me started on how horrifying it is when you first see the Warden of the Gateway to the Netherworld. Let's just say it's a good thing you no longer have bowels or you'd empty them all over yourself.

But hundreds—more?—of times later, I only felt a mild sense of trepidation as I zoomed toward the river that separated this world from the next. Of course, there wasn't really a river; that was a construct of my own mind. So was the image I first saw of the figure that stood at its bank. The image changed according to individual beliefs. If I worshipped ancient Egyptian gods like Mencheres did, I'd see Aken the Ferryman. Right now, I saw the first god I'd ever worshipped—and shuddered.

Then that image dissolved into the reality of a tall man with bronze skin; silver hair streaked with gold and blue; and eyes that flashed so brightly with silver, I couldn't see their actual color. When he saw me, he gave the barest shake of his head, as if disappointed that I'd died *again*. But before I was launched back to the land of the living, I said, "Wait!"

I hoped he'd listen. Sometimes he did, sometimes he didn't.

His hand beckoned me forward. I felt myself zoom up until I faced him. Thankfully, he'd decided to listen this time.

"What do you seek from me?" he asked.

I'd long since ceased being afraid of him, but I'd never felt comfortable with him. Whatever name religions gave him, the Warden
of the Gateway to the Netherworld was not a relaxing figure. "I
need an hour to pass in my world, but no more than two, before
you return me to the ones I marked with my blood."

He didn't smile. That would be too human a reaction, but the
faintest flicker in his expression made me wonder if I'd amused
him. "Do you?"

I'd once begged him for something he didn't give me, so I didn't
know what my odds were with this request. Unlike the other one,
this was small, and hopefully, he was in a generous mood. "Please,"
I said. "This is very important."

He extended a hand and a small, narrow vessel appeared on the
river. "You know the cost of a bargain with me and what you forfeit if you fail."

"Oh, I'll fill your boat," I said with grim purpose.

Without another word, I was zooming backward and the Warden, the river, and everything else faded from my sight. Then
brightness exploded in my vision and I saw the tops of buildings
as if I were falling from a great height. I instinctively braced, but I
didn't have a body, so I felt no impact when I hit one of them.

I went through several floors, everything blurring, before I found
myself looking down on an underground parking garage. Ian was
there, and he looked far more worse for wear than when I'd last
seen him. He had multiple silver harpoons protruding from him
that were secured by chains. No fewer than a dozen vampire guards
held the other ends of those chains. The tips of the harpoons must
have been hooks, because every time Ian moved, they ripped open
large pieces of his flesh.

The Simargl was there, too, chained inside a metal cage. The Nordic vampire stood next to the cage. From the way he kept checking
his watch, he was expecting company soon. Time to crash this party.

I aimed for Ian's shoulder that I'd marked with my blood and
everything went black. Before I could see again, I caught snatches
of conversation.

"Where'd all those ashes come from?"

"They're pouring out of his shoulder! Look!"

"Now something's moving in them."

"It's big. It's coming up out of the ashes. What is it?"

"Holy shit, it—it looks like a woman!"

I brushed my silvery gold-and-blue hair out of my eyes, my gaze finding Ian. For a split second, I saw him through the *otherness* in me instead of my vampire nature. Lights burst from him, hallmarks of the integrity and inner nobility I already knew he had. But darkness also swirled around those lights, and it wasn't only from his brands. Ian had had inner demons long before he made his deal with Dagon.

At that same moment, Ian looked at me. Recognition lit his face, making me glad I'd showed him this appearance before. I'd half expected him to be frightened when he realized I was the creature forming from the ashes near his feet. His captors certainly screamed as if gripped by terror. But elation washed over Ian's expression. Then he bent to yank me into his arms despite the harpoons tearing bigger holes into his flesh.

A spray of his blood hit me. Rage took over. They had hurt him. They had hurt him and he'd let them because I'd told him to go with them. Now, I would avenge every single drop of his blood. I let my hands grip his for the briefest moment. Then, naked except for the ashes clinging to me, I launched myself at Ian's captors.

The good thing about having my former body explode is that it cured me of my hangover. This new body wasn't exhausted or filled with chemicals. That meant I was at full magical and physical capacity. I unleashed my powers like a fireworks finale on the Fourth of July. Truth be told, I might have been showing off a little. Ian had really impressed me with his fighting skills. Now, I was showing him what I could do.

When I was finished, nothing in the garage moved except me, Ian and the Simargl, who was doing circles in his cage in excitement. "Missed you too," I told him, making a mental note to give the Simargl a name as soon as possible.

I pulled a coat off one of the dead guards. The coat was blood-stained, but it was black, so the blood didn't show as much on it. It would have to do until I could get some real clothes. I shook the worst of the gore off it before I put it on. Then I pushed my hair back, wishing I had a clip or hair tie. The long tricolored mass always seemed to swirl around my shoulders as if blown by a hidden breeze when it was down.

Finally, I used magic to blunt the forked edges of the harpoons embedded in Ian so I could remove them without taking out more hunks of his flesh. When they were all out, Ian stared at the dismembered remains of the bodies, at the wreckage done to several cars in the garage, and then, finally, at me.

His former elation was gone. Now, the full weight of everything that had happened was in his gaze.

"I told you I'd see you again," I said in a feeble attempt to lighten the tenseness of the situation.

"That you did." He let out a short laugh. "And then you exploded all over me."

A weird sense of shyness overtook me. Then again, I had exposed myself in the most extreme way possible by doing that, so perhaps it wasn't so weird. Still, I tried to deflect. "It looked worse than it was. You saw your shape-shifter friend temporarily die when she let herself get decapitated by the council's executioner—"

"Stop," he said shortly. "No more lies, half-truths, or omissions. At first, I thought you were a demon-possessed vampire because you could do magic by your will alone, something no vampire can do. Then I tasted your blood and thought you were demon-branded, like me. Thought it was Dagon who'd branded you and that's why you wanted him dead, but now . . . I have no idea what you are. You're right; I've seen demon-branded people 'die' before. They don't spontaneously catch fire and explode. They also don't rise from a pile of ashes that somehow poured from the same spot where you marked me, and their eyes don't glow *silver* like yours did, so for the last time, *what are you?*"

I found myself wishing I was still drunk. It would be so much easier to admit to this next part if I had chemicals numbing my nervousness. "You know about the vampire half. The other half . . ." I gave a hapless shrug. "Depending on the culture or beliefs, there are different names. Demigod. Nephilim. Phoenix. Titan. Hellspawn—"

"Was one of your parents an angel, a demon, or a god?" he interrupted.

Only Tenoch had ever known the truth about me, and he'd exhorted me countless times to tell no one. All those long-ago warnings rang in my head as I said, "I once asked my father what he was because I couldn't figure it out. He never answered me, and he's not the type you press. You'll see what I mean."

His gaze narrowed. "What do you mean, I'll see?"

My swipe encompassed the corpses strewn around the garage. "I couldn't come to you immediately or you'd still be at the hotel with too many innocent people close by. I also couldn't wait too long or they would've delivered you to Dagon. For that kind of precision, I had to make a suitably large offering. My father will be here soon to collect it."

As if that had summoned him, half the garage suddenly turned into blackest darkness, and a ghostly boat sailed over a river that morphed out of nowhere. Ian screamed when he saw the figure at the boat's helm, his pale skin turning dead white.

"It's all right!" I said quickly. "He's not here for you. He's here for them."

Ian's gaze swung back toward me with a mixture of horror and disbelief. "The bloody *Grim Reaper* is your father?"

"What you're seeing isn't what he really looks like. On this side of the veil, you see what you fear."

"I see an enormous cloaked skeleton wielding a huge scythe," Ian said promptly. "That's not what you see?"

I looked at my father, seeing a tall man with silver, gold, and blue hair; strikingly beautiful features; and deep bronze skin. The Warden's true form was so similar to my real appearance, I had to constantly wear the glamoured disguise of a slim blonde Law Guardian to avoid being recognized as his child.

"No, that's not what I see," I said, meeting my father's lightning-like gaze before I looked away. Then I gestured to Ian's former guards. "Your offering, Warden."

My father extended his hand and ghostly visages rose up from the corpses before they were compelled into his boat. None went happily. They all screamed much the way Ian had when he saw my father. The only one who wasn't afraid was the Simargl. He pressed against the bars of his cage as much as his chains allowed, making noises that were similar to happy yips. My father looked at him and gave him the barest nod—the highest form of approval I'd ever seen from him.

"You will care for him," he told me. A command, not a request. "His prior owner treated him in an unworthy manner. I will inform him of the change."

I didn't mind the order. I'd already decided to do that anyway. But I was surprised by that last part. "You know who his former owner is?"

For the second time, I was sure I'd amused my father even though his expression didn't change. "Yes. It is Dagon, and he was just leaving."

Ian and I turned around at the same moment. I couldn't see my expression but it was probably as shocked as Ian's when I saw that Dagon had, at some point, materialized behind us.

$\mathcal{I}$ hadn't seen Dagon in over four thousand years. The demon looked exactly the way I'd remembered: tall, blond, boyishly handsome and with a little smirk that rarely faded no matter what atrocities he was inflicting. That smirk grew when he saw Ian, then dropped entirely when he looked at me. Dammit. I hadn't taken the time to reapply my glamour so Dagon would only see the Law Guardian appearance I'd been hiding under.

"You," he said in astonishment. "I thought by now you *had* to be dead!"

I'd had countless dreams about what would happen when I finally faced Dagon again. The details varied, but they all ended with me stabbing demon bone through his eyes to send him to the fate he so richly deserved. Now, I was caught off guard and unprepared, but I couldn't let him see how rattled I was.

"You of all people should know how hard I am to kill."

Hatred dripped from every syllable. Dagon's smirk returned when he heard it. I fought not to tremble from a mixture of blind rage and remembered despair. Time was supposed to lessen the intensity of all things, yet in that moment, I hated and feared Dagon just as much as I had all those millennia ago, when I'd been nothing more than his favorite prop.

He wagged a finger at me in the playful way people did when they caught a child being naughty. "*You* must be the troublemaker who divested me of my latest soul acquisition. Very clever of you to mute the tether in Ian's brands, but now, it's time for me to take him back."

I moved in front of Ian before either he or Dagon had a chance to twitch. "He's not going anywhere with you."

Dagon's face darkened like a sky full of deadly weather. "Isn't he? You should remember what happens to people who upset me."

"Is that a threat?" My father asked the question in the mildest tone. Dagon still stiffened as if he'd been slapped.

"Of course not, my lord," he said, laughing as if we'd all shared a joke. "That would violate our agreement."

"It would, so you may leave now," the Warden of the Gateway to the Netherworlds replied. Again, it wasn't a suggestion.

Dagon smiled at my father but gave me and Ian a look that promised bloody vengeance. Then, he disappeared.

My father didn't look at me, but I knew he would make sure Dagon didn't pop back up to murder us anytime soon. He might not care for me in the way that mortals cared for their children, but he wouldn't tolerate one of his commands being broken only hours after giving it. *That*, I could count on.

Of course, that command went both ways. Long ago, my father had commanded me never to kill Dagon. I fully intended to go back on that order. And Dagon might not try to kill me *today*, but he would absolutely start plotting my murder now that he knew I was still alive. When it came to our hatred of each other, neither of us was rational or obedient.

My father didn't look at me when he left. He simply turned that boat full of screaming spectral passengers around and sailed back into the unfathomable darkness he'd appeared from. Then that darkness vanished, replaced by the blandness of the garage with the smashed cars and the bodies strewn around it.

I went over to the Simargl's cage and broke it, then unwound him from all the chains around him. As soon as the Simargl was free, he started flying around me in happy circles.

"I'm going to call you Silver," I told him. "Do you like that?" An enthusiastic yip was my answer. Silver it was, then.

I looked at Ian. He still hadn't moved except for his eyes. They raked over me, the body-filled room, and the area where my father had appeared and disappeared. His face was no longer as pale as fresh snow, but his jaw was set so tight, I could hear the cartilage cracking from the strain. The silent tension grew until I couldn't stand it anymore.

"Don't worry, I don't expect you to be okay with this. The vampire race defaults to rejecting people who are a combination of different species." I let out a sharp laugh. "I should know; I've tried and failed to stop the hostilities that have boiled over between vampires and ghouls when 'abominations' like me are discovered."

Ian might have been against Katie's execution, but there was a world of difference between not wanting your friend's child to be murdered and continuing to partner with someone who was half vampire and half of a species that couldn't easily be named. Worse, my powers were everything vampires and ghouls feared when they talked about the perils of mixing different species together.

"It's fine," I went on. "All I ask is that you don't reveal what you know about me to anyone else."

Tenoch would've killed him to ensure his silence. Once, I would've, too. At some point during the short amount of time we'd spent together, I'd started to care for Ian. That was supremely stupid of me, but it was still true.

"We'll go our separate ways," I continued more briskly. "Dagon still can't find you with your brands muted, so you'll be fine if you keep yourself hidden. I still intend to take him down, so you'll really be fine once he's dead."

If I kill him, the pessimistic part of me added, but I didn't say it out loud because I was trying to sound confident. I was also trying not to show how much it would hurt when Ian turned around and walked away. But Tenoch had long prepared me for people being unable to accept what I was. Watching millions slaughter each other over far fewer differences during the thousands of years of my life had proved Tenoch correct.

I was so sure of Ian's rejection, it took a moment for me to register what he was saying. ". . . don't know about you, but I'm starving. Feels like I haven't had a decent meal in days."

"What?" His reaction to this momentous revelation couldn't be something as simple as *hunger.*

He also pulled a coat from a dead guard, shook it so the worst of the gore flew off, and put it on. Then he walked over and gave me a light whack on the ass.

"Half deaf as well as half demigod, hmm? What, your ears didn't fully regenerate along with the rest of you? I'll say it louder, then: Follow me. I'm peckish and I know the perfect place where we can indulge in a feeding splurge."

$\mathcal{I}$ did a warding spell on the Simargl so that Dagon wouldn't be able to track him from his blood anymore. Thank you, Nordic vampire, for spilling that important detail. Then I covered his cage with another dead guard's coat so his wings didn't attract stares when we went outside. Several blocks later, Ian banged on a side door labeled "Crimson Fountain, employee entrance."

The door opened and a young woman with purple hair and dark eye makeup opened the door. "Job interviews don't start for another hour," she began, then stopped when she got a good look at Ian. "But you can wait inside," she added, her scent changing until lust covered the heavy chemical tang from her perfume.

"Grand," he said, walking into the building. I followed, which made the corner of her mouth curl down in disappointment. Then Ian's gaze captured hers and his eyes turned green. "Gather together the rest of the employees and bring them here."

She turned around without another word. Minutes later, about half a dozen people shuffled into the narrow hallway. "Is this everyone?" Ian asked the purple-haired girl.

"So far," she said. "More'll show up after six when the main shift starts."

"Bring them to me as soon as they come in. As for the rest of you," his bright green gaze landed on each until they were all under his thrall. "You don't see me, this woman, or our creature until we tell you that you do. You don't hear us, either. Now, go about your business as usual."

They turned and walked away, some wondering out loud why Dahlia had asked them to come see an empty hallway.

"Cancel the interviews for today," Ian told Dahlia next. "But before you do that, show us the VIP section and turn the music on. It's quiet as a tomb in here."

She nodded, and we followed her through what was obviously a club. I was surprised to see wooden coffins set up around the stage. Then I noticed large glass fangs over the bar, mock headstones making up the backs of chairs, and stakes for some of the beer taps and understood. Now, the cheesy name for the establishment made sense.

"You brought us to a fake vampire bar?"

Ian set Silver's cage down beside the bar, then threw a grin at me. "The owner and I are friendly, though he thinks I'm another poser instead of a real vampire. Doesn't know a bit about the undead world, either, poor fellow. That's why Dagon would never think to look for us here."

He was right. I'd expected us to either flee the city or run to an ally's house. Not go to a club that was a bad stereotype for everything humans normally thought of when they heard the word *vampire*.

"Think it's safe to let him out? Or will he eat the staff?" Ian asked, tracing the bars on Silver's cage.

"Simargls are vegetarian," I replied, offended on Silver's behalf.

"Bring him whatever veggies you've got," he told Dahlia when she came back after turning the music on. She'd turned the house lights down and the club lights on. Now, the club was mostly dark except for multicolored beams that crisscrossed over the empty dance floor and the occasional fog or strobe effect.

"VIP section's over here," Dahlia said, walking up a flight of stairs. After I petted Silver and told him to stay, I followed Dahlia to the second floor. In the far corner, ropes and curtains cordoned a room with long black couches, its own bar, and a great view of the dance floor, if you kept the curtains open.

Ian didn't. He closed them and took his coat off before lounging on the nearest couch. Dahlia's gaze swept over Ian's bare upper body as if he'd compelled her to memorize every detail of how his creamy skin stretched over muscles that rippled with his slightest movement. When she licked her lips, I found myself bristling with what could only be jealousy.

Ridiculous. I'd promised Ian an orgy on my dime as soon as this was over. How could I be resentful of someone merely *looking* at him? But I was, so much that my scent soured, until I might as well have sprayed myself down with a bottle labeled Jealous Bitch.

Ian's gaze touched mine. I quickly glanced away. He couldn't know about my latest irrational flash of possessiveness. By the gods, I still needed to have *some* secrets from him!

"She's obviously into you, so you should start your feeding splurge with her," I said, trying to prove I didn't care about anything that might happen between the two of them.

Ian's mouth curled into a slow grin. Great. He'd probably sensed my possessiveness and was amused by it. *You're being a fool!* I told myself sternly. It didn't matter. After everything that had happened, I was out of the reserves I normally drew from to hide what I was feeling.

But I didn't have to stand here and be mocked for it. I spun around. "I'm going to check on Silver—"

"Wait." It wasn't the command in Ian's tone that stopped me. It was the dangerous amount of intensity in his gaze when I turned back around.

We stared at each other. An electric jolt went through me when his smile faded and naked hunger overtook his expression. "Come back here, Veritas."

The new throatiness in his voice beckoned me more than his words. Once again, the smart move would be to walk away. Instead, I found myself walking toward them as if I'd been hypnotically compelled. I didn't even have Red Dragon to blame my actions on anymore.

His gaze filled with green. I didn't need to see my eyes to know that mine had probably started glowing green, too. An unbearable need swept over me, drowning out everything else. Yes, I should turn around and leave. But I didn't want to.

"Go," Ian told Dahlia, the vibration in his voice telling me he used his power on her. "Close the drapes behind you. Don't come back or even think about us until I summon you."

Dahlia left at once. Seeing her go gave me a brief moment of sanity. I started to follow her, but Ian got up and grabbed me. I stared at the pale hands gripping my arms instead of at him.

"What do you think you're doing?" I asked in a low voice.

"This."

I gasped when he yanked me down onto the couch. All my nerve endings jumped at the feel of his hard body on top of mine. I considered saying what a bad idea this was, but discarded that when his mouth covered mine.

His mouth was firm, but his lips were satin, and his kiss dared me to deny the heat blasting through me. I lost that dare, parting my lips without hesitation. He deepened the kiss, tongue twining with mine until lust made me dizzy. His taste, his scent, the way his hands moved in my hair, the sound he made when he sucked on my tongue . . . I was melting and burning at the same time.

Then I arched against him when he caught my lower lip with his fangs, lightly piercing it. The nip flavored our kiss with the tang of my blood. I scored his lip with my fangs, moaning when I tasted his blood. Ambrosia couldn't compare. I scored his tongue next, then sucked on it. His kiss became even more erotic. That deep inner ache began to throb and my control evaporated. Too much so.

I knew I'd gone too far when he shifted and I glimpsed his back over his wide shoulders. It was streaked with crimson and my hands were also red. At some point, I must have ripped bloody tracks into his skin.

"Sorry!" I said, snatching my hands away.

"I'm not." He grabbed my hands and put them on his back again. "I want more."

He ripped my coat open. I was naked beneath it, and his gaze went molten as it raked over me. "Stunning," he rasped. "Can scarcely believe you're real."

Oh, I was real, and I needed him to never stop kissing me. I pulled his head down and his mouth once again slanted over mine. Then I groaned when my bare chest touched his. His muscles were so hard, so taut, but his skin . . . silk had never felt this luxuriant. I rubbed against him to feel more. Then his hands began to move over me. Everything that had ached now felt like it was burning beneath his touch. I felt more volatile than I had right before I'd exploded. Soon, I was making incoherent noises against his mouth.

He slid between my open legs, then twisted his hips so the bulge in his jeans rubbed me where I throbbed the most. Each sinuous stroke had me arching against him, until I was gripping him with my thighs as tightly as I held him with my arms. I needed to have him inside me. I couldn't wait. There was only one thing in my way—the damn jeans he still wore.

He let out a growling chuckle when I tore at the front of them until dark fabric flew in every direction. Then he sat up and caught my hands. "No," he said, the single word stunning me. "Not until you stop holding back."

What?

"I'm not holding back," I began, only to have him fling me against the couch with such force, it sent me and the sofa sliding across the room.

He stalked over when the wall finally stopped the couch. "Liar. The only time you weren't was when you tore my back up." With each step, his voice deepened. "But after you apologized for that, you haven't drawn my blood since. I won't tolerate your half response. I want all of it, and if you keep holding back," he leaned over, denying me the kiss I sought in favor of nearly yanking my legs open, "I'm going to torture you with pleasure until I break your control."

A wild thrill ran through me that at once became muted with caution. "I can't. I'd hurt you."

"Good," he said with a dark laugh. "Looking forward to it."

I took in a breath to argue. It exploded out of me as his mouth descended between my legs. He didn't tease me with ever-deepening flicks of his tongue the way he had when we first kissed. He devoured my flesh with the same abandon he'd demanded I give to him. My loins clenched with band after band of unbelievable pleasure. I gripped his shoulders as my gasps turned into loud cries.

"Let go," I heard him mutter against my flesh. "Give me all of you."

His tongue had to be made of fire. Only that could explain the way it seared me. I didn't remember falling to the floor, but I must have, because wood replaced the soft leather of the couch. Splinters stabbed my fingers from how hard I dug my nails into it. I didn't register the pain. Not when a new series of deep swirls yanked my back off the floor.

Cries kept spilling out of me, so loud they would have sent the club's employees running if Ian hadn't mesmerized them into neither hearing nor seeing us. Then another series of strokes brought a new rush of ecstasy with the suddenness of a ripcord being pulled. The release I needed was right there—

He tore his mouth away, denying me the orgasm I'd been moments from. "No. Not until you truly let go."

Frustration made my hand whip out faster than I could think.

Then I stared in horror at the bright imprint on his cheek. "I—I am so sorry—"

He blew on my swollen, aching flesh and the instant clench of pleasure stole my voice. "The slap is better, but still not enough." He chuckled before another teasing breath brushed my clitoris like a cluster of feathers. The pleasure only heightened my need, as did the barest flick of his tongue next.

My hands went to his head to urge him back down for more. He caught them, holding them against my stomach. "Not until you unleash *all* you've been holding back. Until then, enjoy the torture." Low, wicked laugh. "I know I will."

He kept bringing me to the edge only to yank me back as if he were the Orgasm Whisperer and knew exactly when to stop. It wasn't long before I considered using magic to make him cease the exquisite torment. At the same time, a darker part of me wanted to let go, the way he urged. The repeated whiplash from passion to denial shredded through the last layers of my control. I was no longer concerned with going too far or hurting him. I couldn't think beyond the need.

I barely registered Ian's growl of approval when the chains broke on the deepest parts of me. Suddenly, I had more than enough strength to yank free from his grasp. I flung Ian off me hard enough to send him smashing into the wall on the other side of the room. Concrete and plaster burst from the impact his body made, and I didn't care. I lunged toward him, almost feral in my need to have him.

He was faster, meeting me in the middle of the room. He grabbed me before slamming both of us against the nearest wall. Another cloud of concrete, dust and debris burst into the air. Then his mouth crushed mine as he yanked my thigh up to his waist. A rough thrust sheathed his full length inside me. My sharp cry mixed with his hoarse shout.

His grip became tight enough to hurt, if I could feel anything aside from the rapturous burn inside. He began to move and pleasure ripped through me like never before. His size, my hypersensitivity to the silver in his piercing, the added friction from it, the thrusts that matched my overwhelming need with blistering ecstasy . . . each withdrawal had me sobbing with denial and each thrust had me crying out for more. I needed all of him. Everything. Now.

Blood flavored our kiss. I didn't know if it was mine or his. Didn't know which of us had taken the other to the ground, either. All I knew was the ferocious pleasure from those hard, deep thrusts that had me tearing at his back in encouragement. He gripped my hips, moving even faster. My climax roared near, leaving me almost rabid. He couldn't deny me this again. He couldn't. I wouldn't let him.

I flipped us over until I was on top of him. Then I gripped his hips so hard, my fingers stabbed right through his skin. I didn't care. I gave myself up to an orgasm that tore through me with the intensity of a killing blow, bowing my back and causing me to scream loud enough to hurt my ears.

Afterward, I slumped over his chest as limply as if I'd been stabbed in the heart with silver. Several moments later, he pushed my hair aside to kiss the exposed curve of my throat.

"Lucifer's hammering hard-on, now *that* was a real shag."

His voice broke through my near-paralyzing afterglow. I looked down at him . . . and gasped. His body was covered in red streaks that could only be blood trails from my nails. But that wasn't what had made me suck in a stunned breath. It was the floor. It hadn't just dented beneath the full frenzy of our passion. In some places, I could actually see all the way through to the dance floor below.

"I am so—" I began, only to have his laughter cut me off.

"If you're about to apologize again, stop. Only a fool would think I'd change anything, and you are no fool."

That was debatable, but now wasn't the time. I started to get off him so he wasn't in danger of falling through if the wrong support beam snapped, but his hands landed on my waist.

"What do you think you're doing?"

I gestured at the obvious. "Getting us out of a hole."

"Allow me," he said, his hands tightening on my hips while he used his power to fly us straight up. Then he flipped in midair until

I was staring up at him instead of down. He was still inside me, still hard, and my eyes widened as those aerial tricks caused new thrusts that didn't feel accidental.

"Didn't you finish?" I'd thought so, but to say I'd been preoccupied would be an understatement.

His grin was accompanied by a twist of his hips that was absolutely no accident. "Do you mean, did I come? Yes. But I'm not nearly finished, little Guardian. Right now, I intend to lose all my control with you, so as you said during our first fight"—a deep thrust bent my spine with bliss—"my turn."

He'd been restraining himself? Then I couldn't wait to find out what he'd be like now. "In that case, like you told me back then . . . come and get me."

Hours later, Ian came into the VIP room, dropping the drape that served as his only clothing. "Club is closed for the night, the last employee went home, the police are gone and the restoration company won't return until tomorrow."

"Good," I said, glad that I was incapable of blushing.

Ian had mesmerized the employees into neither seeing nor hearing us, but that hadn't stopped them from attempting to investigate why the club's walls, floors, and furnishings were being destroyed in the VIP section. They'd even called the police and a construction restoration company in an attempt to mitigate the damage. I might have been willing to ignore a few oblivious employees during the height of our passion, but a few employees, an emergency restoration services crew, *and* a few police officers? No.

Ian had dealt with all of that, *after* bringing me to the most incredible orgasm of my life. I could have helped him erase memories and herd our audience out, except I'd been too busy reeling from the aftereffects. Now, the club was empty of everyone except him, me, and Silver, who was currently perched on one of the club's ceiling beams. I tried not to wonder how long the Simargl had been there. It was embarrassing enough to realize that—for a time—I'd ignored an audience of people without adding my new pet to that voyeuristic mix.

I was now lying on two of the remaining unbroken couches. I'd pushed them together until they formed a serviceable, if narrow, bed. My covers were more of the room's drapes. The deep red fabric rustled as Ian finally joined me. His light kiss on the top of my head shouldn't have made me feel warmer, but it did, as did the arm he slipped around me to pull me closer.

"What time is it?"

I didn't really care, but the question was a buffer from the very unfamiliar feelings swirling inside me. I couldn't decide which was more disconcerting; the thought that he'd goaded me into briefly having sex in front of several strangers, or the thought of how much I hadn't cared at the time. Was I actually an exhibitionist beneath all my hard-won control? Or was his command of my body and emotions so strong, he'd made me one despite myself?

"A little after midnight," he replied, shifting until he faced me. I found that I wasn't ready to look him in the eye, so I promptly closed mine as if I were tired.

I must not have been convincing, since his chest began to vibrate from laughter. "Shields up at full force, I see."

"I don't know what you mean," I said, opening my eyes because I had no other choice now.

His fingers traced my collarbone. "Your whole life, you've hidden what you are, right down to the silver glow in your eyes and the waiflike appearance you glamour yourself with. Yes, I realized *this* was your true appearance when you rose from the ashes wearing it. So, in a very short period of time, you've revealed your true looks, your real scent, your lineage, your powers and now, your passion. You're feeling exposed, so it's understandable that you're trying to emotionally cover up again."

I flinched at his dead-on accuracy. With a sardonic smile, he turned me into spooning position and then pulled me back against his chest. Now, his too-knowing gaze was out of view.

"Better?"

I didn't respond even if an inner knot of tenseness did ease. Yes, not having to look at him helped, but it didn't compare with everything else. He was right; I felt supremely exposed. If I wasn't so physically sated, I might have even gotten up and gone for a walk in an attempt to regroup.

He sighed as if he could feel my continuing struggle. "Would it help if I told you one of my deep, dark secrets?"

"Yes," I said at once. I knew so little about him, and here he knew more about me than anyone had in centuries.

His laughter tickled the back of my neck. "Very well, here is something only Mencheres knows about me: My real name isn't Ian."

*T*hat shocked me into sitting up. "What?" Had absolutely *nothing* been right in his dossier?

"It's true. Not even my best mates know it. They met me as Ian when we were convicts on our way to the New South Wales penal colonies. I was too seasick to tell them that wasn't my real name. Would have died from dehydration on that voyage, too, had Crispin not shared his meager food and water with me, then browbeat Charles and Timothy into doing the same."

"So that's why you hate boats," I murmured, remembering his comment at the private airport back in Poland.

"Oh, indeed. No one celebrated the invention of flight more than me. With planes available for intercontinental travel, I never had to set foot on a heaving ship again."

I'd already told him too much, but for some reason, I revealed something else. "I'm afraid of fire," I confessed. "That's why I felt the same about the invention of electricity. But if your name isn't Ian, why did everyone think it was?"

A pensive tone entered his voice. "In seventeen eighty-eight London, Ian Maynard murdered a prostitute and was sentenced to twenty years' hard labor in the Australian penal colonies. But Ian never set foot on the *Alexander*. I was switched for him the night before the prisoners were shipped out."

"Why? And how did they get away with such a switch?"

"Greed." His tone was nonchalant, but his scent soured. "Ian's father bribed the guards to ensure my protestations fell on deaf ears. Can't blame them. The guards' choices were facing a rich man's wrath for speaking out or pocketing a goodly sum for staying quiet. They made the wise choice."

"You're very forgiving," I said, feeling all the anger he didn't over the greedy guards' actions.

"They didn't betray me." Steel edged his voice now. "I reserve my anger for the ones who did. I didn't *accidentally* end up at the prison the night of the switch. I was led there under false pretenses. You see, my father was also Ian's father, but Viscount Maynard only considered Ian worthy of saving since he was his legitimate heir. I was merely the regrettable result of a dalliance between him and his former scullery maid. Still, we were nearly the same age and we looked similar enough, so Viscount Maynard knew he could get away with the switch."

I closed my eyes. Such cruel class distinctions had faded in recent centuries, but I well remembered when they had meant the difference between life and death. "I'm sorry. That was unforgivable of him."

"I thought so, too," he said dryly. "Especially when he convinced my mother to go along with it." At my sharp intake of breath, he added, "Her initial betrayal was at least understandable. My father threatened to turn her and her new husband out into the street. They were his tenants, so he had the power to evict them, and it was winter. If the cold didn't kill them, starvation would, and she was pregnant to boot."

"What a monster," I said with hatred. One of the true joys of my job was serving justice to people like Viscount Maynard.

"Yes, which was why my ma stayed quiet." He paused for a moment. When he spoke again, his tone was rougher. "What I didn't find out until much later was that after the switch, she couldn't bear it and told the magistrates. My father dismissed it as the ravings of a madwoman and spent more money silencing anyone who might believe her. Then he evicted them as promised. She died from pneumonia before the babe was born. I didn't know, of course. I was shipped away by then. For nearly two decades, I hated her for her betrayal, and that whole time, she was dead because she'd tried to save me."

I closed my eyes. Few things were as crushing as the weight of a loved one's death. That weight was only made heavier when compounded by guilt. I'd ripped myself to pieces wondering if there was anything I could have done to pull Tenoch back from the darkness that caused him to take his own life. From the pain in Ian's tone and the way his body braced as if absorbing invisible blows, he was still punishing himself over his mother's death and his mistaken hatred of her.

"It wasn't your fault." Those words had been said to me many times about Tenoch. I hadn't believed them, but I'd still needed to hear them. Maybe Ian did now, too.

A scoff left him. "I didn't throw her out to die, but I did almost everything else. I should have been the one screaming about the switch all the way from the jailhouse to the penal colonies. But my father told me no one would believe me, and I was cowed by his position, the guards in his pocket, and the belief that I, a commoner, couldn't triumph over my 'betters,' as the gentry was seen back then. So I stayed quiet."

"You might not have been able to win," I said gently. "Courts favored the rich and powerful then." They still did, far too much. "Plus, your father was a ruthless man. He probably would've had you silenced if you'd spoken out."

"What did playing it safe and deferring to those in authority get me?" he countered sharply. "A murder sentence, a hellish imprisonment, and a dead mum I'd hated before I found out that she'd been far braver than I."

So many things about him made sense now. I'd wondered how someone so loyal and honorable at his core could also be such a hell-raising, law-breaking, manipulating bastard. Now I knew. Ian had molded himself into the exact opposite of the man he'd been back then because he blamed that man for his imprisonment and his mother's death. Was that also why Ian would die for his friends, but he continually kept them at arm's length? Did he not believe that he deserved their love, too?

I wasn't going to push by asking. When someone showed you their scars, you didn't poke at them to see which one hurt the most. "Tell me your father paid for what he did," I said instead. "Tell me he died violently and painfully."

He let out an appreciative sound at the vehemence in my tone. "Two decades later, when I returned to London, I interrogated him to find out the rest of what happened. Then I tore his throat out."

Good. "What about your brother?"

He sighed. "I didn't have to kill him. Oh, I wanted to since he was *thrilled* about the jailhouse switch despite our being friendly for a bastard and an heir. But Ian's brush with the law and our father shipping him to relatives in France wasn't enough to curb his sadistic ways. Eventually, he murdered the wrong prostitute and was killed by her lover."

Justice served, I thought, but kept that to myself, too. "After you escaped the penal colony, you decided to keep the name that had been forced on you. Why?"

He was silent for so long, I was about to withdraw the question. But then he said, "I suppose for the same reason my mate Charles calls himself Spade—the tool he was assigned back then. Some things, you never want to forget lest you lose the lesson learned with them. My lesson was realizing who I was. Thought I knew when times were easy, but it's who you are when things are at their worst that's the real truth. It's why I enjoy pain, in point of fact. You either feel it or you don't—no lies, no broken trust, and no self-delusion. Back then, I *thought* I wasn't a murderer like my brother. Turns out, I was. When I accepted that, I kept Ian's name as a reminder."

"Who did you murder?" I asked softly.

I felt him rest his head on his arm. I wanted to turn around, but I stayed facing the other way. Maybe he needed the illusion of privacy now the way I had before.

"The prison colony overseer. He fancied me, and he was a nasty sod who didn't bother about my failing to return his interest. After the third or fourth rape"—his shoulder lifted in a shrug, as if the number no longer mattered to him—"I decided to kill him. Knew I'd hang for it, but I didn't care. One night, I lured him outside the camp under the guise of wanting his attentions. Then I slit his throat and ran. Thought the other guards would catch me, but when days passed and they didn't, I knew I'd gotten away. Then I knew it didn't matter. I was going to die anyway. You've heard the rest of the story."

Yes. Mencheres had found him and Ian's boundless loyalty to his sire had been born. "Thank you for answering my question," I said in a steady voice. "But I disagree with your reason for keeping your brother's name. You weren't a murderer like he was. You were an avenger of wrongs. If I were the one choosing your name back then, I would've picked Aequitas."

"The Latin concept for justice?" I felt him laugh, then I felt the brush of his lips on my back. "Sometimes, little Guardian, you are truly adorable. I am as far from 'just' as a person can be. I would have only agreed to that if I were being ironic."

"Like me calling myself the Latin word for truth, when everything about me is a lie?" I noted.

His laugh was lower now. "Yes, and I take my hat off to you. I thought *I* was a rebel, but you are the very definition of the word."

"You're not wearing a hat," I muttered.

"No, I'm not," he said, punctuating his point by pulling up the fold of drapery between us. I closed my eyes when I felt his bare, luscious body against mine. Only minutes ago, I'd been more than sated, but now, hunger rose as if I'd been long denied.

Why wouldn't I have known that sex with him would be addictive? He didn't have an endless stream of women and men chasing after him for no reason. But I couldn't afford to crave him this way. That was almost as dangerous as our perilous circumstances. He hadn't only found an entry into my deepest secrets; I was afraid he'd also cracked a door into my heart.

"What's your real name?" I asked, hoping his rejection of the bald question would put brakes on my emotions.

I felt him stiffen in all the wrong ways. I thought my deflection worked and he was about to leave. Then he said, "I'll tell you on the condition that you never call me by it. I chose to keep the name Ian long ago and Ian I'll remain."

"Agreed," I said, curiosity getting the better of me.

"Killian." He said it with a touch of bemusement, as if he'd forgotten what it felt like for that name to cross his lips. "The name I was born with was Killian."

I absolutely *should not* tell him this next part. Should not, should not . . . oh, screw it. "The name Tenoch gave me was Ariel. He picked it because that was the name of the town he rescued me from." I let out a small laugh. "Now, everyone who hears 'Ariel' thinks of a fictional mermaid. Even if I hadn't been forced to change my name for secrecy long ago, I still would have changed it because of *that*."

"Tenoch gave it to you? You don't remember the name you were born with?"

I closed my eyes and saw only fire; the earliest memory I had. "No. I was too young when Dagon's people burned my village. When I rose from the ashes, they took me to their master, and Dagon only ever called me 'girl.'"

I'd long wondered if the reason I burst into flames and turned into ashes every time I died was because that's what had happened the first time. Or maybe, it's what would happen to anyone with my lineage. I didn't know. I was the only one of my kind, to the best of my knowledge.

Now the hands that settled on me were comforting instead of sensual. "That must be why you're so determined to see Dagon dead."

My laugh was bitter. "It's not, actually. I wouldn't risk the thousands of new years I could live by going on a probable suicide quest just to avenge *myself*."

His pause sounded surprised. "If not yourself, then who are you trying to avenge?"

The thousands of people whose screams still echo in my ears.

But if I told Ian that, I'd have to tell him the rest, and I couldn't. The memories hurt too much.

"Why am I telling you any of this?" I wondered out loud. "I don't know what it is about you that's gotten me to tell you secrets only Tenoch has known. I didn't even tell Xun Guan what I really was, and she's been my closest friend and occasional lover for centuries."

His snort rustled my hair. "You might have known Xun Guan longer than I've been alive, but she's not a true friend. If she was, she wouldn't have made you prove your claim about me. She would have let it go. People who value the law above all else might be admirable, but they make terrible confidants. If your other friends and former lovers are like her, it's little wonder you shared your secrets with me. Circumstances might've forced you to reveal some of them, but you told me the rest because you know I need you, so you know I won't betray you. And since I'm a scoundrel who's done far worse, you also know I won't judge you."

"You're far less scoundrel than you claim. In fact, I'm going to have to rewrite your *entire* dossier once this is over."

He chuckled. "Don't you dare. I've worked very hard to build my terrible, sleazy reputation." Then his laughter faded and his tone turned serious. "There's another reason, of course. The very real possibility that both of us will be dead soon. That's why you're sharing some of your most closely guarded secrets. Same reason I shared some of mine with you. When time is short, anything less than honesty feels like a waste of effort."

How true that was, too.

"I still would like to know why you're risking your life to kill Dagon," he said, his tone softer now. "But if you don't want to tell me, or if you simply can't, I understand."

Part of me did want to tell him, surprisingly. He must be right. After Tenoch died, I'd lost the only person who'd known everything about me and had accepted me anyway. I hadn't realized how lonely I'd been until I'd found someone else I could share my secrets with. And yes, time might be short indeed, so clinging to my secrets might be the very definition of wasted effort.

But I also couldn't bear to relive the most horrifying aspects of my past. Not now. I needed to keep them buried. Dangerous though Ian was to my heart, I knew he could wipe the past and everything else from my mind.

"I don't want to talk anymore," I said, turning around and pressing my mouth to his.

He responded at once, as if he knew how desperate I was to escape the memories that chased me. Soon, his mouth, hands, and body claimed my complete attention. This time, I didn't need any prompting to release all my control. He'd already proved that he could take everything I had, and I gave it without restraint.

As for the club . . . well, that turned out to be more fragile. Still, that's what insurance was for, right? In case it didn't cover all the damage, I'd arrange for a check to be sent to the owners later. It would be the best money I'd ever spent.

We left the club at dawn. As a vampire, that was my least favorite hour to travel, yet at the moment, it was also the safest. With the sun out, we didn't have to worry about Dagon sneaking up on us if he decided to ignore my father's warning so soon. And the bright rays of light now elicited a smile from me instead of how I'd recoiled from them yesterday. What a difference a lack of hangover made. And lots of sex.

I dressed in clothes I'd found in the club's Lost and Found. They didn't match, but it hardly mattered. Ian was wearing a police uniform. I doubted he'd found that in Lost and Found, so I surmised that one of the officers who'd showed up at the club last night must have left wearing a lot less than he'd arrived with. I could only imagine the story Ian would've implanted in his head to explain the lack of clothes, too.

Silver walked by our side, leashed as if he were any other pet. I'd glamoured him so his wings and feathers were invisible. Now, he only looked like a smaller version of a gray Samoyed.

I'd glamoured myself, too, using the appearance I normally wore. The waif, to hear Ian describe it. Yes, it was less beautiful and curvy than my true form, but Tenoch had given me this appearance, using his biological daughter for the template. I'd kept my skin color, but I still considered wearing his daughter's face and form one of the highest honors of my life. Tenoch had loved her so much, he'd remembered every detail of her even thousands of years after her death. He'd shared his beloved memory with me to help conceal me from Dagon, my former captors, and the rest of Dagon's followers. Even before he'd made me a vampire, Tenoch had treated me as if I were family.

"Bloody hell!"

Ian's curse turned my head around. He held the new mobile he'd somehow acquired to his ear. His lips were compressed into a thin line as he listened. I couldn't make out the words, but I thought I recognized Mencheres's voice. It sounded as if Ian were listening to a recorded message. Then Ian suddenly hurled his phone to the ground so hard, it shattered.

"What's wrong?" Had Dagon done something horrible to one of Ian's friends? That would be just like him.

"Xun Guan," Ian snarled.

I blinked. "What about her?" She wouldn't hurt anyone . . .

Ian stomped on the remains of his phone as if he hadn't already destroyed it enough. "The jealous bitch voiced so much dismay over our supposed marriage, word of it reached Mencheres. Now, he's demanding to know what the devil is going on, and if I ignore him, we'll have *two* people hunting us."

I knew countless words in hundreds of languages, but "Oh, fuck!" was what flew out of my mouth.

Ian gave me a frustrated look. "Exactly." Then he muttered another string of curses, ending with "Mencheres will tell Crispin, then Crispin will tell Cat, and Cat will tell *everyone*. Might as well start shopping for a bloody wedding band now."

"*Fuck*," I said with even more vehemence. "That means Dagon will hear about it, too!"

Ian shot me an irate glance. "As if I care what he thinks."

His sharp wits must have been dulled by his horror over being outed as a supposedly married man. "Dagon now knows I'm alive, but he doesn't know what identity I'm hiding under. He *does* know that we've partnered up, so how long do you think it will take him to figure out that I'm really Veritas once he hears you've suddenly married a Law Guardian?"

Ian's brows came together in the darkest of frowns. "Everything you've done to hide yourself—"

"Exposed," I said, shuddering. "Just like that." *Dammit, Xun Guan! How could you?*

But it wasn't her fault. I shouldn't have let Xun Guan get close enough to me to hurt her this way. I'd known her feelings were deep, and I'd still sought comfort in her arms from time to time. Like Ian, she'd also sensed that I'd been holding back, both in bed and out of it. But I'd never dropped my guard with her. My refusal had hurt Xun Guan deeply, as had my disavowal of serious relationships. Now, my supposed about-face by marrying a virtual stranger must have been too much for her. I had only myself to blame for her talking to others about her pain.

Still, all the people I needed to get justice for didn't deserve to have Dagon beat me because of this. Ian didn't, either, and he needed me to ensure his victory. The clock might be winding down on my alias, but the game wasn't over yet.

"We'll deal with Mencheres by playing the happy couple, then we'll have to move fast to kill Dagon."

"How?" Ian asked bluntly. "Even if we could fool Mencheres into believing our marriage was genuine albeit supremely idiotic, our plans for Dagon required time. We don't have that now."

"I know!" My brain ached from all the ideas I thought up and immediately discarded. My distress must have been palpable, because Silver whined and pressed himself against my leg. I bent to pet him while trying to figure out how we could compress our original, elaborate plan into a much speedier version.

Ian knelt next to me. "Didn't mean to snap at you. None of this is your fault."

"No?" I said, with a humorless laugh. "It's not one of your ex-lovers that blew our plans all to hell."

"Could've been," he said, flashing me a sudden grin. "Statistically, it *should* have been. Despite your vast age, you've probably limited yourself to a mere four or five lovers a year. I've frequently gone through that number in a single night, so my exes doubtless outnumber yours."

Since he'd vastly *over*estimated my lovers, he was right. "I do remember what you were doing when I found you," I said.

"Eh, that." Ian's wave dismissed the carnival-themed orgy. "Wasn't even really enjoying myself."

"I agree. You looked more miserable than anything else."

His brows went up. "'Miserable' might be stretching it . . ."

I sighed. "Come on, Ian. You thought you only had a hundred weeks to live. You chose to spend that time not with your friends, or members of your line, or even strangers who found you attractive. Instead, you spent it with people you paid to be there. That had to be horribly lonely, making that orgy only a few steps up from self-flagellating on the misery scale."

A sardonic smile twisted his mouth. "How like you to ignore the surface and see what's beneath. Most people don't bother. You're wrong about one thing, though. Being with my friends would have been more miserable. Then, I'd have to think about how much I'd miss them. Still, with time running short, I did want more memories of what it felt like to have people touch me without meaning me harm. Knew it would be some of the last I'd get since I had less than two years before Dagon came to collect my soul. 'Course, the orgy only served to make me feel more alone. May as well have been slamming doors in an empty house just to pretend the noises they made were other people's voices."

I touched his face. "I know what it's like to medicate pain in unhealthy ways. I sometimes get judgy and forget that, but when I was recovering from my worst trauma, I did things that don't give me room to criticize you or anyone else."

He covered the hand I held to his face with his own. "Perhaps one day, you'll tell me about your worst trauma."

I glanced away, catching a glimpse of his sardonic smile again before he dropped his hand. At once, I missed his touch, but I was still unable to open up the way he wanted me to.

"So, Xun Guan's actions aren't your fault," he said, going back to his original point. Silver picked up on my inner turmoil. He whined again, rubbing his head against me. I fluffed the feathers near his wings, then paused when I felt something bumpy. Then I plunged my fingers deeper to see what it was.

The bumps were scars. Anger burned through me. I couldn't imagine the damage Dagon must have done to leave permanent scars on a creature that healed nearly as well as I did. Thank all the gods that the Nordic vampire had been loose-lipped. If not for him telling me about Dagon's blood-tracking spell, Silver would be back in the cruelest of captivities, all so Dagon could profit from a creature that was created to be cherished—

"Silver!" I cried out, leaping up in excitement.

That startled the Simagyl so much, he flew back until his new leash stopped him. I began to soothe him at once, all while Ian eyed me as if I'd lost my mind.

"I'm not crazy," I announced, then laughed when the couple nearest us overheard that and did a double-take. Yes, I suppose that was hardly a ringing endorsement of anyone's sanity. "I know how we can bring Dagon to us as soon as we want."

"Cut off your warding spell on my brands," Ian replied.

I waved at his crotch. "Not that, though that would do it, too. Still, then Dagon would know it was a trap since you'd never *accidentally* do that. But if I let the blocking spell on Silver's blood dissipate, Dagon will be able to trace him again. He knows Silver's with us, and Dagon's arrogant enough to believe his magic poked a hole through my spell. If Dagon thinks he overpowered my magic, he shouldn't expect a trap."

Even better, my father couldn't punish me for breaking his command. Dagon would strike as soon as he saw me. Then, whatever I did to protect myself could legitimately be called self-defense.

For a split second, alarm passed over Ian's face. I couldn't imagine why, but then it was gone as if it had never been there. "Arrogant or no, Dagon is no fool. He'll still come in force. We'd need all our combined strength to kill him, plus several spelled mirrors at the ready."

Why did anything he said have the ability to surprise me anymore? "You're intending to use the mirror trap on Dagon?" I certainly had been, but I hadn't shared that with Ian.

He gave me an amused look. "Why do you think I tested it on you first? Believe me, there were many other ways I could have won that bet between us."

"You think?" I said, grinning because I had hope again.

He leaned down. "Not think," he murmured. "Know. Just like I knew I had to have you even when I despised you for what I thought you'd done."

His nearness was distracting enough. When his mouth slid to the most sensitive spot on my throat, I almost forgot what we were talking about. When he lightly bit it, desire shot through me like an arrow fired from a high-tension crossbow.

"I'd never murder an innocent," I managed to gasp out. "Just because Katie was born different doesn't mean she was born wrong. Actions, not existence, define character."

"I couldn't agree more." He growled against my skin before a slow lick made me shudder. "All my instincts told me that about you, yet I'd seen you at that execution. Couldn't reconcile it with what my gut told me until your drunken confession."

More and more, I was glad I'd gotten completely wasted the other night. That also was very much *not* like me, but here I was, an apparent proud binge drinker.

"Stop," I said, pushing him back reluctantly. "We have work to do. Call Mencheres and try to settle him down. Once we have him taken care of, we'll move on to getting those mirrors ready for Dagon."

A slight grin curled his mouth. "Any more orders?"

Dozens of explicit ones instantly raced through my mind. Ian inhaled as if tasting the air. "I miss your true scent when you're aroused. This one smells the way you look: boring and sweet. But

when your glamour drops and you are as you were meant to be"—
another inhalation brought his mouth to my throat again—"your
scent reminds me of spring rains during a lightning storm—wild,
pure, deadly and stunningly beautiful, just like you are."

I closed my eyes, letting his voice, words, and nearness wash over
me. I'd never had someone affect me on so many levels. The part of
me that loved it greedily gulped at every mystifying sensation. But
the logical part said that all of this would only turn to pain. Worse,
I knew the logical part was right.

Ian needed me now, but when he didn't, he'd be gone. He'd made
no pretense about that. He might be enjoying the perks of our being thrown together, but I was the only one feeling things on a
deeper level. That had to stop, before Xun Guan wasn't the only
one nursing a confused and wounded heart.

"Save your compliments for later," I said, opening my eyes.
"We've got too much work to do now."

Now Ian's smile was also part smirk. "Love raising those shields
back up, don't you?"

When they were the only things protecting me from an onslaught
of emotions I alone was feeling? *Yes.* "I don't know what you mean,
but don't you have a call to make?"

"So I do." He went to the person nearest us, gave him a few
flashes from his gaze, then walked back holding his mobile phone.
Once he punched in Mencheres's number, it was answered on the
second ring. "Mencheres," Ian said in a bright, chipper voice. "Got
your fifteen messages."

"Is it true?" I was standing so close to Ian, I could hear Mencheres
clearly. The former pharaoh had never sounded more upset. "Did
you actually get *married*?"

Ian winced but said, "Seems good news travels fast," in the lightest of tones. If I hadn't known how much he hadn't wanted news of
this sham to reach Mencheres, I never would have guessed what it
cost him to confirm that.

Silence for a full, very uncomfortable minute. Then Mencheres
said, "Are you still in New York City?" in a tone so flat, I was

rattled. Mencheres being upset was one thing. His sounding this cold usually meant that people were going to die.

"For the moment," Ian replied. "But we're leaving soon—"

"I am already here," Mencheres interrupted. "I flew in as soon as word of where you were and what you did reached me."

Ian rolled his eyes. "Of course you did." Then he shook his head at me as if to say, *parents, what are you going to do?* "We'll stop by. Staying at the Ritz? Or the Waldorf?"

"The Ritz," Mencheres replied crisply. "Penthouse suite. Come now, and do *not* bring her with you."

Her? I didn't even merit being called by my name? Mencheres's normally faultless manners pre-dated chivalry by so many thousands of years, I'd often wondered if he'd been the one to invent it. Now I was "her." He must have been truly furious.

"See you shortly," Ian said, and hung up.

I gave him a look after I double-checked that he'd truly disconnected the call. "You know I'm coming with you, right?"

Ian's laughter was as careless as the tone he'd used when confirming the marriage he'd never wanted. "As you reminded Xun Guan, where one vampire spouse is, the other is allowed regardless. But you do need to change." His gaze took in my mismatched clothes and too-big shoes while letting out a *tutting* sound. "Can't have you seeing your new father-in-law looking like a street sweeper."

"Unless I compel someone to switch their clothes with me, I don't see how my outfit can improve. We left our wallets back in the hotel room those vampires trashed, remember?"

"Don't you know a troll that owes you a truckload of gold?" he countered.

"He doesn't owe me," I corrected, but Ian was right. I'd never intended to pick up the gold Nechtan promised me, but it would be a lot easier to convert some of that into cash at a local pawn shop than it would be to get the new identification I'd need in order to access my accounts. Cash would also be harder to trace us with. Nechtan it was, then.

"Let's swing by Central Park."

$\mathcal{I}$t only took pawning one of Nechtan's lake offerings for both Ian and me to look much nicer. I pawned a few more items for traveling money, then stored the rest at a warehouse I hastily rented. Driving around in a truck filled with gold left us primed for more trouble than we already had. But as soon as we stepped through the doorway of Mencheres's penthouse suite, I knew this would be much worse than meeting a disapproving in-law. Ian saw it right away, too.

"What is this, an intervention?" he demanded of the three men and the single woman who were lined up around the hotel's doorway. "You look as if you're poised to attack."

"We are if you try to leave," Mencheres replied in a bitingly smooth tone. "And I told you not to bring her."

"'Her' is here anyway," I said, irritation making me ignore the terrible grammar of the statement.

I recognized all of them, though I didn't remember meeting the tall, lanky vampire with the black, spiky hair before now. From Ian's dossier, I knew he was Spade, real name Charles DeMortimer, married to a human, of all things. He might be dressed as if he was attending a fancy brunch, but he held himself with a fighter's coiled poise. Dangerous, though not the biggest threat in the room. Mencheres was, and after him, his co-ruler, Bones.

Bones and Cat had changed their appearance. Bones's short, curly dark hair was now ash blond and so long it concealed parts of his handsome face. Likewise, Cat's eye-catching crimson locks were now such a drab shade of brown, the box of color it came from must've been labeled "Eh, Who Cares?" She'd also styled it so that one side fell all the way forward, shielding almost half her face. Glamour would've been an easier, more effective disguise, but to each their own.

The last time I'd seen them had been at their daughter's supposed execution. When I met Cat's wintry gray gaze, I immediately upgraded her dangerousness above Bones. He might be older, yet icy spikes didn't dig into my spine when I looked into Bones's eyes. Cat must still have access to the most dangerous magic of all—grave power. Only a few people in the world could wield it, and it was nearly unbeatable. With how Cat stared straight through me as if I were already slain on the ground, she was about to kill me with it.

No wonder Mencheres had said not to bring me! If I'd have known Cat and Bones were here, I wouldn't have come. I'd want to slaughter me, too, if I were them. Now, I had to do something drastic unless I wanted bodies to start hitting the floor.

"I know your daughter's still alive," I said bluntly. "It was a shape-shifter that was decapitated, not her. You have nothing to fear. I will continue to keep her secret."

For some reason, the person who appeared most shocked was Spade. He gaped at me as if I'd just pulled a lightning bolt out of my ass. "But you're a Law Guardian," he sputtered.

"Yes," I said with all the pride I still felt in my job. "And the laws were originally made to protect people, not to oppress them. Some have been twisted over time, but none state that mixed-species children are illegal. Only fear and bigotry have made that claim, and I have no duty to uphold those."

Cat's gaze flicked to Ian for an instant before lasering back on me. "Is this bullshit, or is she for real?"

Ian grunted. "Reaper, you have no idea how real she is on this topic. Katie's secret is safe with her. She gave you the sword coated in Denise's blood to ensure that, remember?"

"Shut it, Ian!" Spade snarled.

Ah. *Now* Spade's shock made sense. The human Spade had married was named Denise, but from Ian's comment, Denise wasn't merely human. She was also the demon-branded shape-shifter. "Your wife is safe from me, too," I told Spade.

"I don't believe you."

The softly spoken words came from Mencheres. He hadn't moved, but all at once, the air became charged with so much energy, it was painful. "I have seen firsthand how you helped imprison and kill many whose only crimes were being different. Why should I think you've changed?"

Ian's brows rose as he glanced at me, seeing if I'd deny Mencheres's claims. "It sounds worse than it is," I began.

The air around me suddenly compressed as if it had turned into a massive fist. My bones broke and I felt a new, ominous pressure on my neck. Was he really threatening to decapitate me? If he did, as soon as I came back from the dead, I'd hit him with a spell that would make him regret it for the next hundred years!

"Stop this at once," Ian ordered in a furious tone.

At the same time, I choked out, "Damn it, Mencheres, allow me to prove it! Or have you forgotten I gave *you* the benefit of the doubt when the council was screaming for your head?"

Whether it was my reminder or Ian's directive, the punishing pressure ceased, allowing my bones to stop snapping like dry twigs. "Speak," Mencheres said shortly.

Ian put his arm around me, his glare telling Mencheres everything I was thinking about his treatment of me. But like many new members of a family, I had to suck up some insults for the greater good. Still, as I healed, I ground out a curse in Sumerian that Ian chuckled at because of course he was able to translate it. Then, with a muttered grumble, I dropped my glamour. What was revealing one more secret? I might as well start telling everyone I passed on the street the truth about me, too.

Mencheres drew in a breath when he saw silver replace my ordinary blonde hair, with streaks of gold and blue woven through it. Then he made an incoherent sound when I grew several inches and my body filled out into curves and muscles that strained every button and seam on my elegant pantsuit. I knew the moment my face changed to its true visage. That's when my real name slipped from his lips and he took a step backward, which seemed to shock Cat and Bones more than my new appearance.

"Ariel," Mencheres said in a stunned whisper.

Ian looked intrigued. "You recognize her in her true form?"

"Yes." Mencheres still sounded slightly dazed. "Ariel is the most powerful witch I ever encountered. She also helped me funnel countless practicing vampires, witches, mages, and demon-kin to safety during the Great Purge."

"That's what it was called when the council wrote new laws oppressing anyone who wasn't a 'normal' vampire," I clarified. "I was only an Enforcer back then, but it still gave me access to information on upcoming raids. I shared that information with Mencheres, only he believed it came from a trueborn vampire-witch named Ariel and not the new Enforcer known as Veritas."

Mencheres shook his head as if to clear it. "But you, as Veritas, still rounded up and arrested many."

I shrugged. "Only the ones who used their inborn power or skills to harm others. There are always bad apples, Mencheres. I gave those to the council. Then the council believed they'd succeeded in decimating the 'dangerous' parts of the population. If they hadn't, the raids would have continued, plus I wouldn't have been trusted with more high-level intelligence."

Ian began to laugh. "*That's* how Nechtan knew you! This whole time, you've been working for the council while using their information against them. I am *so* hard for you right now."

I looked, and no, he wasn't lying. I must not have been the only one who decided to get visual confirmation. Bones cleared his throat in a pointed way.

"Now's not the time for that, Ian. Despite these unexpected revelations, we all came here for a reason. That reason hasn't changed, even if my intention to murder your wife has."

All humor—and erectness—left Ian. "You intended to do *what*, Crispin?"

"Kill your new wife," Cat repeated bluntly. Then she shot me a half-apologetic, half-defiant look. I returned it with a hard one of my own. New family or no, I didn't take death threats lightly. "We thought she was using you to try to get to Katie," Cat went on. "I always wondered if she knew more than she'd let on at the execution. I'll never forget the look she gave me when she handed me that sword—"

"You couldn't translate 'shut up and take it'?" I muttered.

"—and unless there was an extreme ulterior motive, why would a Law Guardian marry *you*?" Cat continued, turning her attention to Ian. "You're allergic to monogamy, following the law, *and* telling the truth! I mean, I love you and all—"

"I can see that," he interjected sarcastically.

"—but you're the last, and I mean *last*, person a stick-up-her-ass Law Guardian would want to marry." I bristled at that, not that Cat cared. "And for the life of me, I can't imagine why you'd marry *her*," Cat went on. "We came here to figure out if she blackmailed you with one of your many crimes since the Ian I know would never willingly marry."

"I would have said the same about Crispin once," Ian replied, pinpricks of emerald gleaming in his gaze. "Or Mencheres, or even Charles, yet here we are, married men all. In truth, I should blame you lot. You must have weaponized matrimony and made it airborne."

"You see?" Cat turned to Bones. "Who says that sort of thing if they're happily married?"

Ian rolled his eyes. "Did you think an exchange of blood and some vows would change who I am? Nothing will, and if Veritas accepts that, my oldest friends should, too."

Spade made an exasperated noise. "We are your oldest friends. That's why we know you wouldn't choose to bind yourself with unbreakable vows. You gleefully mock them instead."

I'd heard enough. "If you truly knew Ian, you'd know he has more honor than the rest of you would dare aspire to."

Cat's eyes bugged. "We're talking about *this* Ian, right?"

They had no idea what Ian had sacrificed for them. "Yes, *this* Ian!" Then my voice thickened with everything he still wouldn't tell them despite his silence possibly costing him his life and his soul. "The one any woman would be proud to call her husband, and the same one any smart person would be honored to call their friend."

"Did she just call us stupid?" Cat whispered to Bones.

"I believe so," Bones drawled.

Spade stared at me as if I fascinated him. "I've never seen someone shagged into a state of witlessness before."

"Then I pity your wife," Ian snapped before I could give my own rude rejoinder. "Up your bedroom game, Charles, before Denise finds someone who will. More importantly"—his fangs came out as he snarled the rest—"the next person who insults her will get their mouth shoved up their own arse."

A look of amazement crossed Bones's features. "You're genuinely offended . . . on someone else's behalf."

He said it as if he couldn't believe the words were crossing his lips. Then his dark brown gaze turned stony.

"I can believe you indulging in a serious fling, but marrying? That's falling off your promiscuity wagon so hard, you've shattered the earth's crust. This is barely early days of dating. How long have you two been together? Weeks, at most?"

Ian gave him an irritated glare. "Refresh my memory, Crispin. Did you fall in love with Cat the first night you met her? Or did you hold all the way out until the second?"

Bones glanced away. "That's not the same."

Ian snorted. "Yes, there's the very marked difference of how our dear Reaper kept trying to kill you back then. That said, we're all old enough to know straightaway when someone is merely more of the same, or truly special." His look my way lasted only a second, but it felt as tangible as a caress. "As soon as I had my first real encounter with Veritas, I knew no one else could compare. More importantly, I knew she was mine."

I forced a smile while it felt like I was being mercilessly squeezed on the inside this time. He was only saying it to sell this sham, but gods help me, I wished it were true. It was for me. Dangerously so. I'd known in an hour how unique Ian was and he hadn't stopped surprising me since. Worse, in a mere two weeks, I was possessive of him in ways I'd never experienced before, had shared nearly every secret I had with him, and had found him increasingly fascinating and irresistible. Could this be what people felt when they were falling in love? If so, it was more powerful than any magic I'd ever encountered.

Spade leaned closer to Mencheres. "You said Ariel is a powerful witch?" he asked in a low whisper. "Maybe she used a spell to force him into *thinking* he wanted to marry her . . . ?"

I was debating turning him into a proverbial toad when Ian flew at him. "Warned you, mate. Now, pucker up!"

Then he froze in midair, his hands on Spade's ankles as if he'd been about to grab them to flip Spade's ass up and his head low. Cat raised a brow at Bones, but he shook his head.

"Enough," Mencheres said, revealing it was he who'd used his power to stop Ian. "Spade, you do not want to see what Ariel can do when she's angry, and also, you were being very rude."

"Seemed to be a fair question," Spade muttered.

"Sure, why *wouldn't* everyone assume I'd used witchcraft to force Ian into marrying me?" My voice was withering, probably because Spade had had the right idea, just the wrong persuasion method. If I didn't know that they were acting out of genuine concern for Ian, I'd show them some real witchcraft right now. "It's what every new bride wants to hear, isn't it?"

A strained pause, then Cat said, "Maybe we should all start over, hmm? This isn't what we thought it was, obviously."

"Indeed," Ian said in an icy tone. "Now, let me down."

Mencheres grunted. "Not until you renounce your threat."

"Charles needs to apologize first." Ian's voice was tight, either from continued anger at Spade, or from being frozen with his head at ankle level while the rest of him was at a slant.

Spade let out an elegant scoff. "I was concerned enough to drop everything to make sure you weren't being coerced into matrimony. If I was overzealous toward that end, I apologize."

"Not to me, you simpleton," Ian ground out. "Her."

"Why bother having a name at all?" I said irritably. "I'll just call myself Her from here on out."

"Speaking of, do you prefer Veritas or Ariel?" Cat asked.

"Veritas," I said, putting my glamour back on for emphasis.

When both Mencheres's brows rose, I realized I'd forgotten to mime using tactical magic or cover what I was doing with a verbal spell first. Thankfully, the rest of them didn't seem to notice the significance.

"Then, Veritas," Spade said, emphasizing all three syllables of my name. "I apologize for the unintended slight."

"Apology accepted," I said, which I meant as much as Spade meant his ground-out mea culpa. To Ian, I added, "Seriously, I have no desire to see what an ass sandwich looks like."

Ian looked at Mencheres. Mencheres released his telekinetic hold and Ian dropped to the floor. He got up with far more grace than he'd fallen, a casual swipe dusting off his shirt and pants. Then he looked at Spade, smiled with teeth, and said, "Hope you weren't hungry."

I wasn't the only one to stifle a laugh. Cat did, too.

"Well, it seems like this intervention has turned into a party," Cat said, her tone becoming markedly more cheerful. "Let's break out the booze! Mencheres, I hope your mini bar has gin and tonic. I don't know about the rest of you, but all this near-slaughter stuff has made me thirsty."

After more polite interrogation disguised as get-to-know-you conversation, I was ready to leave. All the liquor in the hotel couldn't take the edge off being on the receiving end of countless appraising looks, veiled trick questions, and endless false smiles. It took all of my control to keep from telling them not to bother. Ian's friends might not be actively trying to kill me any longer, but it was clear they still didn't trust me. They shouldn't, either, though not for the reasons they believed.

Thank the gods Ian also wasn't entertained, and he wasn't shy about showing it. After the second hour, he stood up, announced that he was bored and said we were leaving.

I didn't cheer, but it was close.

"Well, mates, it's been grand," Ian said in a tone that implied he felt the opposite. "Before we go, a reminder that Veritas's real identity as Ariel needs to be kept in strictest confidence. After all, were it to become known, the council would torture the shite out of her, then who knows what other secrets she'd be forced to reveal?"

Cat stiffened and Bones's eyes narrowed while Spade visibly flinched. Once again, I almost cheered. With that single remark, Ian had reminded them that if they betrayed me, they also endangered the ones they loved most. Even Mencheres wouldn't be safe, considering his history with me as Ariel, although he appeared the least concerned. In fact, he smiled at me.

"This should prove to be most interesting," he murmured.

I didn't know what he meant by that, but Ian said, "Until again," and escorted me to the door. I hesitated over my form of farewell. I couldn't say that today had been a pleasure. Not even I could pull off that momentous of a lie.

"It was nice not having to kill any of you," I settled on.

Ian laughed and winked at his friends. "Definitely an original," he told them.

I was surprised when Cat hugged me. She must have caught it in my expression because she grinned when she let go. "Sorry, but where I come from, you hug your family. Ian is Bones's cousin, so that makes the two of us family now, too. Don't edge away, Ian. You know you're next," she added, and grabbed Ian.

Cousins? I knew Ian considered Mencheres as a surrogate father, but I hadn't realized any of them were related by blood. I met Ian's eyes. His brow only arched as if to say, *Your dossier knew nothing, as I told you.*

I'd ask him about being related to Bones later. Now, I just wanted to leave. When Cat finally let Ian go, we did.

We took the elevator to the first floor. There, we picked up Silver from an empty room we'd mesmerized an employee into letting us use. We'd left Silver there since it would have been a bit much for Ian to show up with a new wife *and* a new pet, especially one that looked like a winged dog.

"That was as much fun as getting head from a shark," Ian commented as we left the hotel with Silver on his leash.

I let out a grunt of agreement. "How much you want to bet they're following us right now?"

"Undoubtedly, but don't fret. I intend to lose them in the tubes."

"You mean the subway?"

He flashed me an impish grin. "Yes. Ready for some fun?"

I must have been, since I found myself grinning back. "Oh, yes. Even if they somehow manage to keep up, I still want to pay them back for the miserable afternoon."

He laughed. "Then hold on to Silver and let's do this."

WE ARRIVED IN Trenton, New Jersey, as the sun was starting to set over the Delaware River. We'd given Ian's friends the slip somewhere back in New York. We'd lost them after jumping from moving train to moving train so many times, I'd actually gotten dizzy. But it had been that giddy sort of dizziness that reminded me of children spinning in circles so they could laugh when they fell down. Ian had a knack for reveling in the moment no matter his overall circumstances. His joy was infectious, reminding me that somewhere along the way, I'd lost that. Finding it again felt like rain soaking into a drought-dried land.

How I would miss him when this was over! I'd had more fun with Ian than I'd had in . . . I didn't want to remember how long. Right now, I didn't want to do anything except savor the moment. Soon, and only if all went exactly as hoped, we'd both go back to our separate lives.

Ian kept a brisk pace as we went through an urban area of Trenton. After several minutes, Silver started to lag behind. I picked him up, murmuring, "Poor boy, I know you're tired. It's been a long day for you."

"Just a few more blocks until we reach the bazaar," Ian said. "Shouldn't take us long to get what we need there."

"What are we buying? Mirrors?" We could have done that at one of the many shops we'd passed, but maybe Ian had a special type in mind.

"Magical supplies to power our spells. This bazaar doesn't have the best stuff, but we can't risk stocking up at one of my houses. If Dagon knows where they are, he'll have spies staking them out."

"I can power the spells," I protested.

He gave me an amused look. "Your abilities are indeed impressive, but we can't have you drain yourself on spells. You won't have enough time to rejuvenate. All Xun Guan's wailing over losing you moved up our timetable, remember?"

I disputed the "wailing" part but I couldn't forget the rest. In fact, I was glad I'd left my mobile back in that demolished New

York City hotel room. It was probably blowing up from texts about my surprise "marriage" to Ian from fellow Guardians and some council members, too.

"Guess I need to drop my glamour before we get there," was all I said. "I can hardly go to a magic bazaar wearing my Law Guardian appearance."

"Not without causing a panic," Ian agreed, flashing a grin my way.

I found myself smiling back as I dropped my glamour, once again feeling my clothes stretch to accommodate the changes in my height and curves. For so long, I'd associated my real form with negative connotations. My silvery blonde hair with its gold and blue streaks was a constant reminder that my blending of species was considered an abomination to most vampires and ghouls. But Ian didn't look at me with any of the disgust Tenoch had feared people would show if they knew what I was. Quite the opposite. Green pinpoints of desire began to appear in his eyes.

"Perfection," he murmured.

Silver broke the moment by making happy little yipping sounds while sniffing several times. He must have caught the change in my scent, too. Guess Ian wasn't alone in preferring my real appearance. Suddenly, I wondered if some of Silver's happiness could stem from him knowing others of my kind. *Were* there others? Too bad Silver couldn't talk to tell me.

Five blocks later, Ian stopped. "Here we are."

I saw nothing but the underpass of a bridge in front of us, the river to our left, and an empty lot to our right. Whatever had stood in that lot had been torn down so long ago, only the foundation slab remained. But there had to be more here.

"What's the trick to penetrating the glamour around this place? Another gift to a bridge troll?"

Ian grinned. "Nothing so extravagant. You simply need to work a spell. It should present itself soon."

A black cat jumped out from behind a bush near the underpass. It hissed at us, which made Silver quiver.

"Don't worry," I told him. "It's just a cat . . ." My voice trailed off as I saw the large nameplate on the cat's collar.

"'I am a dog,'" Ian read aloud, snorting. "They've made the spell too easy. Must be catering to any sort these days."

His fingers moved as if he were rolling an invisible coin between them. When he was finished, the cat had morphed into a dog. Now, Silver's wings began to wiggle in a friendly way.

"You can't play with it," I told him, sighing. "It might not be nice." Or an animal at all.

Before I was done speaking, the area around us changed. The empty lot all the way to the underpass beneath the bridge was now filled with booths, people, lights, and noise. So much noise.

"Best deal for a love spell here!"

"Grow your cock three inches in one dose!"

"Look twenty years younger overnight!"

"Lose all the weight you want with our new potion!"

"It sounds like a bunch of late-night infomercials come to life," I said, wincing. I remembered bazaars from ancient times, when they were commonly situated at the intersections of trading routes. Back then, they were one of the few ways you could experience different cultures. If I closed my eyes, I could still hear the sounds of people speaking long-dead languages, smell the delicious scent of meat from countless cooking pots, and see the blaze of fires that were the only illumination against the night.

Ian snorted. "They have the tourist-trap vendors in front. The real quality magic dealers are in the back."

The booths weren't merely lined up on either side of the orb-lit path. They were also above it. Some vendors sprinkled samples of their concoctions onto people below the way perfume hawkers at malls used to spritz unwary passersby. The layout reminded me of an advertising gauntlet. I doubted anyone had escaped with the full contents of their wallets intact.

We made our way through the vendors, ignoring the shouts directed at us from all sides and the dusting of spells from above. One briefly changed my hair color to brown, then red before it went back to my natural silvery-and-streaked state. Another dusting of magic powder gave me gigantic breasts that popped the buttons off of my jacket before it wore off. I ignored Ian's grin at that spell, saying "no" very firmly to the vendor.

The crowds abruptly thinned as we approached the latter part of the vendors. The air changed, too. Faint hums of magic now felt like drumbeats along my skin. Ian was right. This section contained the real power.

"May, my lovely one," Ian said, walking over to a booth covered in fine silks instead of the plastic coating that was common for the other vendors. "It's been far too long."

A regal-looking woman with red highlights in her ebony hair rose. "My beautiful one." She greeted Ian, leaning over the table that displayed her wares to accept Ian's kiss on each cheek. "It has indeed been too long. And who is this?"

"Ariel," I answered before he had to figure out which name to call me. Then I extended my hand. "Pleased to meet you, May."

She shook it. Her dark brown skin was warm, marking her as human, but the power tinging her aura denoted her a trueborn witch. There was also something in her gaze that made me believe she was much older than her mid-thirties appearance. Either she'd helped herself to some of the bazaar's anti-aging spells, or she regularly drank vampire blood to stave off the effects of time.

"Charmed," she said, then politely returned her attention to Ian. "What are you seeking tonight?"

"Six of the most potent spellbinders you have," he replied.

"Six?" Her brows rose. "You must be intending to do something very dangerous or very lethal."

Ian's smile was instant. "Both."

She paused, then shrugged. "Very well, but as always, if you are caught with these items, you did not get them from me."

"Don't fret, May." Ian's voice rang out with impish humor. "Law Guardians don't scare me."

I rolled my eyes. He couldn't resist, could he?

After a large amount of gold changed hands, Ian had six carefully packaged binding objects in six different bags. "Remember, don't allow the naked elements to touch each other until you're ready to use them," May said in parting.

"Pleasure doing business with you, as always," Ian replied.

We were making our way back through the congested section of the bazaar when I felt a familiar, distinctive brush of power. "They found us," I muttered to Ian.

"I know. Determined, aren't they?" he noted without a hint of surprise.

Then a familiar voice shouted, "There you are!" so loudly, we heard it above the many vendors hawking their wares.

Ian turned at the same time I did. Cat gave us a merry wave as she pushed through the throng of shoppers between us. Bones was behind her, his expression as intense as Cat's was falsely cheerful.

Inwardly, I sighed. You could run from family, but it seemed that you couldn't hide.

*I*t feels like it took *forever* to get here," Cat said in a chipper tone when she reached us. "But wow, is this place ever worth it! I didn't know magic users had their own version of a flea market. I am *so* getting that boob-booster spell. It'll be fun having double D's for a night, or maybe I should try—"

"How did you find us?" Ian interrupted her. "I know we lost you in the tubes."

Cat gave him an arch look. "Oh, you did, but I have two words for you: tracking devices. I slipped one in both your pockets when I hugged you. You guys really went all out with the train hopping, didn't you? It looked exhausting. That's why Bones and I sat back and had some drinks while we watched the blips on our cell phones."

I shifted Silver until I was holding him with one arm. Then I began searching my pockets. Sure enough, I found a tiny, flat device no bigger than a ladybug in my front pocket. I hurled it toward the nearby river, cursing the entire time. Karma was quick to get me with this one. Just the other day, I'd tricked Shayla into hugging me so I could track her. Now I'd been had the same way.

Ian handed me his remaining pouches of gold. Then he ripped his pockets completely off, hurling their contents and the material to the ground. He wasn't taking a chance that Cat had slipped more than one tracker on him, it appeared.

"Clever," he told Cat with his own fake grin. "I would've felt a spell, but I didn't think to check for bits of tech."

"Older vamps like you seldom do," Cat assured him.

Bones drew abreast with Cat. He gave a measured look around the market before his gaze landed on Ian. "Unusual spot for a pair of honeymooners, isn't it?"

"Says you," Ian replied at once. "I have half a dozen magical sex toys in these bags."

I also didn't miss a beat. "I like it twisted. Real twisted."

"Stop the pretense," Bones snapped. "You're not here for mystical bedroom props. Mencheres and Charles are combing through their allies trying to see if any of them knows what you're really up to, but I wanted to give you another chance to simply *tell* us."

"C'mon, Ian," Cat said, dropping her false cheerfulness. "Something's going on. Whatever it is, we want to help."

I glanced at Ian. We really *could* use their help. Bones could use his telekinesis on Dagon if the mirror spell failed. Bones might not be strong enough to completely immobilize him, but he could slow Dagon down, and that might make all the difference. Moreover, Cat siphoned abilities from every vampire she drank from. She could be telekinetic herself from drinking Bones's blood. She could also drink from Vlad and manifest fire, too. Or drink from the voodoo queen Marie Laveau to add grave power to that, and the list went on.

If I had friends this powerful, I'd have already enlisted their assistance. But Xun Guan was my dearest friend, and she'd be appalled at how many laws I was breaking. Mencheres was the only other person I might have considered reaching out to, but Ian had made me swear never to tell him about Dagon. Everyone else powerful enough to help that I'd trusted was dead. There was a price for living as many years as I had. That price was burying most of my dearest friends.

"Ian?" My question was clear in my tone. But when his features remained as hard as flint, I had my answer.

"As I've told you both," Ian said in an acid voice. "Nothing is wrong, aside from my being interrogated, followed, and interrogated again. Blimey, Crispin, I treated you less suspiciously after *you* got married, and you might recall that our relationship was at its lowest point back then."

Bones's flinch was almost imperceptible, but I caught it. Cat did, too. She linked her arm in his and gave Ian a measured look. "Bones thought he was protecting me back then. If you were him, you probably would have done the same. But we love you, Ian. You know that. And we want to help. Let us, please."

Bones gently pushed Cat away to move closer to Ian. Then he raised his hand as if to touch him, but dropped it with a sigh.

"I have no excuse for betraying you. Oh, I gave myself many at the time, but I should have trusted you. I didn't. Don't make the same mistake I did. Believe me, I've regretted it ever since. You're not just my friend, my sire, and my cousin. You're also the closest I've ever had to a brother. You know that, don't you, mate? I'd do anything for you, so tell me what's going on and *let* me."

Ian's expression softened. He even sighed as if not knowing where to begin. I laced my hand in his and gave an encouraging squeeze. He squeezed back, then looked at Bones.

"Crispin," he began. Then his eyes narrowed at something over their shoulders. At once, tension thrummed from him. "Go away," he finished, his voice changing to growl. "Now."

Bones looked as startled as I felt by Ian's sudden nastiness, but he planted his feet. "I'm not leaving until—"

"Then we are!" Ian snapped.

Now I saw what had alarmed Ian. Two demons were shoving people out of their way as they headed toward us. From their expressions, they recognized Ian. From Ian's expression, they weren't friends. How had the demons found us? Or was this simple bad luck? These weren't the first demons we'd seen at this bazaar. The place was crawling with supernaturals. But they were the first that clearly wanted to start trouble we didn't need.

I tightened my one-armed grip on Silver. Then Ian and I shot into the air. We couldn't go high, though, as we were still beneath the overpass.

"If you don't stop, Ian, I will stop you!" Bones shouted. He and Cat had flown right after us.

Power squeezed me in the next instant. Dammit! Bones's telekinesis was as strong as I'd thought it was. He must have used more on Ian than me because Ian dropped like a stone. Only my quick grab kept him from falling into the crowd. Worse, the demons had almost reached us. One leap and they'd be able to pull us down. And my magic wouldn't work on them. Like trueborn witches and warlocks, they were immune.

But Cat and Bones weren't. I threw a spell that exploded like a flash-bang grenade in front of them. It startled them enough for Bones's power to slip. When it did, Ian and I hurtled toward the other end of the overpass. We'd barely touched the open sky when that viselike power slammed both of us again.

We fell with a thud just meters from the end of the bazaar. Now, I couldn't move at all. Neither could Ian. Even Silver seemed frozen in my arms. A nearby whoosh had to be Cat and Bones coming for us. We needed a massive distraction to break free, but I couldn't hurt Cat or Bones. I also didn't want to hurt anyone at the bazaar. What, then?

The river! I focused on it and pulled with all of my will, but I didn't just yank power from the water this time. I tore thousands of liters of the river itself free, then hurled it all at Cat, Bones and the demons who were almost upon us.

The water slammed into them, flinging them in different directions. It also tore through part of the bazaar, scattering booths and people alike, though I tried to limit its damage there. As soon as I felt Bones's hold on me crack again, I lunged toward Ian, but he was already reaching for me.

We surged into the sky, Silver shaking the water off his feathers like an angry duck. I felt Bones's power grab us again, but we were too far away for it to stop us. I flung a stronger flash-bang spell in his direction and that invisible pressure vanished. There were drawbacks to a vampire's supernaturally enhanced eyesight and hearing, namely making flash-bang spells that much more effective.

Even temporarily blinded and deaf, I wasn't worried about leaving Cat and Bones with the two demons. Not with how lethal they were. That's why I would have been glad for their help with Dagon. If the demons at the bazaar tried anything, they'd be dead too fast to regret it.

"Head east!" I shouted to Ian, flying faster.

He kept pace with ease. Soon, we were too far away for Bones's power to reach us. If Cat and Bones did extricate themselves from the river mess in time to give chase, I wanted us to be close to more water so I could use its power to stop them. There was an entire ocean on the other side of New Jersey. That was more than enough.

ater, we watched whitecaps froth on the ocean from a private residence near the Atlantic City Boardwalk. The homeowners hadn't intended for their house to become an Airbnb, but while we had lots of cash, we didn't have new identification. Plus, a hotel would also be the first place Cat, Bones, or the demons would look for us, not to mention hotels weren't demon proof. So, after a few flashes from Ian's gaze and a generous amount of spending money, the husband and wife decided to take an impromptu weekend vacation.

I was tired after the fiasco at the bazaar. This had been a very long day, but we still had work to do. Our bags from the bazaar were spread across the living-room couch. Silver lay next to them, his wings folded around his head until only the tip of his nose was visible. He'd fallen asleep after a large meal of sautéed vegetables. For Silver, the night was over. For us, it might be just beginning.

"I suppose we should start doing prep work on the spells," I said with a sigh.

"Or," Ian said in a smooth tone, "you could tell me why you neglected to mention that you're telekinetic in addition to your other abilities."

Of course he wouldn't leave the events at the bazaar alone. "I'm not telekinetic," I began.

"You're claiming the river suddenly became sentient and had an uncontrollable urge to go shopping?"

I ignored his sarcasm. "Telekinetic vampires can use their powers on anything. I can only manipulate water, and this ability has nothing to do with my being a vampire."

Interest gleamed from Ian's gaze. "Go on."

I spread out my hands. "That's it. My other nature allows me to draw power from water and also move it around short distances. Nothing else."

"When's the last time you tried to do something else?" At my pause, his mouth curled knowingly. "That's what I thought."

"You don't understand." Now my voice was quiet. "My other nature is"—*Dangerous. Uncontrollable. Possibly heartless.* "Unpredictable," I settled on. "So, I keep it locked away, but like anything in a cage, it can poke its fingers through."

His brows went up. "Your abilities with water are what happens when you pull on your other nature's metaphysical fingers?"

It almost sounded like a fart-joke analogy, but whatever. "In short, yes."

He came closer. "Have you ever considered that you're being irrationally fearful of your other half?"

I gave him a pointed look. "You've seen my father. Tell me there's anything irrational about fearing *that.*"

"Valid point," he said, giving me a quick grin. Then, surprisingly, he reached out and began to undo the remaining buttons on my jacket. Talk about a change of topic.

I caught his hand. "I, ah, don't think that's a good idea."

"Not bored of me already, are you?" His accompanying chuckle said he knew the answer was no.

I gave a meaningful glance around. "All this stuff is very breakable unless I hold back, and you don't prefer that."

"I don't," he said at once.

"And it wouldn't be right for us to trash this couple's house," I added, in case that hadn't occurred to him. We'd already left quite a trail of destruction in our wake.

He traced a finger over the belt in my slacks before unbuckling it and slowly drawing it free from the loops. "There are other ways we can both be satisfied." He pulled the belt free and circled it around my wrists. "Repeatedly."

I laughed despite my instant surge of desire. "You know a belt won't be enough to restrain me."

He leaned down, his mouth brushing mine as he tightened it on my wrists. "An ordinary one? No. One infused with magic? Yes."

A tingle went through me before it was muted by echoes that still managed to reach me even through four and a half millenniums. "I'm not sure about trying that."

He leaned back enough to look at me. "Don't tell me you've never mixed sex with bondage before?"

"Not willingly," I said with a note of grimness.

He took the belt off my wrists at once. "If I'd have known, I never would have held you down last night."

I let out a soft sniff. "If I hadn't wanted that, I would have stopped you. I can still freeze time, remember?"

"Yes." His voice deepened. "But you don't need a spell. Saying no will do, unless you'd prefer another safety word."

"I don't know any." My tone turned wry. "I've never needed one before. The few times I lost control with people when I was young, I knew to stop when I heard screams followed by variations on 'arrgh, my back, my *back!*'"

His chuckle rolled over me with the same effect as a potent intoxicant. "Good thing I heal almost instantly and I love it when you're rough, so no fears of that with me."

I looked down at the belt hanging loosely in his hand. Did I trust him enough to bind me? I had no doubt he'd use a strong-enough magic to make the ties unbreakable.

He saw where I was looking and tossed the belt aside. "Forget that. There's an entire beach outside. Not even you can do irreversible damage to sand."

I glanced out the window. Moonlight now touched upon the water, giving it a lovely, silvery glow. But there was also snow, an icy wind, and more importantly, the knowledge that I'd be letting ancient wounds restrain me more than magical ties ever could.

He started to propel me outside, but I stopped him. "Wait," I said. "Pineapples."

He shrugged. "Not the first fruit I'd pick to add into sex, but if that's what you fancy—"

"Not that." I shook my head at the thought, then retrieved the belt he'd thrown aside. "My safety word." I held his gaze as I placed the belt in his hands. "I want it to be 'pineapples.'"

He didn't ask if I was sure, which I was glad about. I didn't want to be questioned as if I didn't know my own mind. All he said was, "How far do you want to go with this?"

I considered that. "No beatings, humiliation, or insults." Some people might enjoy that, but I didn't. "And since I'm not sure if I'll like bondage, keep it vanilla, as they say."

His eyes started to change, bright emerald replacing their island-shallows color. "Anything else?"

"We put Silver in another room." I wrinkled my nose. "I don't want him watching us again."

His laugh was a low, anticipatory sound. "Is that it?"

"No." This hadn't come up before, but I wasn't about to leave it to chance. "No one else except the two of us."

Something flashed in his eyes, gone faster than the brief illumination from a lightning strike. "Vanilla or no, I intend to spend all my energy on you, so neither of us will have anything left for anyone else."

With that, he yanked me close, his mouth covering mine while his hands did absolutely wonderful things to my body. Tomorrow, I'd worry about how much I felt when I was in his arms, but right now, I just wanted to feel more of it.

"Now," he murmured against my lips. "Let's get started."

$\mathcal{I}$ was in the bedroom, my hands tied behind my back with the belt that now felt stronger than the mythical vibranium. I was still wearing my clothes, which surprised me because whatever Ian had in mind, nakedness would be required at some point. I also wasn't on the bed, but that was less of a surprise. Ian seemed to find beds too limiting during sex.

He'd left me here while he went downstairs to do . . . something. I was tempted to see what it was, but when I tried to move, I realized the belt wasn't the only thing he'd spelled. I could move my legs to shift position and stretch them, but I couldn't walk. I tried to hop next. It didn't work. I could bounce in place, but I couldn't move forward or backward.

He'd only been gone a couple minutes, but I began to feel uneasy. What if I'd made a colossal mistake letting him render me essentially helpless? As his friends had repeatedly pointed out, we hardly knew each other. I might *feel* like I could trust him, but I of all people knew the treacherousness of someone caught in a demon's deal.

What if he'd maneuvered me into getting trussed up so he could deliver me to Dagon? Ian knew how much the demon hated me. He could probably negotiate better terms on his deal from Dagon or be released from it entirely if he presented me to the demon like a wrapped-up gift. And I'd deserve all of Dagon's laughter for falling right into such a trap.

"Here we are," Ian said, coming back into the room. In one

hand, he held a mixing bowl containing different cooking utensils, of all things. He tutted when I craned to see what was in his other hand. "No peeking or you'll spoil the surprise."

"It better not be a summoning spell."

My voice was low, but he heard it. His gaze narrowed as he set down everything he'd been holding and came over.

"I'd say I was insulted," he bit out, "but since I have set other people up in similar ways, that would be hypocritical."

I felt even more uneasy now. The word *pineapples* hovered on my lips, not that it would do any good if my fears were founded. Ian let out a harsh sound as he stared at me.

"Don't bother with the safety word. I'm well past being in the mood now." Then his fingers executed a complicated set of swirls and the belt fell from my hands. "And for the record, if I *had* been intending to betray you to Dagon, I wouldn't have chosen a private residence he couldn't enter. I also wouldn't have left you alone long enough to consider that this was a trap, and I wouldn't have used a summoning spell. You'd only thwart me by freezing time when you saw it. But if I sliced off that warding spell while shagging you from behind, you wouldn't notice what was happening until it was too late."

Everything he said made so much sense, I winced. "Yeah, that'd do it."

Even so, I couldn't help myself; I tested my arms and legs. They moved as normal and relief swamped me, followed instantly by guilt as Ian turned on his heel and left.

"I'm sorry," I began, hating how inadequate those words were as I hurried after him. "I don't know why I said that—"

"Because you were thinking it," he threw over his shoulder. "You desire me, but beneath that, you still consider me to be a lying, manipulating killer. You're half right. I do lie and manipulate and kill, but I only do it to other liars, manipulators, and killers. I don't harm those who've never harmed me, and it's not my fault that that list has precious few names on it."

"Your friends and your dossier say otherwise." It flew out before I could stop it. Then I was so appalled, I slapped my hand over my lips as if I could force the words back.

He whirled so fast, I ran into him. "Your precious dossier," he said in a blistering tone. "Did it tell you Cat murdered my longtime friend and very nearly killed me the day we met? Yet I didn't repay her as she deserved. I merely kidnapped her mates and blackmailed her over them. Wouldn't even have done that had Crispin been honest with me about her. I gave him every freedom while he was under my line, and how did he thank me? By betraying me in front of both our lines. He's right; if he'd simply *told* me he loved Cat, I wouldn't have come between them. I would have found a gentler way to avenge my fallen friend."

"What about Spade?" I asked in a much softer tone.

A scoff. "Even two hundred years can't diminish Baron De-Mortimer's inherent snobbery. He still sees me as a conniving commoner, so that's how I treat him over small, insignificant matters. But when he needed help taking down a Red Dragon dealer after Denise, or when he was possessed by a bloody demon controlling his every action, I was there for him."

"And Mencheres?" I almost whispered.

He looked away. "He's frequently given me the rough edge of his tongue, and I can't count all the instances he's put me in his tele-kinetic version of 'time out.' But he's always stood by me. That's why, when I saw Vlad murder him, I summoned Dagon and sold my soul in order to bring Mencheres back."

Shock hit me. Yes, a video of Vlad supposedly murdering Mencheres had circulated on the Internet, but it had been debunked almost immediately. "You believed that was real?"

Ian's mouth twisted. "I was there. Didn't find out it was a sham until after I dealt away my soul. Dagon had a grand laugh telling me how I'd sold it for nothing, because the bloke Vlad beheaded was only glamoured to look like Mencheres. But you know demon deals. No backsies, even if you've been tricked."

My shock ebbed, replaced by the most poignant kind of sadness. "I was there when Vlad told Mencheres about the fake video, but no one mentioned what you'd done because of it."

"Only Leila knew, at first." He flashed me a humorless smile. "Dagon froze time as soon as I summoned him, but Leila's a trueborn witch, so it did nothing to her. She saw the whole thing, including Dagon revealing that Mencheres's death was a ruse. Knew she'd tell Vlad about it, so I made sure the pair of them were indebted to me by finding the necromancer who'd tied himself to Leila. That bought her and Vlad's silence, ensuring Mencheres wouldn't hear about what I'd done."

Vlad owes me, Ian had said after arranging for Vlad to send his private plane to us. Yes, the Impaler did, and far more than plane loans and other favors could repay.

"Now," Ian said, his tone turning hard. "If you don't want me to leave and never return, tell me who betrayed you so badly that you were convinced I was going to barter you to Dagon only five minutes into being bound and alone."

I didn't know what startled me more; the abrupt change in topic, or his threat. "What?"

"Has to be a betrayal," he went on in that flintlike tone. "I know from personal experience what a rape panic attack is, and it wasn't that. I gave you time alone to see if you could tolerate being restrained without those kinds of flashbacks, but you were dead calm . . . and convinced I'd betrayed you. Why?"

I cast about for anything to say except the truth. "You'd really leave? That would destroy our plans to kill Dagon!"

His jaw tightened until I heard a cracking sound. "For a smart girl, you do ignore the obvious at times. *You don't need me for that anymore.* You're right—if you mute the spell on Silver's blood, Dagon will come, which now makes my presence optional instead of necessary."

I knew my mouth was open. Knew I should shut it and say something measured and rational, but the thoughts swirling in my head were anything but. Worse, they all culminated into a cry of *Wait, don't go!* that was so desperate, I was afraid if I tried to say anything else, that's what would come out instead.

A harsh smile curled his lips. "I'll take your silence as my answer." Then he spun around and strode down the stairs.

"Wait, don't go!"

I shouted it with all the feelings I'd tried to suppress. Hearing them so clearly vocalized horrified me. I couldn't pass that off as concern over losing his fighting skills. My voice had been too raw, too revealing, too *honest*. He'd know how I felt about him now. He'd have to be deaf not to.

He stopped at the foot of the stairs. I closed my eyes. I couldn't bear to see the pity on his face when he turned around. I'd let him know I'd fallen for him as if I were a modern schoolgirl texting him all the details about my crush. Stupid, stupid, stupid! I'd well proven the saying that there was no fool like an old fool.

"Dammit," I sighed, sinking down to sit on the stairs. "Can we both pretend the last five minutes didn't happen?"

"No." His tone was so sharp, it made my eyes snap open. He'd turned around and was now staring at me with the oddest mixture of amusement and dangerous intensity on his face.

"Care to elaborate?" I said in a tone as sharp as his. I might be wrecked inside, but I'd be damned if I'd show him more of that than I already had. "I can't tell from your expression if you're about to laugh at me or rip my throat out."

Suddenly, he was in front of me, pulling me up with a roughness that tore my jacket. "Neither. I'm going to fuck you until both of us scream."

Ian kissed me so hard, all the feelings I'd failed to suppress transformed into desire. I kissed him back while a new frenzy of emotions exploded inside me. I didn't care if this was stupid or too soon or dangerous or would leave me heartbroken. I *needed* him like I'd never needed anything before.

We fell onto the stairs so roughly, the breath I'd gasped in was knocked out of me. Then I ripped at his clothes until his bare skin touched mine. I had to feel him to prove I hadn't lost him yet. My hands raced around his back and shoulders, reveling in the muscles beneath his silky skin. Then I buried them in his sunset-colored hair to press him closer.

His mouth was bruising, as were his hands as they tore my clothes from me. Then his mouth went to my neck. I cried out as his fangs sank in deep. Heat burst inside me as the juice from his fangs entered my bloodstream. Then his slow, strong suctions increased the pleasure, stunning me with their intensity.

He gripped me tighter, his fangs sinking in again to send more of those incredible surges through me. Good gods, I hadn't known it could feel like this! It had hurt when Tenoch bit me to turn me into a vampire. I'd never let another vampire bite me since. I couldn't. My blood would've outed me for what I was.

Ian propelled my mouth to his neck. I hesitated. I'd never drunk from a vampire, either, since I couldn't offer reciprocity. Then his new, deeper bite knocked the hesitation out of me. I sank my fangs into him, moaning when his blood slid down my throat. With the brands, his blood was now the most potent of wines. Every swallow sent delicious fire through my veins.

Desire maddened me. Each rub of his skin made my flesh oversensitized, and every new bite between us had me shuddering with pleasure. Finally, I tore my mouth away to shout "Please!" in whatever language came to mind first.

His mouth left my neck to sear over mine. Then he slid between my legs and I felt the glorious burn of a silver-studded thrust. Even as he started to pull out, I gripped him with arms and legs to force him deeper, crying out when that roughly buried him all the way inside me.

The sound he made was worth the ache. With his size, I would've needed more gentleness for it not to hurt, but I didn't care. I arched against him and he began to move as if the passion boiling over in me was spilling out into him, too. That ache increased, but so did the pleasure, until both made me scream so loud, he paused and tore his mouth from mine.

"Don't stop!" I said raggedly.

Concern creased his features. "Felt you tensing. This is hurting you."

"I don't care."

Everything I felt was bared in my gaze, but I didn't look away. All I did was tighten my legs around him to tell him in another way that I wanted more of those hard, deep thrusts despite the slivers of pain. They were an outlet for everything I couldn't bring myself to say out loud.

"I care," he said vehemently.

He kissed me, but he didn't move the way I wanted. He stayed buried deep while he began to undulate his hips, his pelvis rubbing against my clitoris with an erotic caress.

That fullness combined with the instant starbursts had me crying out against his mouth. He continued those sensual rubs while his hands moved over me until the rest of my nerve endings felt raw from pleasure. It was all too much. I came with a cry his mouth couldn't completely muffle.

Ian reared up and his hands left my hips. Oddly, he fluttered his fingers in the air as if counting something I couldn't see. Then he touched his mouth before reaching down to glide his fingers over my clitoris.

"Say yes," he rasped. "You have to accept this spell for it to work."

"What spell?" I murmured, still tingling from the orgasm and the feel of his fingers.

"Say yes," his voice deepened, "and I'll show you."

"Yes . . ."

I glimpsed his smile before his head dipped. Then I let out a shocked gasp as I felt his mouth in two places at once. His tongue tangled with mine while at the same time, I felt it twisting over my clitoris. He was still inside me, and the combination of incredible fullness plus sinuous laves had me shuddering.

I moved against him, wanting him to feel the same pleasure that was cascading through me. He let out a low chuckle as he stopped caressing me to hold my hips immobile. Those magically mirrored flicks and delves turned post-climax tingles into new throbs of arousal as he kissed me until I couldn't remember anything except his taste. He still wasn't moving inside me, but the undulations I couldn't stop myself from making stretched and stroked my inner walls while every phantom lick sent more shards of pleasure into me.

"Gods, I love this spell," I moaned against his lips.

His laugh was wickedness at its most tempting. "Agreed. The only real crime is that it's illegal," he teased before his mouth once again slanted over mine.

I could barely think through the ecstasy. I ran my hands over his back and ass, loving the feel of his sleek skin over those hard slopes and ridges. Then I raked my nails deep, feeling his shudder all through me. I glided my breasts against his chest before pinching his nipples hard enough to elicit a moan. Hearing it made my loins clench almost as much as those endlessly erotic licks, so I did it again, harder. With a throaty chuckle, he stopped kissing me to bend his head to my breast.

I cried out when his fangs pierced the tip. With the spell, I felt it in my nipple as well as in the throbbing apex between my legs. A long moan tore from me as the juice in his fangs bathed my breast and my loins with the sweetest of heats. He sank his fangs into the tip of my other breast next, pinching my bitten nipple at the same time. Merciless pleasure slammed into me.

My skin felt too tight, my nipples burned, and I was now so wet, I could feel it on my inner thighs. When I was crying out in near sobs, he finally began to move with all the unrestrained passion I'd demanded from him.

Pleasure razed me from the inside out. This time, his roughness had me begging for more in ways I'd be embarrassed about later, if any part of me could still think. I came with a climax that left me shaking. I was still in its throes when he flipped us and slid down to bury his head between my legs for real this time.

The stairs crumbled beneath my grip. He yanked me closer, tongue swirling, flicking and delving so deep, I felt dizzy. His fingers were busy elsewhere, doing things I hadn't known I liked until that moment. Then he sucked on my clit until I thought I'd go insane, but that was nothing compared to when his fangs sank in and stabbed even more incredible rapture right through me.

I came so hard I must have actually blacked out. The next thing I knew, he was on top of me, moving in a way that had my back arching with lingering rapture. I felt worn out, but I wanted him to feel the same incredible sensations I had, so I mustered my energy and tightened my inner muscles with all my strength.

He gave a shout, and I gloried in every one of the deep spasms that came next. After the last shudder left him, he fell against me as if his own body weight was suddenly too much for him to support.

*A*fter several moments, I realized I was breathing every so often; a vampire's version of hyperventilating. My blood felt like it was tingling, so if my heart was still capable of beating, it would have been hammering. That wasn't all I felt. From the various things jabbing me in the back and legs, we must have broken this section of the staircase, too.

Gods, sex with him was going to cost a fortune, if I didn't want to leave a trail of ripped-off people behind me. But I didn't move. No amount of splinters could compare to the warm, residual sensations from that climax. It felt as if thousands of little sparklers were still softly going off beneath my skin.

Ian finally lifted his head and balanced his weight on his arms. He smiled before lowering his mouth to mine. His kiss was lingering, as if he was savoring the taste of me. The spell must have worn off, because I only felt it on my mouth this time. He stopped when he felt the tears that had started to slide out my eyes.

"What's this?" he asked, touching one of the trails. Then concern drew his brows together. "Still too rough?"

I let out a low, barely audible laugh. "Not at all. You're going to make a world-class masochist out of me, it seems."

The briefest smile touched his mouth before his expression turned serious again. "What, then?"

I stroked his face, fingers running over his dark red brows, high cheekbones, chiseled jaw, and full, firm lips. He was so beautiful. If

I stared at him too long, I'd be overcome and not say what I had to say. That's why I dropped my hand. I'd intended to hold on to this last secret forever, but it was time, too, for this one to fall.

"You asked who betrayed me. Her name was Ereshki."

I felt him tense, but his tone was light when he said, "Another former lover?"

How much easier this would be if that's all she had been. "No. She was my friend . . . or so I believed for a long time."

He rolled over until he was lying next to me instead of pressing me against the broken stairs. "Why did she betray you?"

I took in a deep breath. "To get free from her soul bargain . . . with Dagon."

His irises had softened back to turquoise after his climax, but at that, they blazed bright green. "Tell me everything."

To distract myself from the pain these memories would cause, I started toying with the plywood pieces bursting out from the broken part of the stairs.

"Fenkir and Rani are the demons who burned my village and first murdered me. They did it because Dagon had tasked them with convincing people to give up their gods in favor of worshipping him. If the village refused, Fenkir and Rani could get nasty. Back then, Dagon was trying to make a name for himself as a deity because he can draw energy from people if their devotion is radical enough. Did you know that?"

"He told me something of the sort once," Ian said. "Didn't believe him because he's a lying, self-glorifying sod."

"That he is," I agreed. "But he wasn't lying about that. From the little I know of demon rules, they're allowed to influence humans, but they're not supposed to use their *powers* on them to inspire worship. So, Dagon couldn't freeze time, teleport, or use his other tricks to get human populaces to think he was a god. That's why he was so delighted when Fenkir and Rani brought him an unkillable toddler. Now he had a great prop for his 'I'm a god' act that got around the rules."

Ian scoffed. "How did *your* abilities help him get worship?"

"He claimed credit for them. Fenkir and Rani would take me from village to village to sacrifice me. Then, Dagon would say he's the one who resurrected me after I rose from the ashes."

Not a muscle moved, but the scent of Ian's fury enveloped me. "Where was your terrifying biological father in all this?"

"At first, he didn't know I existed. Children between his kind and humans are rare, he said, and his affair with my mother was very brief. But people only see the Warden of the Gatekeeper to the Netherworld when there's bad news about their afterlives. So, when my father kept catching glimpses of me between my murders and my resurrections, he knew I had to be his. Our shared blood was the only reason a child would ever be drawn to his part of the underworld."

Ian's body felt as if it had turned to marble. "He knew what was happening to you, yet he didn't save you and Tenoch did. Glad to hear the damned see your father after they die. Gives me a chance to tell him what an utter bastard he is."

"He couldn't find me on his own," I began.

"Rot," Ian said curtly. "He's Aken the Ferryman to Mencheres, and Mencheres summoned him to find Kira when she was in danger for the express reason that he sees *everyone*."

"Not me." My voice was grim. "His kind is 'blind to their blood,' as he put it. He also couldn't get help from his fellow whatevers because fathering a child with a human is apparently a no-no. He needed someone else to find me, but not a human, since humans aren't strong enough to go against demons. Couldn't be a demon, since then Dagon would probably hear about it. That left vampires and ghouls, but my father didn't have any friends among their kind. It took him a while before he settled on Tenoch and learned enough about him to trust sending him after me."

"How long?" Ian asked, his tone edged with steel.

I sighed. "Seasons aren't as distinct in that part of the world. I also don't know exactly how young I was when Dagon took me. You've seen what I look like without my glamour. I was probably in my early twenties by the time Tenoch rescued me."

"Two. Decades." The air around him actually began to crackle, reminding me of the buildup to what happened when Mencheres was in a fury. "You were slaughtered over and over for two decades, but you said before that you're not trying to kill Dagon for your own vengeance. Why the bloody hell *not?*"

I closed my eyes. This part is what haunted me no matter how much time had passed. "I wasn't the only one who was murdered. Dagon channeled the most energy when his worshippers made human sacrifices. In every new village, Fenkir and Rani would tell the people what a great god Dagon was and how they could prove it because Dagon could raise the dead. Then, they'd kill me in whatever way they thought would impress the villagers most. When I rose from the dead . . . the villagers usually believed in Dagon, and they celebrated their new god by doing what he commanded, which was to sacrifice some of their people to him."

I opened my eyes, not wiping away the tears that now streamed through them. "The worst part was, for many years, I believed in Dagon, too. Oh, I hated him because my life was horrible. I also feared him since I knew he could make it worse. But I was too young to remember that Dagon hadn't been there the first time I came back from the dead. Dagon told me he was the one who kept resurrecting me, and he could do things no one else could, so I really thought he *was* a god. That's why," my voice broke and for several moments, I couldn't speak. "That's why I backed his claims," I finally whispered. "I told the people he was a god and that they . . . they should do what he said."

Saying it out loud made all the memories come flooding back, crushing me beneath their weight. I covered my face in my hands and cried in a way I hadn't let myself cry for centuries. *So many innocent people, murdered. So many families, broken when their loved ones didn't return from the dead the way I had.* Then worse, Fenkir, Rani, and Dagon would tell the families it was their lack of faith that prevented the resurrections, and what would be required to push their faith to the necessary level? More sacrifices.

"Don't you dare blame yourself." Ian's voice cut through the guilt that, as always, felt as if it would destroy me. "Dagon brutalized an innocent child into aiding his deception, but it was *his* deception. Not yours. What you went through is so horrifying, I'm amazed you're not still broken from it. Don't you dare shoulder any of his guilt. He deserves *all* of it."

"He does deserve to pay," I said, swiping at my eyes. I didn't agree that I was guilt free, but I knew that much, at least. "That's why I don't care how many more lifetimes I could live if I leave Dagon alone. I won't do it. Those people deserve their justice. They've waited too long as it is."

He reached over, taking my hand and lacing his fingers through mine. Such a simple gesture, especially considering the far more graphic things we'd done. But in that moment, it felt more intimate than everything that had come before it.

"You won't fail." His voice vibrated from his intensity. "People like you have the rarest form of bravery. Friends and lovers might be willing to die for each other, but that's partly selfish. Risking everything for people you don't know is real bravery. You made all those people Dagon killed yours to avenge when you didn't have to. Then you became a Law Guardian so you could funnel more persecuted people to safety while also punishing those who abuse others. All this puts you right under the council's nose, but you did it anyway. You are awash in that rarest of braveries, Veritas. Dagon doesn't know it, but he doesn't stand a chance against you."

$\mathcal{I}$ squeezed his hand, new tears spilling out that weren't from anguish this time. Oh, how I had needed to hear out loud that I *could* beat Dagon! Even more, to have someone other than me believe it was possible.

"Thank you," I said softly. "You have that bravery, too, you know. Oh, you'll say it's selfish because you care about Mencheres and the rest of your friends. But you'd rather risk death than risk them in this fight. That's bravery and loyalty at its most unselfish."

He squeezed back, though he refused to acknowledge any nobility in his actions, of course. Then he let me go. "You never said how Ereshki fits into all this."

The breath that escaped me was too bitter to be a laugh. "Even with how brainwashed I was, it did occur to me to question why I was the only person who came back from the dead. Eventually, I questioned it enough to tell the villages *not* to listen to Dagon. Fenkir, Rani, and Dagon tried every torture imaginable to make me stop, but I refused. Between that and word traveling about other villages deeply regretting their brief stint at Dagon worship, converts and sacrifices were way down. Then one day, Dagon brought Ereshki to my cage."

I could still picture her: long black hair, skin the same desert-sand color as mine, and clear brown eyes that crinkled at the corners when she laughed.

"He said he'd prove he was a god, then he slit her throat. I'd seen so much death by then, I was numb to it . . . until her throat healed and she came back, alive. Dagon told me Ereshki was special like me because we both had *true* faith, and if only others would, too, there would be no more death at all—"

"I literally *cannot wait* to kill him," Ian snarled, leaping up to pace at the bottom of the ruined staircase. "I knew Dagon was a bastard, but I had no idea about this. I only thought he swindled the greedy or the corrupt out of their souls the way other demons do."

I was touched that Ian was taking this so personally. He might not care for me the same way I cared for him, but he obviously felt something, to be this upset on my behalf.

"That's what Dagon's been reduced to now. It's why he hates me so much. Eventually, when my father got the whole story, he punished Dagon by forbidding him from building up his followers among humans again. That cut Dagon's power source, and he's blamed me for it ever since. But back to Ereshki. She came back from the dead because she was demon-branded, not that I knew it. I thought she was my friend. I—I'd never had one before, and I loved her more than words can say. It broke me when I overheard her talking to Fenkir and Rani one day and discovered she'd only been pretending, to keep me in line. I didn't even get a chance to confront her about it. Tenoch found me that night."

Ian stopped pacing. "The first person you trusted was a demon-branded bitch who tricked you into re-believing in the sod who continually murdered you?" A humorless laugh left him. "No wonder you had a betrayal flashback when you let another demon-branded person bind you."

"I'm sorry," I said softly. "I really *don't* think you're like her. I never would have told you everything if I did."

"Tell me one more thing. Tell me Tenoch killed everyone violently and painfully once he found you."

A smile ghosted across my lips. He'd used the same words I had when he'd told me about his father. "My father wouldn't let him, since that would make Tenoch a target for other demons. He did tear Fenkir, Rani, and Ereshki into lots of pieces, but that only slowed them down long enough for Tenoch to whisk me away. I assume Dagon killed them for letting someone steal me, since I've never seen them since, and believe me, I've looked. After that, Tenoch took me to my father. It was the first time we 'met,' aside from the glimpses I'd caught after I died. The Warden told me about demons, vampires, my mixed heritage, and everything else."

"That must have been quite a shock," Ian said steadily.

"Oh, it was." Another bitter laugh. "I was beyond traumatized, both from what had happened to me and from what I'd helped Dagon do to others. Plus, like you, I also blamed my father for not doing more to get me out of that sooner. Not that he cared. The Warden doesn't feel the way we do, or he doesn't consider me worthy of his deeper feelings. But he did ask Tenoch to look out for me, and that was his greatest gift. Tenoch saved me in body, mind, and spirit. Then he replaced every minute Dagon robbed me of by turning me into a vampire. He also taught me magic and how to use *all* my powers. Tenoch wanted to make sure I knew how to protect myself from anyone else who would try to hurt me or use me for their own purposes."

At that, I got up and went over to Ian, taking both his hands. "That's why I understand exactly why you sold your soul to save Mencheres. I tried to give the Warden mine in exchange for Tenoch's life after he committed suicide. The Warden said he couldn't because Tenoch hadn't crossed through his part of the underworld on his way to his next life. That's the good news, even though I've missed Tenoch every day since then."

Ian clasped my hands before pulling his free to settle them on either side of my face. "Of course you did, but you're not alone any longer. You do realize that, don't you?"

I glanced away, a snort escaping me. It was better than the muffled sob rising in my throat. "It's okay, Ian. I'm under no illusions about us. Even if we win, you're not the 'stick around' kind of guy. You're the guy people sigh wistfully about when they're later with the person who *does* stick around."

His grin was pure him: more than a little dangerous and more than a lot enticing. "Oh, there are vast multitudes sighing over me, don't you doubt it. But you know how Mencheres used to be able to see the future? I have something like that, too."

"You do?" I asked in surprise.

A nod. "Several years ago, I started getting *feelings*. I'd suddenly know the person I was with was going to rob me, for example. Dismissed it as lucky hunches at first, then paranoia when I felt it with Crispin. But after Crispin's betrayal, I started paying attention. Turns out, the feelings were never wrong, but they didn't happen every time. A heads-up would have been appreciated before I sold my soul to Dagon, but did my paranormal ESP warn me then? *No.* That's when I understood why Mencheres always considered his gift more of a curse. When you can't count on it, it can feel more taunt than blessing when it does finally happen. Take yourself."

I stiffened. If his ability only caused him to have premonitions about bad things happening, this would hurt.

"The first time I saw you, you were moderating a duel Crispin was in and you nearly executed Cat for saving him—"

"That was *not* my fault," I interrupted. "Everyone was warned that if they interfered, they'd die. Cat torched the head off Bones's opponent in front of four Law Guardians and hundreds of witnesses. She could've flash-fried his internal organs to help Bones. Or cooked his spine, or something else that wouldn't have been seen. But no. She goes for the most visible display of duel interference *ever*—"

"The woman has no subtlety," Ian agreed, laughing. "But to my point, I saw you then and felt nothing. Saw you months later during the ghoul uprising and felt nothing then, too . . . until I watched you tear through a group of ghouls 'til they were no more than blood in the wind. Made me so hard, I almost tripped over my cock on my way to kill the ghoul in front of me."

"Romantic," I said in an acerbic tone, but a fluttering had started inside that I was having a difficult time controlling.

A quick grin. "Indeed. Felt nothing when you rudely interrupted my orgy, either, except rage when I recognized you as the Guardian who'd been at Katie's supposed execution. Then we fought . . . and I felt the same thing I'd felt when I watched you tear through those ghouls years before."

"Something long and hard?" I supplied, adding, "I remember it hitting my foot when I was trying to hold you down."

"Not that, though that, too," he said with another unrepentant grin. Then it faded as he said, "I felt that you were mine. Rattled me so much, it kept me far away from you on that battlefield years ago. Feeling that toward anyone was a shock, but feeling it toward a *Law Guardian*?" He shook his head. "I wanted no part of it, so I made sure not to cross your path again. Had every intention of getting away from you when you ambushed me at the bordello, too, though I was curious to see what you intended with your 'surprise prostitute' act. Yes, I recognized you straightaway, not that I let on, until you arrogantly announced that we were leaving. Then you muted the beacon on Dagon's brands and I knew I had to partner with you or give up on saving my soul. But I had my disgust over Katie to hold me in check. When you eliminated *that,* I had nothing to stop me from realizing why I'd felt one way toward you sometimes and so very differently at others."

He ran his hands over me, his touch affecting me almost as much as the words I couldn't believe I was hearing.

"You were always hiding before, either under your glamour or your rigid, law-worshipping act. When you dropped it fighting or binge drinking or rescuing flying demon dogs or telling me you'd never have sex with me while lust swam in your eyes"—his voice deepened and he pulled me hard against him—"I saw the real you, and every time I did, I knew you were *mine.*"

I kept opening my mouth but I couldn't seem to speak. That's why I continued to stare at him, waiting for him to say something that made sense. This didn't. Neither did the joy bursting through me, lighting me up on the inside as if I'd swallowed the sun. I wanted to believe him, but did I dare? Could I risk what I'd feel if I did?

"If you're lying to me, I will kill you," I found myself saying.

Then I bit my lip enough to make it bleed. Gods, what was wrong with me? I was the worst at this. The absolute *worst*.

Ian grinned before leaning down to lick the blood off my lip. "I know, it's a lot to take in. Never thought you'd be this happy, did you? Or this *lucky*. Blimey, go ahead and envy yourself. Countless other people will, I assure you."

A laugh escaped me even as my eyes became so shiny, his image started to blur. "You might be the most conceited man I've ever met, and I've met millions of them."

His low, seductive laugh coincided with his hands settling on my hips. "Then I deserve a spanking, don't I? Here, I'll start things off."

With that, he smacked my ass several times in quick succession. I looked down as if feeling it wasn't enough and I needed visual confirmation of the pink handprints to believe he'd actually done it. Seeing it, he laughed again.

"Never been spanked before? You have so much catching up to do. We'll start now."

"Wait!" I said when his mouth swooped down. He paused, mouth barely brushing my lips. "You've said these . . . these *amazing* things, but I haven't told you how I felt."

"Veritas." The way he said my name made me shiver. So did the look in his eyes when he leaned back so I could see every nuance of his expression. "You told me everything I needed to know with how you shouted after me not to leave before."

Once again, I felt supremely exposed, as if he'd pulled back all my defenses and stared directly into my soul. But this time, I didn't turn away, drop my gaze or attempt to cover up.

"Good," I said steadily. "Because I meant it."

Then I whacked his ass hard enough to make my hand sting. His laughter chased after me as I flew up the stairs and tossed a "Come and get me!" over my shoulder at him.

"Right behind you," he chuckled, and flew after me.

*T*hat's the last one," Ian said after I heard the rustling sound of fabric dropping behind me. "You can turn around now."

I did, seeing a heavy black drape over the tall mirror behind me. Similar drapes covered more mirrors on the other three walls of the small room. Having mirrors on every wall would have looked suspicious, except for the kind of room we were in.

Fifty years ago, this mirrored fun house might have been bustling with laughter and activity. Today, it was one of many abandoned shells. Brush and other overgrowth advanced on the former amusement park like a surrounding army on a doomed city. Graffiti covered the structures that still stood within, and the half-rotted skeleton of the wooden roller coaster reminded me of a sad, ghostly sentry looming over the entire park's remains.

Ian had picked this place for our ambush. I, too, would have chosen somewhere quiet, abandoned, and at least a few miles away from regular populaces. But it wouldn't have occurred to me to choose an actual mirrored fun house to trap Dagon with a bunch of spelled mirrors. My sense of humor wasn't that twisted.

Ian's was, and I had to admit, the irony was growing on me. After scouting out the area to make sure this tiny slice of western Pennsylvania was as Ian remembered, we'd started our work. First was rebuilding the fun house enough to make it suitable for our needs. It didn't take much since we weren't attempting to return it to its former dubious glory. We only needed it to be functional for our trap. Dagon shouldn't be wary of finding a few mirrors left in it, and catching him by surprise was the most critical part of our plan.

Next was the park itself. I wanted a few surprises waiting for Dagon and whatever backup he brought, if things didn't work as hoped for in the fun house. Finally, I had to get Silver ready. I did the magical equivalent of a locater beacon on the Simargyl, plus I embedded a tiny GPS chip beneath his skin. I had no intention of letting Dagon recover him, but I wouldn't leave Silver's fate to chance if the worst happened.

I also explained to Silver that I wasn't giving him back to Dagon; I was making sure Dagon couldn't hurt him anymore by luring him here. I don't know how much the Simargl understood. But I had to try anyway.

It took three days to get everything ready. As the sun set on the third day, we were finally done. I put my hands on Silver and willed the former warding spell I'd placed on him to weaken, allowing Dagon to once again locate Silver by tracing his blood. Then, I went to find Ian.

He was right outside the fun house, watching as the sun cast dying mauve and purple beams through the ruined theme park. He wore all black, as I did, and both of us had two demon-bone knives apiece in sheaths attached to our belts. The knives also had steel on the backside of the blades. Now there was no danger of them breaking when smashing through other bones.

They weren't our only weapons. We also had silver knives in case of vampires and a short sword for ghouls, plus many spells in place around the park. Despite all this, pre-battle jitters had set in. So much of my life had led up to this. Was Ian experiencing the same nerve-frying mix of worry, resolve, anger, hope, and fear?

Then again, he might be feeling something else. The other day, he'd reminded me that I didn't need him anymore. He'd said it as a challenge, but what if he was second-guessing his role in this? If Dagon got out of our trap, I'd come back if he killed me. But if Ian died . . . he wouldn't only lose his life. He'd also lose his soul.

The thought filled me with the kind of sickening dread I hadn't felt since I was human. It wasn't worth the risk. "Dagon should feel his tether to Silver returning soon, but you still have time to leave," I said. "In fact, you *should* go. You've already done more than enough. Let me take it from here."

He turned around and laughed. "And miss Dagon's expression when we trap him in those mirrors? Not a chance."

I stared at him, suddenly terrified I'd never see him again if he stayed. "Ian, really, you should go—"

He pressed a finger to my lips. "Stop. Your concern is touching, but if I didn't want to be here, I wouldn't be. Now, get Silver in position. We don't know how quick Dagon will be."

Arguments and outright pleas trembled on my lips, but I forced them back. Ian might be far younger than me, but at two hundred fifty plus, he was more than old enough to know his own mind. If I kept going on about my fears, I'd rattle us both into being less than our fighting best. We couldn't afford that. Tonight was too dangerous as it was.

That's why I nodded, smiling before kissing the finger still pressed to my lips. "Try not to tire yourself out, then," I said in as careless a voice as I could manage. "I have plans to celebrate Dagon's death that involve *lots* of your stamina."

He laughed again. "Same to you, little Guardian."

Then he kissed me, hard, fierce, and astonishingly passionate considering our circumstances. When he stopped, my mouth wasn't the only part of me that throbbed. His slow smirk said he knew how he'd affected me, too.

Not to be outdone, I grabbed his cock, squeezing until his eyes lit up with green. "Now I won't be the only one impatient for our victory celebration," I taunted before letting go and leaving to take care of Silver.

His low laugh promised sweet revenge later. My spirits lifted, shoving down my earlier fears. We *would* win tonight and both of us would survive to celebrate it. We had to.

Once I had Silver safely concealed behind a small, swinging door the Simargl could also use to exit, if need be, I took my position behind another blind door on the opposite side of the room. Ian came in and flew up to his spot, concealed above a sheet of painted plywood in the ceiling. Once we were safely out of view of the mirrors, I pushed the lever on the pulley system we'd set up. The drapes rose, exposing the mirrors. Now, we waited.

An hour ticked by. Then two. Then three. By the fourth, I was tempted to leave my position to stretch my legs, but I didn't. We'd wait until after dawn if need be. Once the sun was up, the chances of Dagon appearing dropped dramatically. But night . . . night was his playtime.

A little past 1 A.M., I heard a whoosh as if a gust of wind had blown into the fun house. It was followed by a wave of power and the sulfur smell all demons had. I clamped down on my aura, squelching all hints of my supernatural energy. At the same time, I readied myself to let my power burst free. Dagon hadn't frozen time yet, but he would. It was his favorite trick.

Footsteps sounded, then I heard, "Fun house, eh? 'Mirror, mirror, on the wall, who's the fairest of them all?'" in a singsong voice.

Dagon's voice. Yes! I'd been worried that he'd send someone else out of an abundance of caution. He hadn't, so his arrogance was everything I'd hoped. We'd set up more mirrors at the front of the funhouse, some broken, some not, but all unspelled. I wanted him to think nothing of the mirrors in this room when he finally reached it.

"Where's my little fluffy money bag?" Dagon was still using that singsong voice, only it sounded closer now. My hands tightened, one on the remote drapery switch I'd been holding this entire time, the other on the bone knife. "I know you're in here. Come out, come out, wherever you are . . ."

Silver's whine was a thin, soft sound filled with fear. Dagon's footsteps quickened. "There you are," he said, all merriment gone from his voice. His footsteps were now right outside the room. Silver whined again, sounding desperate.

"Come here, you little—" Dagon began.

Magic flooded the room, drenching me with its power. Dagon let out a snarl that quickly turned into a howl. Ian told me the mirror spell came in two modes: silent and sound. No contest as to which one I'd wanted. I wouldn't have even needed the full-body splash of magic to know the trap had been sprung. Not with Dagon's howl turning into a scream of pure rage.

Listening to it felt better than therapy. I'd waited over four and a half thousand years for Dagon to pay for everything he'd done. Today, his bill finally came due.

I pressed the button on the remote control, hearing fabric swish as the counter-weight system we'd set up dragged the drapes back up to re-cover the mirrors. I came out of my hiding spot to see Ian already diving down from his ceiling perch. He rammed his bone knife into Dagon's left eye with such force, the tip of his blade came out the back of Dagon's skull.

I didn't pause to savor Dagon's new scream. I slammed my bone knife into his other eye, putting all my rage, guilt, and grief into the blow. My hand went all the way through Dagon's skull and into the mirror behind him. It shattered as the double blow sealed Dagon's fate. His eye sockets turned into blackened, smoking holes that burned my arm from its close contact. I didn't care. His final, enraged scream was drowned out by the rest of the mirrors exploding as the spell ended with his death.

Shards of glass ripped through the room, slicing into me from head to toe. I didn't feel the pain. I was too filled with relief as I watched Dagon's body start to shrink and deflate, almost like when vampires died and their bodies aged back to their actual years. By the time Ian yanked my arm from Dagon's skull to swing me around in joyous circle, Dagon's body resembled a man-sized piece of beef jerky.

"Break my back and baste my balls, we did it!"

Ian's shout coincided with my burst of laughter, as if my happiness was too great for my body to contain. Finally, it was over! All the pain, the planning, the thousands of years of waiting while fighting despair thinking Dagon might never be brought to justice . . . finished. Maybe now, at last, all of Dagon's victims could rest in peace.

I don't know if Ian kissed me or if I yanked his head down to mine. Either way, our mouths were pressed together with all the jubilance of our combined victory. Dagon's victims weren't just avenged; Ian was also *free*, his soul his own again. I was happier than I'd ever been.

Then a voice hit me like a thousand icicles suddenly shoved through my veins. "This is so sweet, if I had a heart, I'd cry."

Ian shoved me back, putting himself between me and the owner of that voice that should not, *could not* be there.

"Hello," Dagon purred. "Miss me?"

Dagon winced when he saw the corpse. "I told Rani to watch out for a trap, but he didn't think either of you were smart enough to set up anything he couldn't get out of."

That dried-up demon husk was *Rani*? "You glamoured him to look like you."

Dagon's smile was all teeth. "Got the idea from your friend Vlad since glamour worked so well on Ian the first time. You know what they say about fooling someone twice, boy." He tossed his blond hair before wagging a finger at Ian. "Shame on *you*."

Ian smiled back. "Here's a saying I fancy more: If at first you don't succeed . . ."

"Try, try again," I finished. We'd known the mirror trap might not work. That's why Ian and I still had another bone knife, and we also had a whole theme park full of surprises.

Without warning, Dagon's power blasted from him like a bomb going off. It froze time in the room, rolling over me before catching Ian in its pitiless grip. Just as fast, I let mine loose, releasing Ian from his paralysis before Dagon could take so much as a step toward him.

"I don't think so." I barely recognized my own voice from the growl that came out of my throat. Dagon stared at me as if he'd suddenly seen a stranger, too. Then he laughed.

"Look at you, girl! Full of power now that you're all grown up." Then he took in a deep sniff and laughed again. "From your scent, you've been mixing your work with play, too. Not that I blame you. I couldn't resist Ian, either."

I swung a horrified glance at Ian. "You didn't?"

Dagon took advantage of that by leaping around Ian to slam a fist into my stomach. The impact knocked me through all the remaining walls in the fun house and into the Tilt-A-Whirl behind it. I hit that hard enough to crack my skull, then shook my head to clear it as I looked back at the fun house.

Ian and Dagon burst through its roof. They were grappling in midair, each landing punishing blows on the other. Dagon tried freezing time again. I blasted his spell apart before Ian even slowed down. Then I grabbed my second bone knife, about to fly toward them when a fresh sizzle of power hit my back like a swarm of stinging hornets. I whirled around to see who it was and . . . what the hell?

Dagon was behind me! I spared a glance to confirm that another Dagon was still in the air fighting with Ian. He was. The demon had indeed arrived with reinforcements. As an extra trick, he'd glamoured all of them to look like him. Now, I didn't know which was the real Dagon. Didn't matter. We'd just kill them all.

This Dagon grinned before disappearing in a clear attempt to teleport the rest of the way to me. I tightened my hand around the bone knife and flew at the spot where I'd last seen him. Seconds later, he appeared back in that same place, frowning.

Surprise! I thought nastily. The complex web Ian and I had spent days casting over the entire park meant demons could teleport into it, but they couldn't teleport within the park's limits again.

I slammed into him, shoving my knife into his eye at the same time. The force smashed us both through the Tilt-A-Whirl I'd recently cracked my head against. Its heavy steel frame tore as we hurtled through both sides of it, the jagged metal ripping into my flesh. The double impact was so violent, I missed when I aimed for the demon's other eye.

He punched me in the head. My vision went dark and horrible crunching noises exploded in my skull. I managed to tear away before he landed another one, flying blind until my eyes healed enough to see again. When they did, everything was still blurry. I blinked until I saw a shadowy image of the demon running beneath me, something large in his hands.

Carousel pony, I realized as he hurled it at me. I dodged far enough for it to miss most of me, though its legs struck my shoulder with a glancing blow. I blinked rapidly, trying to force my vision to heal faster.

"Did you lose something, girl?" the demon taunted in Sumerian, holding up a small object this time. A few more blinks and I saw it was my demon-bone knife. But that wasn't what made me feel as though I'd been hit by a car.

His voice and scent was the same as Dagon's. The glamour Dagon had used had been thorough. But the way this demon said 'girl,' with one more syllable than the ancient language called for . . . I remembered a demon who used to pronounce it that way.

"Fenkir," I said, hate slicing deeper than the metal had.

Dagon's face grinned back at me, but the one eye that wasn't blackened out and smoking . . . I knew the person staring back at me from that eye, no matter what color and shape it came in.

"Girrrrllll," Fenkir said, deliberately dragging out the only word he and the others had called me back when I'd been their captive. "This time, when I kill you, you'll stay dead." And he wagged the demon-bone knife at me.

I'd never been murdered by demon bone through the eyes before, so it was possible. Perhaps they knew my father was actually a different sort of demon.

I wasn't about to ask. I also wasn't going to let the fear of permanent death stop me. I only paused to cast a split-second glance Ian's way. He and Dagon were still trading blows that leveled everything in their path, but Ian didn't seem to need my help at the moment. And I *really* wanted to show Fenkir how far I'd come since I had been the traumatized, broken girl he'd last seen.

I held my arms out. Wind began to blow my hair around as the power I summoned spilled out into the air around me. Fenkir cocked his head, squinting with his one eye as he watched.

"Are you too much of a coward to come down and fight?"

"Don't worry. I'm coming."

The power built, fueled by memories I finally freed because they gave it fuel. When it grew enough to make my skin burn as if something inside was trying to claw its way out, I aimed that power right at Fenkir and released it.

He screamed. A pitiless part of me enjoyed hearing it. *Told you I was coming. Here I am.*

Then he ran. My power continued to laser into him with concentrated beams. His legs became sluggish. I flew at him right as he tripped. He rolled when he fell, holding the bone knife in front of him while an expression I'd never seen before crossed his features.

Panic.

If I were Fenkir, I'd pause to savor that expression on my victim's face. Then, I'd take my time torturing that person, instead of delivering a clean kill. I'd also laugh, while promising to stop if he or she begged me pathetically enough. But of course I wouldn't, and I would laugh again as I continued the torture. That was Fenkir.

It wasn't me. I landed on him with all the force I could muster. It broke my legs, but it shattered his rib cage and spine. The momentary paralysis made it easy for me to rip the bone knife from his hand. Then I stabbed it through both his eyes even though one was still blackened and smoking. I was off him again before his body had a chance to start deflating.

Fenkir loved drawing out the pain before he killed people. I just wanted justice served. For him, it finally was.

I yanked the bone knife out of Fenkir's eye and flew back toward the fun house. Ian and the other Dagon were no longer there. They'd moved their battle near the rusted Paratrooper ride. Two of the mock metal parachutes were torn from their perch when Dagon threw Ian into them. I flew faster and grabbed Ian's arm, spinning him around before he could fly back to attack again.

"Not here!" I urged in a low voice.

Enough of the bloodlust left his gaze for him to nod, but Ian also had actual blood all over him. I hoped some of it was Dagon's.

From the crimson lines streaking the demon, it could be. But was this really Dagon? Or another glamoured demon?

I had to find out. "Fenkir's gone to be with Rani," I called out. "Hope you don't miss him too much."

Fury lit Dagon's features. Then it cleared and he laughed. "Such a shame. He was so looking forward to getting another piece of you. You remember how Rani and Fenkir used to love taking turns? I never understood how they bore all your *sniveling* enough to enjoy it, but enjoy it they did."

Yes, this was the real Dagon, and his smirk made those memories all too vivid. He'd worn that same expression countless times while I was being abused. Those memories had fueled me with Fenkir, but now they cut me. I couldn't let that happen. I had to lose the despair and keep only the rage.

"Know what I remember, Dagon?" Ian's tone was scathingly bright. "How you panted after me for weeks before I agreed to spend the night with you. Didn't turn out how you'd hoped, did it? When it was over, you still had blue balls, and I had your egg-sized blue diamond. Looks smashing on the mantle of my favorite house, by the way."

Dagon's expression became mottled with rage. "Fuck you."

Ian flashed a savage grin. "Oh, you tried. And failed."

Dagon tore off one of the remaining paratrooper pods and hurled it at Ian. He ducked it with a crowing sound. "Still sore about that, hmm? You should be, I'm magnificent. Ask her."

"*That's* why Dagon's been hunting you for decades?" I let myself laugh out loud at the demon's palpable humiliation. Dagon had tried to wound me with the past, but while I'd dealt with that, Ian had made sure Dagon's strategy backfired. "Wow, you got fucked, all right," I went on mercilessly. "Just not how you wanted, and let me assure you—you missed *out*."

Ian grinned, continuing to fly toward the wooden roller coaster while Dagon chased after us. "Diamond's valued at millions," Ian called out to me. "Still wasn't worth cuddling and kissing him to get close enough to steal it."

We were almost at the roller coaster. Dagon was still furious, but he'd slowed down from his single-minded pursuit of us. I needed to get him mad enough to keep following.

"When we leave here, we're selling that diamond and donating the money to charity," I told Ian. "We'll even make the donation in Dagon's name so everyone can thank him for it."

Ian laughed. "Still treating what's mine as yours, I see."

I raised my voice to make sure Dagon caught every word of what I said next. "Embrace your new state of matrimony, honey!"

That did it. Dagon zoomed toward us, his body upright as if rage kept his spine ramrod straight. I flew around the roller coaster, Ian right behind me. Dagon was *almost* in the blast zone. A little closer . . .

He stopped as if he felt exactly where the blast radius of the salt bombs was located. Then he held out his arms in much the same way I had when I'd channeled the energy to make Fenkir stagger. I'd use that tactic on Dagon if he weren't too strong for it. Plus, I still had to conserve my power in case he tried freezing time again.

But that wasn't what he was doing. Moments later, a shockwave hit me, though not from a time-pause attempt. It had been from the force of three dozen demons instantly teleporting into our area. Ian ground out a curse while I stared at them in dismay.

I looked back at Dagon in time to see him smile. "You didn't think it would be easy to kill me, did you?"

*B*ugger." Ian said the single word with all the vehemence I felt. Then, he gave me a light push toward the horde. "You need to hold them and Dagon off by yourself for a few minutes. Something I have to do."

"That's more important than *this*?" I sputtered.

His smile was a tight flash of fang. "Like you told me before, you have to trust me without arguing for once."

With that, he flew off, leaving me, Dagon, and the newly arrived demons staring after him.

Dagon began to laugh so hard, it sounded like he pulled a muscle from it. "He left you to save his own skin! Ah, girl, I'm enjoying your expression so much, I think I'll let Ian have a head start." Then he whistled at the demons. "Bring her to me alive!" To me, he added, "You stole my last Red Dragon source, so I'm going to use your blood as my new one, and that's only one of many, many plans I have for you."

"Then like Ian, I'll have to disappoint you," I snapped before turning toward the horde. Eeesh. Nearly two score against one was terrible odds, no matter my strength.

I set my jaw and zipped the bone knife into one of the many pockets in my cargo pants. I couldn't risk sheathing it in my belt because the belt could be torn free, and I couldn't risk it being pulled from my hands again. Not when I still needed it to kill Dagon. Besides, they'd been told not to kill me and they felt like average soldiers to me, not upper-echelon demons. There were other ways to level the playing field than risking my only demon-bone knife.

I flew over to them, staying out of their reach but only just. Ian had said he needed time. I'd give him as much as I could. True to Dagon's taunt, he hadn't chased after Ian yet. No, he seemed to be settling in to watch the show with me and his demons.

"Go on, try to teleport up here to get me," I taunted them, then laughed at the multiple failed results. Their attempts ate up only a couple minutes, though. I needed something more dramatic to hold their attention longer.

"I'm guessing none of you can fly, but can any of you jump high enough to reach me?"

That resulted in several more attempts, some of them forcing me to fly higher in sudden aerial leaps. All the while, I kept up the taunts with comments like "Almost!" and "You were so close!" while getting closer to the Enterprise. It was a ride shaped like a Ferris wheel when it was upright, but was now abandoned on the ground—like a huge, multi-spiked metal wheel.

"I'm getting bored, so I'll make it easier for you," I said, landing dead center in the middle of the rust-coated ride.

The demons vaulted over the remaining gondolas and countless metal arms that anchored the gondolas to its base. I sent my magic out, not in a blast that would have warned them but in drips that coated the ride slowly enough to let two of the fastest demons jump me before it was even half finished.

I defended against the worst of their blows, but I didn't fight back when even more demons joined in. All my energy was focused on spilling out more magic in non-alarming drips. Pain exploded everywhere. The blows were too fast to heal between them. Soon, my head sounded like a bag of stones grinding together, I was blind from the blood, and I fought not to puke up my pulverized organs.

But my projection of helplessness galvanized the demons. From the sounds, all of them were probably on the sprawling ride now. I could hear them shouting as they tried to force their way through the others to get their turn to beat me. When I felt my magic reach the end of the enormous wheel, I dropped to my knees and pulled the pin on the spell. Most of my magic wouldn't work on the demons, but it worked fine on inanimate objects.

The wheel burst apart as thousands of pounds of metal instantly turned into high-velocity shrapnel. I was so covered by demons, not a single piece tore into me. From the chorus of screams, the shrapnel hit everyone else. When the demons around me fell back in a belated attempt to shield themselves, I shot straight up so fast, only a few pieces of shrapnel hit me. Then I took out my bone knife, waited a few seconds until the shrapnel was no longer whirling about with tornado-like speed, and flew back down to stab out every eye I could.

I was knee deep in demon corpses when something slammed me from behind. I hurtled into the demon in front of me with enough force to flatten us both. I looked down, seeing the ragged metal edge of a sizeable pole protruding from my stomach. It had gone right through me and into the brown-haired demon I'd landed on.

My body was pinned, but my arms were still free. I stabbed the demon's eyes out before someone yanked my bone knife away. More agony exploded as the pole was lifted with me still on the other end like a skewered fish. I gritted my teeth hard enough to bite off a fang as I shoved myself forward with all my strength. It felt like the pole had been made from razor wire, but I didn't stop until I fell off the other end. Then I whirled, spitting my fang at the demon who'd done this to me.

Dagon looked at the fang and arched a brow. "I've never cared enough to ask before, but do those grow back?"

"I'll have two to bite you with in no time," I promised.

He took the pole he'd impaled me on and hurled it again. Instead of aiming for me, he skewered the demon next to him. Everyone's eyes bulged, mine included.

"When I said bring her to me, it wasn't a suggestion," he told the demons in a blisteringly cheerful voice. "If you make me get her myself, why do I need any of you alive?"

I was grabbed from behind before I could twitch to fly away. Then the demons tore into me as if their lives depended on it, which they now knew they did. Soon, it took all my strength to stay conscious and keep my limbs from being ripped off. Pain drenched me, far past my ability to concentrate enough to cast a spell. After a while, I wasn't even sure if I was still standing. *Whatever Ian had left to do*, I found myself thinking dazedly, *it had better fucking dazzle me when he gets back!*

Then power hit me with the suddenness of a rogue wave. The beatings stopped as the demons looked around to see what had caused it. I tried, too, but there was too much blood in my eyes to see. "What?" I heard Dagon say. He sounded surprised. Was that a good thing or a bad thing?

I swiped at my eyes and turned toward Dagon's voice. Several hard blinks later, I saw Ian flying toward us. He was about thirty meters away, surrounded by small, pale objects that circled him in the air. At first, I thought it was a flock of tiny white birds. When I blinked again, I realized they were bones. Human-looking ones. They were moving around Ian in faster and faster circles. Ian's lips were moving, too, but he was too far away for me to hear him. He must be doing a spell. Why? Ian knew that Dagon was too powerful for most spells to work on him.

The bones suddenly exploded, forming into a pale cloud around Ian. As soon as they did, Ian stabbed himself in the chest with one of his silver knives and twisted the blade. If not for his demon brands, that would have killed him. Blood flowed out and shock filled me. I only knew *one* type of spell that required bones turning into dust and blood from the heart. A grave magic spell.

"Ian, don't!" I shouted.

He ignored me while his blood coated the powdered bones until the cloud that surrounded him was red. From the curse Dagon muttered, he knew what type of spell Ian was attempting, too. More power blasted through the air as Ian began summoning the darkest of energies from beyond the grave.

Gods, he must be trying to create a wraith. If he did, not even Dagon could stand against it. But grave magic was far more likely to kill its caster than be successful. That's why even I had never attempted it. Ian's brands might prevent the spell from killing him, but it could hurt Ian so badly, he wouldn't be able to fight off a weak demon, let alone Dagon. I had to make sure Dagon didn't take advantage of that weakness.

But to do that, I needed to get through these damn demons! Seizing on the distraction, I ripped the arm off the nearest one while he was still looking up at Ian. Then I stabbed it fingers-first into his eyes when he swung back around. He screamed as both of them were pierced from his own twitching appendages. He fell onto me, eyes still smoking as he died. Demon bone was demon bone, whether or not skin was still attached to it.

I held him in front of me as a shield while tearing off more of his bones to use as weapons. I wished I still had my machete, but at some point, one of the demons had ripped it from me. They no longer swarmed me from the front now that I had a weapon that could kill them. But there were still two demons clinging to my back, so I couldn't fly away yet.

I threw myself backward, trying to get them off me by brute force. When I fell on them, I stabbed blindly at whatever was behind me. I ended up killing one out of sheer luck. With only one more clinging to me, I managed to get in the air, but then another demon snatched my leg and anchored me to the ground. Out of the corner of my eye, I saw Dagon fly into Ian, punching, kicking, and stabbing him with a frenzy bordering on maniacal. Ian only protected his eyes as he fought, and all the while, his lips never stopped moving.

A familiar power blasted out from Dagon. Just as fast, I blocked his third attempt to freeze time. Then a brutal blow returned my attention to the demon on my back. I let myself drop out of the air, using all my momentum to give him the full force of our landing. Blood shot up around us but he held on, teeth and claws tearing into me. I stabbed at every part I could reach while looking for something else I could use. In moments, more demons would pile on top of me. I didn't dare deplete more of my strength with another elaborate spell. I had to keep canceling out Dagon's spells against Ian.

A demon running toward me leapt over a pile of metal shards between us. Yes, that! I sent a quick spell to fling the metal into his eyes and into the demon's eyes behind me. The shards blinded the running demon, and I tripped him when he came near. He fell on top of me. I slashed my makeshift bone knife through his eyes, then flung him at the next demon hurtling toward me.

His body knocked him down. I took that split second to flip over and stab the eyes out of the demon beneath me, then leapt to my feet. I'd hacked my way through two more demons when Dagon's laugh made me whip my head up again.

The red cloud around Ian had formed into two figures that were now clear enough to identify. *Fenkir and Rani,* I realized in disbelief. Ian had used *their* bones for this spell?

"You fool!" Dagon chortled. "Don't you know wraiths are made when the rage of a murdered person is yanked from their bones and given form? But I didn't kill Fenkir and Rani. You're raising creatures that will attack *her*!"

Dagon was right. Wraiths went after their murderers and no one else. Why would Ian raise wraiths from Fenkir and Rani's bones? They'd go straight for me as soon as the spell was finished, if Dagon didn't kill Ian first!

Trust me without arguing for once.

Ian's words were a reminder I didn't want in my appalled state. But I couldn't ignore the fact that Ian had trusted me when everything he'd known would've urged him not to. I did owe him the same, even if everything *I* knew screamed at me to run for my life before he finished that spell.

But if this ended up killing me, I'd make sure my first words to Ian after I came back from the dead was *I knew this was a bad idea!*

hatever happened, I couldn't afford to be incapacitated when Ian was done with that spell. I yanked a hunk of breastplate and rib from the demon body nearest me. Then I wrapped my hand around it so the rib bones poked out between my fingers. With that and the long, thin radius bone in my other hand, I started slashing at every demon near me.

They fought back just as viciously, now ignoring Dagon's order not to kill me. They even used the same method I had and tore bones off their dead companions for weapons. I was slashed, stabbed and sliced countless times, then healed only to have it happen again. Adrenaline, determination, and fury numbed most of the pain. The rest made me stagger as I tried to force them back far enough so I could fly away. Above all, I protected my eyes. Everything else, I could heal or come back from. I still didn't want to test the theory that I couldn't come back from *that*.

The demons around me were suddenly flung aside so hard, many landed on their asses. My brief exultation vanished when I saw why. Two filmy forms streaked toward me. Icy power burst from them with such tremendous force, it cleared everything in their path. *Oh, fuuuuck!* was my single thought. Then the wraiths made from Fenkir and Rani's bones ripped into me.

Time evaporated. So did distinct sensations. I didn't have separate body parts like two arms, two legs, a torso and a head anymore. Instead, I was one exposed nerve that was being endlessly shredded, scorched with icy fire and shredded again.

Then that unbelievable agony vanished. I came to, gasping—gasping!—while healing from wounds that had left no marks. Almost tentatively, a black-haired demon stepped out from the group that had gathered a few meters away, watching me. Then a shrill scream yanked everyone's attention upward.

Ian floated near the top of the wooden roller coaster. His arms were raised above his head and blood poured from his mouth and eyes. But he wasn't the one screaming. It was Dagon, because the two wraiths were now tearing into him.

Holy and unholy gods, Ian had actually done it! I hadn't known wraiths could be redirected from the person who murdered them to someone else. Now, I was seeing it with my own eyes. The demons seemed transfixed by it, too. They watched as the wraiths stabbed their bodies through Dagon in endless loops that had the demon convulsing so hard, his arms and legs broke.

So that's what they'd been doing to me, I thought numbly, almost pitying Dagon the horrifying pain. Almost.

Then Ian's hands moved, the gestures too fast to track. The wraiths began carrying Dagon toward the roller coaster. As if that broke the trance, the dark-haired demon resumed his path toward me, but he kept glancing up. Clearly, he'd rather keep staring at what was happening to Dagon than try to kill me, but he kept coming for me nonetheless.

I attempted to fly away, cursing when I couldn't. The wraiths' attack must've taken too much out of me. It took all my effort to scrounge around for more demon bone. I must have lost mine when the wraiths ripped through me. If I didn't find some, I'd be in trouble. Soon, more demons would get back to trying to kill me, once they stopped watching the wraiths and Dagon.

I'd grabbed a handful of what looked like half-crushed shin bones before throwing them away when they folded, too broken to be lethal. Then, incredibly, I saw *my* demon-bone knife a few meters away, the gleam from its steel-reinforced back practically winking at me in the moonlight. One of the demons must have torn it free from my pocket while fighting me. Instead of picking it up, he had left the knife on the ground.

I lunged for it right as the black-haired demon coming after me saw it, too. Both of us scrambled to grab the knife. It skidded out of our grasp as our struggles knocked it away.

"Now!" Ian's shout jerked my head up. "Detonate, detonate!"

I shoved the demon off me to grab the bulky object in the pocket of my cargo pants. Another demon jumped on my back, tearing into me with something that burned as if I was being splashed with acid. I didn't defend myself, keeping my focus on pressing every part of the detonator within my pocket. It felt broken from the various fights. I wasn't sure if it still worked, but I had to try. After a few frantic seconds, I felt a dip in the metal and pushed inward, hard.

Explosions rocked the roller coaster as our salt bombs went off. There were so many, they turned the air white. We'd also spelled them to increase their distance and velocity. Dagon's new shriek when salt blasted into him was sweet music. More salt bombs near the roller coaster's base shot out far enough to strafe the demons surrounding me. Their screams soon drowned out Dagon's. I took advantage of their writhing to force myself free and grab my bone knife. I still couldn't fly, but I managed several jumps as the wooden skeleton of the roller coaster toppled over, the base crumbling with the detonation.

"Bone knife!" Ian shouted. "Now!"

I had one, but how was I going to get it to him? I still couldn't fly! But even scalded all over with salt while being strafed with wraiths, Dagon had started to struggle. I had no idea how he managed it. He must be far, far stronger than I'd realized. Ian had clearly used everything he had to wield the grave magic enough to do the unthinkable and force the wraiths off me and onto Dagon. Now, he looked as if he couldn't hold himself aloft in the sky much longer.

"Hold on!" I shouted back. "I'm coming!"

I pulled extra energy from the only water source I could find: a left-over sewer tank buried beneath the park. It didn't have much in it, but I took everything. Then I flung myself into the air without knowing if I'd rise or splat to the ground.

I rose. Ian let out a roar when he saw it. Then he managed to fly over to Dagon and get so close, the wraiths' carnage tore into him, too. Right as I reached them, he flipped Dagon over so the demon was facing me.

Dagon's screams were white noise. All I was focused on was his eyes. I hit one at full force, my momentum driving the bone knife deep into his skull. His shriek ruptured my eardrums, causing instant deafness. I ripped the knife out and rammed it into Dagon's other eye without hearing his new scream. Smoke burst from that, too, and I saw rather than heard Ian's shout.

Then Ian's arms fell away, and he dropped from the air. Dagon dropped, too, both eyes still smoking as he hit the ground very near to Ian. Both men hit hard and didn't move. Then light burst from Dagon, and the wraiths disappeared. His body also began shrinking into itself, proving he was finally, truly dead.

I couldn't celebrate. I was too worried about Ian. I flew down, landing hard enough to crack the ground next to him. Then I touched Ian's back. He wasn't moving. I was struck with fear over what I'd find when I turned him over. He'd landed on his stomach, his arm flung over the part of his face that wasn't pressed into the concrete. He felt cold, gods, so cold! What if Dagon had done something as a final, cruel taunt? What if he'd spelled himself so that if he died, Ian died, too?

"Ian." I ran my hand along his back, gulping when he didn't move or speak. "Ian, wake up!"

He rolled over and my heart jumped as if struck with a thousand volts. Then he sat up, his forearm still pressed against his forehead. "Remind me never to attempt grave magic again," he moaned. "That hurt too much even for me to enjoy."

I grasped his free hand and pressed it to my chest. I would've hugged him, but I was afraid that would cause him more pain. "You're really okay?"

What a stupid question. He'd just said he wasn't. But I needed to hear his voice again, even if it was only to answer my ridiculous query. What I should be doing is finishing off the rest of the demons before they ceased being incapacitated from the salt bombs. Not sitting here clutching Ian's hand while unable to look away from his face.

And I would do that. In a minute.

"Mostly." He gave me a faint smile. "Twisting the wraith spell to send them after Dagon still has me all sixes and sevens, but I'll recover. Good thing it worked."

"Yes, good thing," I breathed. "Though you should never have attempted it. That spell could've gotten you killed in several different ways."

His smile faded. "We were outnumbered, Dagon wasn't taking our bait, and he was more powerful than either of us anticipated. It was a choice of possible dying versus absolutely dying. Given the choice, I'd always rather go down fighting."

I brushed my lips over his knuckles. "So would I." Then, even though it was the last thing I wanted to do, I released his hand. "Speaking of fighting, those demons screeching over their salt wounds aren't going to kill themselves. Stay here. I'll be back after I take care of them."

This time, his smile looked more like the usual Ian: half teasing, half enticing. "Give me a moment, and I'll join you. Can't have you tiring yourself out. We have a celebration to—"

His smile froze and he stopped speaking so abruptly, I looked back at the demons to see if one of them had gotten up and started doing something threatening. But no, they were all still writhing on the ground more than thirty meters away.

Then I looked back at Ian—and screamed.

His right eye was now black and smoking.

$\mathcal{I}$ an's head drooped and he listed to the side. That's when I saw the hilt of a bone knife sticking out of the back of his head. Dagon—how? HOW?—was rising up behind Ian. His eyes, healed back to their icy blue color, stared right at me as he shoved another blade into the back of Ian's skull.

"Don't!" My scream broke from sheer panic. "Please, stop!"

Dagon did, though his hand remained on the knife that was half-buried in Ian's skull. Shudders wracked Ian, filling me with relief and rage. Those shudders meant the second knife hadn't bitten too deeply yet. He still had a chance.

A little smile played on Dagon's lips as he leaned over so he could see me fully past Ian's shoulder. "What will you give me if I don't kill him, girl?"

". . . n't." Ian's harsh grunt was barely coherent, but his remaining eye blazed with green and his expression translated it plainly. *Don't.*

". . . eave . . ." Ian forced out, his stare drilling into mine. ". . . by . . . owr' . . . s'ell . . .'ing . . . us . . . I . . . commaaaaan . . . ou . . ."

I choked back a sob as I pieced together what he was trying to say. "You can't command me to leave by the power of the spell binding us. I got out of its hold almost two weeks ago, when I killed the body it was tied to."

Incredibly, a smile ticked the corner of Ian's mouth. ". . . 'eat'd," he said, approval clear in the broken word.

Tears overflowed and I didn't care that they made Dagon grin. "Yes, I cheated. I didn't trust you then, so I wasn't about to make a deal I couldn't get out of."

Dagon tapped the hilt of the bone knife. Anguish flashed across Ian's face before he tried to conceal it. "If you want him to live," Dagon purred, "you'll make another deal, girl. Only this one, you won't get out of."

Of course Dagon wanted my soul, my abilities, my subjugation, or all three. Could I stall him while I siphoned enough power to free Ian? There was no lake, pond, or other water source nearby. But if I stretched my senses, I might be able to find one farther away that I could tap into. I had to try.

"*How* did you survive getting your eyes stabbed out? You couldn't have been playing dead. The wraiths vanished as the spell broke with your death and your body started decomposing. I had no idea you were so powerful. Do other people know?"

His laugh was his delighted one, chilling me because it usually heralded horrible things to come. I tried to ignore it as I sent my senses outward, skipping over a dried-up well that had once been used for this park but wouldn't help me now.

"Almost no one does." Dagon's tone was as carefree as a child's. He even shifted to make himself more comfortable. Then he tapped the knife hilt again as if to warn Ian not to move. "I suppose I have you to thank for the idea."

"Me?" What felt like it used to be a stream was now dried into the merest trickle. Damned climate change. I pulled what little I could from that and kept searching.

"All your dying and coming back." For the barest instant, hatred filled Dagon's expression. Then his bright smile was back. "Such incredible power, wasted on a half-mortal brat. Still, if one as pathetic as you could beat death, I could, too. Demons already had access to the right power source. We'd just been transferring it instead of harvesting it."

Power source? Did he mean the magic that all demons inherently had? But demons didn't transfer magic. They enhanced their abilities with it . . . though they did transfer something else.

"Souls?" I asked, so sickened by the prospect, I stopped searching for water for a second.

Now his laugh sounded genuine. "Very good!"

Then his laughter cut off and his deceptively youthful features twisted with all the rage that his eons of living had allowed him to store up.

"And you cost me two: one to harvest for my resurrection, one to heal my body so I wasn't trapped inside a half-rotted corpse. Souls aren't as easy to come by anymore, girl. People are more loath to bargain them away. I also have to send *some* up the chain, or I'll draw suspicion. That's why you're now going to sell me yours, unless you'd rather see your lover die?"

Dagon tapped the knife hilt again, harder. Ian's features tightened until his cheekbones stood out in sharp relief and his jaw looked carved from steel. His gaze lasered on me, not a hint of pleading for his life in it. Instead, defiance blazed out.

Don't you dare! that look said. *Sod Dagon and his filthy deals!*

I understood that rage. Oh, how I understood it! I also hated the idea of giving Dagon anything he wanted, especially—especially!—this. But as I stared at Ian, I found myself unable to tell Dagon I wouldn't do it.

There are ways out of deals like this, I rationalized. Ian had almost gotten out of his deal, except for Dagon's surprise resurrection trick. For all I knew, my father might be able to help me get my soul back, too. Furthermore, *I* didn't stay dead after I died. Dagon would have a much harder time trying to collect a soul from someone who couldn't be killed. I still had a chance if I did this. If I said no, Ian didn't.

"I'm sorry," I whispered to Ian. "I don't want to, either. But I can't . . . I can't just let you *die.*"

Dagon began to smile. That rage and tightness left Ian's face. His expression filled with a wistful sort of tenderness that made no sense considering our terrible circumstances.

"... ud've ...'uv'd ...'oo," Ian said, struggling to get each syllable out. Then, he closed his eye.

"What?" I asked softly.

I was still trying to translate what he'd said when Ian slammed his head backward, the violent motion ramming Dagon's knife all the way through his remaining eye.

$\int$moke burst from Ian's ruptured eye. At once, his body began to collapse into itself, that silky ivory skin turning to leather that cracked and split until his features were unrecognizable. Horror froze me into immobility while my mind screamed endless denials. Then pain roared through me, until I felt like my bones had been replaced with a storm of knives.

"*That* spoiled my plans," Dagon said disgustedly. "I was going to kill him after you agreed, then laugh at you while I reneged. Ah, well." His hands clamped around Ian's head. "At least he's still good for something else."

He sealed his mouth over the back of Ian's head and inhaled deeply. Something bright flashed for an instant before a glow appeared in Dagon's throat. He dropped Ian's head, swallowed that glow, then belched as if he'd just shotgunned a beer.

"Mmmm. His soul was taste-eee."

Something broke inside me. Not grief; that waited beneath my pain and rage, patient and far deadlier than both. No, it wasn't that. All but one of the chains that held down the thing Tenoch warned me about for thousands of years had just snapped.

You cannot control the full power of your other nature, Veritas. It's too strong. Siphon away bits of it if you must, but always, always keep the rest of it chained. Promise me.

Several of those chains had snapped when Tenoch died. Only my promise had kept me from breaking the last few. Now, only one strained against the force surging beneath it. I might have thrown more chains over it. I'd promised Tenoch I always would. But Dagon kept smacking his lips, mocking my pain with the same malevolent joy he'd shown me and countless others.

And at the same time, I realized what Ian had been trying to tell me when he'd said ". . . ud've . . .'uv'd . . .'oo."

I hadn't understood the garbled words at first, but now, they blazed across my mind with crystalline clarity.

Could have loved you.

Ian had fought to get those words out. He'd fought again when he denied Dagon the final taunt the demon had intended. Ian must have known Dagon's offer to spare him was no more than a cruel trick, despite my being too desperate to see that.

Given the choice, I'd always rather go down fighting, he'd said mere minutes ago. From the moment I'd met him to his very *last* moment, he'd proven that.

Now he was gone. Murdered by the same demon who'd stolen far, far too much from me. A demon who was still smacking his lips as if trying to draw out the very last drops of my pain for his delight. *Could have loved you . . .*

"I could have loved you, too," I said out loud, ignoring Dagon's surprised "Huh?" in response.

Then I snapped that last chain myself.

Power crashed into every part of me. It gushed until my skin split, healed, then split again, as if my body was too small to contain it. My vision went black, but it didn't matter. All at once, I could *feel* everything around me. More than that, I could feel the thrum of water from numerous sources, some very near, some several kilometers away. The energy in the water called to me, twining around that ever-growing force as if begging to be a part of it.

I didn't attempt to fly, but I was suddenly in the air. Dagon grabbed me, trying to pull me back down. My eyes opened, bathing him in brilliant beams of silver. He let me go, dropping to the ground. Then he began to back away, slowly.

"Girl," he said in a lower, almost cautious tone.

I concentrated on the water closest to me, marveling that I had never considered using it from these sources before. Why hadn't I? It had been right within my grasp this whole time.

"That's *not* my name," I growled.

Then I ripped out all the water from Dagon's body. It came out bloody, but so much more powerful than what I'd find in an ordinary pond or stream. I stripped the considerable energy from it, ignoring the way Dagon's scream turned hoarse as his throat and the rest of him instantly desiccated. Then I kept the bloody water floating around me without needing a second thought to do so.

That had been easy. What else could I do?

The demons. Their screams choked off into odd, hissing sounds as their bodies abruptly went dry. Now I had a *lot* of water at my disposal. I pulled the energy out of it and played with the remainder. Some I turned into steam and scalded the dry flesh off Dagon and the other demons. Others parts I kept swirling in the air around me.

But the steam rehydrated Dagon and the other demons more than I preferred. I stopped scalding them to rip out both the old and the new water they'd healed enough to regenerate. I was focused on pulling all the energy from it when I sensed something hurtling toward my eye.

I froze it into place without thinking about whether I could. I just . . . did. Then I looked at the bone knife I'd just encased in ice. It floated mere centimeters from my eye, its sharp point still red. A glance down confirmed it was one of the same knives that had killed Ian. Dagon had ripped them from Ian's head, keeping one while throwing the other at me.

I stared at Ian's remains through the force that had overtaken me. It registered my grief, but in an insulated way, filtering the facts through while leaving emotions behind. Dagon had murdered the man I considered mine. He had also tried to murder me. I would punish him for that. I would also punish all who'd helped him do it. It was what they deserved.

I started with the demons, sending the water hovering near me down in a rush that coated the ground around them. Then I pulled it back up, making sure the demons saw the new articles it contained. They tried to run when they saw the pieces of bone from the skeletons of their slain, but their bodies were too dry, so they could only shuffle. A few tried to teleport out. If they weren't so weak, it would have worked. Ian was dead, so every part of the spell fused in his magic would have died, too. But I'd ripped too much water and energy from them to teleport.

I turned the water containing demon bone into jagged bits of ice. Then I rammed that into their eyes. Their screams reached a near-simultaneous crescendo before silencing with a finality that gave me a sense of resolution versus satisfaction. After they were dead, I pulled all those bits of bones out of their eyes and covered them with more ice. Then I aimed those new pieces at Dagon, who was trying to fly and couldn't.

"I don't know how many extra souls you have in you to burn through before you stay dead," I told him in a calm voice, "but I'm going to find out."

Dagon spun around, holding both hands over his eyes to protect them. "If you kill me, you'll *never* see Ian again!"

I yanked the last bits of water out of the dead demons and used it to form an ice shield that knocked Dagon down when it hit him. I piled more ice on top of him, skipping only the parts that contained demon bone shards. Those I poised over him in every direction he might attempt to escape. After all that, I floated down to him.

His hands were still over his eyes. That was fine. I didn't mind stabbing the ice weapons through them. "You already made sure I'd never see Ian again when you killed him and swallowed his soul. You have nothing left to threaten me with or bargain with me for, demon."

The ice I'd piled over him kept Dagon from moving his arms, but his fingers flicked in the general direction of Ian's corpse. "If a harvested soul has the power to bring me back from the dead, it can bring him back, too."

He *was* attempting to bargain. How interesting. "You're saying you'd harvest someone else's soul to resurrect Ian?"

His tone grew crafty. "Demons like me have the power to transfer souls from one place to another. Why *couldn't* I resurrect Ian by harvesting the power from someone else's soul, then put Ian's soul back in his body and use another one to heal him good as new? But kill me, and you kill Ian's last chance to be alive again."

My laughter was knives sharpening against each other. Even insulated by the incredible power of my other nature, grief found its way to me. "You probably could do all that. But you won't. I almost took your word about saving Ian's life earlier. Look how that turned out for me."

More slivers of pain slipped in, drawn by the grief spreading like poison through me. Talking about Ian was dangerous. It fueled my vampire half, which was screaming and beating against its new cage with all its might. I could drown that half with more of this power. I should do that. It would insulate me from its weakness, grief, and pain. When had it ever brought me anything except those three?

"I can bring Ian back," Dagon said, sounding desperate now. "Only me. Kill me, and Ian stays dead forever."

The demon would say anything to save his own life. Pathetic. Why hadn't I killed him already? Why wasn't I sending the bone-encased ice knives into his eyes right this moment?

. . . *could have loved you, could have loved you, could have loved you . . .*

The new cage housing my vampire half shattered. So did the ice knives. Water and bits of bones rained over Dagon as all my pain, grief, hope, love, fears . . . everything that was *me* roared back on top. It shoved my other nature beneath it, winding countless chains over it to keep it down. Gods, it *burned* to feel everything again! For a moment, I didn't think I could stand it. At once, that powerful numbness tempted me. *If you let me free*, it promised, *I will protect you from all this.*

I couldn't. Not if Ian still had a chance. I channeled all my scorching feelings at it, their intensity forcing it back and forming ever more chains over it.

"I don't trust you, Dagon, but there is someone who might be able to do everything you said," I found myself saying.

Dagon peeked out from behind his hands, eyes widening at the water and bone fragments now covering him. "Don't bother." Even soaked with bloody water, his laugh was a dry wheeze. "Your father doesn't care enough to help you."

"He might not," I agreed, continuing to shove my other half down and fling every inner chain I had over it so it wouldn't control me again. "But I'm going to find out."

$\mathcal{I}$ jumped on Dagon before he healed enough to attempt tele-porting. The web around the park had fractured with Ian's death since his magic had powered some of it. Then I grabbed two larger pieces of demon bone from the many shards around him. Before he could react, I stabbed one through his eye and held the shard over his remaining eye. Dagon screamed, cursing and threatening me in more languages than even I knew about how I'd regret this.

I ignored him as I twisted the blade in his smoking, blackened eye socket. Slowly, blood began to drip out. I kept twisting until I had the amount I needed. Only blood from someone at the edge of death would work for this ritual. Then I left the knife in his eye socket to give myself a free hand. I wet my finger in his dripping blood, then began drawing the first of a dozen symbols that would summon the Warden of the Gateway to the Netherworld.

Yes, I could kill myself to get to him faster, but that would mean leaving Dagon alone and giving him a chance to escape. I wasn't doing that. Not with Ian's soul inside him.

Each time I finished a symbol, white-hot pain shot through me. That pain grew until it felt as if I'd submerged my body into a pool of fire. By the ninth symbol, I was trembling from it, and I fought to keep those shakes from my hand. Each symbol had to be flaw-less, or I'd need to do this all over again.

Dagon shifted beneath me, almost causing me to miss a stroke in the tenth symbol. I shoved the bone shard closer until it nicked the jelly in his eye. "Don't think I won't kill you before I let you leave. And if you burn up Ian's soul to resurrect yourself, I'll stab your eyes out a thousand times if needed until I know you'll stay dead."

"Fool," Dagon hissed. "This will gain you nothing even if you do succeed. Ian never cared for you. He only pretended to, so he could use your affection to his best advantage. That's what Ian does. He did the same to me, remember?"

A month ago, I would have agreed with Dagon. Now, I knew better. I let out a grunt as I finished the tenth symbol. "Are you trying to talk me into killing you this instant instead of waiting to see if I can save Ian? If so, don't bother."

"I'm trying to speak sense to you," he snapped. "Release me. I'll take my life as reimbursement for my murdered men and count the score even between us. That is the best deal you could possibly make."

"I don't think so." I began drawing the eleventh symbol. More agony sliced into me, and my vision briefly went dark. When it returned, Dagon had tilted his head. Now his eye was a centimeter away from the bone shard instead of beneath it.

I shoved it back until a pearl of crimson touched the tip. "Move again, and you're dead."

Then I tried to clear my mind from the merciless pain. One more symbol. That's all I needed. My hand shook as I wet my finger in Dagon's blood. It still shook when I began to lower it to draw. The blood wavered, about to spill and ruin the spell. I held it over Dagon's chest so if that crimson drop fell, it wouldn't mar the other symbols.

What if I couldn't do this? I had never attempted to summon my father this way before. I only knew this spell because Tenoch had forced me to learn it. It was how he'd summoned the Warden after he'd first rescued me. If I had to start over while in this much pain, I'd never be able to complete this ritual!

But . . . I could use my other nature to finish this last symbol. Pain wouldn't register to me then. Nor would the fear I felt over what would happen to Ian if I failed. I could do that. I only had to let my other half back on top for an instant—

It surged against its chains, sensing freedom. I felt one of them snap and I shuddered. Then I threw more over it with force of sheer will. Tenoch had warned me what would happen if I ever fully let this nature out. Looked like he'd been right. I'd siphoned power as needed from it before, but now that it had gotten a taste of being in control . . . nothing less would probably satisfy it.

And I shouldn't *have* to need it to complete this ritual! Tenoch had done this when he first saved me without having a more powerful other nature. Mencheres had done it once, too, though he denied it to avoid being punished by the council. Ian hadn't, but he'd mastered a grave magic spell well enough to redirect the wraiths from me to Dagon, all without needing a half-celestial nature of indeterminate origin for help.

If they could do those things with vampire power alone, *I* could, too. I wouldn't risk everything simply because using my other nature was easier at this particular moment.

I took a breath to steady myself, giving Dagon one last warning glance. Then, whole body shuddering from geysers of agony going off inside me, I forced my hand steady as I dipped it into Dagon's blood again. What I'd had before was now drying.

"You're going to fail," Dagon snarled.

I didn't reply. I slowly, carefully drew the final symbol without making a mistake. That was all the response he deserved.

The bodies nearby and the splintered remains of the roller coaster around us vanished. A river cut through it, dark as deepest despair. A long, thin boat rode on it. For a moment, I saw two Dagons: one at the helm, and one beneath me.

Then the figure at the helm changed, morphing from the false god I'd been tricked into worshipping as a child into the being that had fathered me. His silvery hair with its gold and blue streaks rustled in a wind I couldn't feel as that lightning-like gaze met mine. Then he took in the bone shards on Dagon and around me.

"I see that neither of you have obeyed me," he said in the mildest of tones. But the waters that weren't really there rippled as if his anger was a strong current.

"Father," I said, choosing the form of address I never used to his face. Then I got off Dagon since he wouldn't dare try anything now. "Dagon has taken someone precious from me. I need your help to get him back."

He said only, "Who murdered all these?" with a glance at the shards littering us and the many skeletons I now couldn't see.

"She did!" Dagon said at once. Then he got up and flung the excess bone fragments off his clothes for emphasis. "She killed every last one of my loyal servants!"

"Who you brought with you so you could kill me," I countered.

His icy blue gaze had regained most of its arrogance now that he no longer had a bone knife against his only remaining eye. "No. I told them *not* to kill you. Deny that, if you dare."

"Did I forget the part where you were trying to enslave me to use my blood as your latest drug trade?" I said caustically. "He came for the Simargyl," I told the Warden, who watched us silently. "You revoked his ownership of Silver and gave him to me, but Dagon used a trace on Silver's blood to ambush us. I killed those demons in self-defense." Mostly true.

"You *lured* me here!" Dagon sputtered. "You had traps—"

"Enough." The Warden's command made Dagon clamp his mouth shut. I would have enjoyed that, but I was too desperate.

"Dagon killed my companion." I fought the lump in my throat as pain of a different kind strafed me. Not physical, yet in its own way, more intense than what I'd felt when I'd been drawing the symbols. "But you can bring him back."

The Warden gave me a diffident glance. "If you're referring to the man who was with you before, he did not pass through my section of the Netherworld."

"No, he didn't," I agreed. Dagon glared at me, silently warning me to say no more. "Dagon kept his soul inside him instead of sending it on."

The Warden was silent again. Moments turned into minutes. I

wanted to demand he say something, but I didn't. Dagon wasn't the only one who kept glancing at the waters beneath the Warden's boat. They weren't rippling anymore. They were roiling.

"If that is true," the Warden finally said, "all I can do is free his soul to send it to the destination meant for it."

"No," I said at once. "Dagon tricked him into dealing it away. If you send his soul on, you condemn him."

"I condemn no one." Was that a hint of weariness is his tone? "I only guard the gateway to the side of the netherworld assigned to me. Whoever passes through it has already sealed their own fate."

I was about to rail at him. Then I remembered what I'd felt when my other nature had been in control. That half came from him, so it stood to reason that it was a milder version of his mentality, psyche, whatever. If so, sentiment meant nothing. I'd have to use something else to sway him.

What would resonate with the Warden, if emotions were irrelevant? Balancing the scales? My other half hadn't felt grief over Ian, but it *had* taken offense at being robbed of what I considered mine. It had also felt that killing Dagon and his men was the appropriate response. If my father had a similar sense of obligatory recompense, maybe I could shift it . . .

"I brought you valuable information about Dagon hoarding souls, and you give me nothing in return," I said. "Your unpaid debt to me stands that much taller."

"Oh?" The faintest hints of disbelief—or was it scorn?—tinged the Warden's tone. "What unpaid debt?"

"I am your progeny." Modern speech failed me in my urgency. "Dagon had me raped, tortured, and murdered for decades, but you gave him the lightest of reprimands by disallowing him further human worship. That is your oldest debt to me. Dagon took your obvious disregard for your progeny as weakness and began keeping some of the souls he was supposed to deliver through your part of the netherworld. Moreover, when he found out I was still alive, he ignored your command and set out to re-enslave me. Even if I also disobeyed your command, I did so after *thousands of years*.

Dagon's contempt of you is so great, he disobeyed you mere days after discovering I still lived. And now I get no recompense for bringing all this to your attention?"

The Warden's silver gaze landed on Dagon. The demon took a step backward—and my father's hand rammed into his chest, disappearing inside Dagon's body. Dagon shuddered, his single eye glowing such a bright shade of red, I thought it might spontaneously combust.

"She speaks the truth." The Warden's voice rose until it boomed as he withdrew his hand. "You *are* filled with souls."

Now I knew my father's voice sounded like thunder when he was angry. Dagon dropped to his knees, either in fear or pain since he continued to shudder as if my father's hand was still feeling around inside his chest. "My lord Warden, I—"

I clutched my hands over my ears at what came out of the Warden's mouth. It was too loud, too awful, too *crowded*, as if every voice trapped in the worst part of the Netherworld had screamed all at once. Then he shut his mouth and that horrifying sound was replaced with silence heavy enough to suffocate.

*Y*ou have indeed done well," the Warden said, turning to me. It was praise I'd never heard from him. "Dagon will be punished. You will never see him again."

In that moment, I was genuinely afraid of him. Whatever my father was—a lesser god, different sort of demon, former or current angel, other type of celestial being, ancient alien for all I knew—his power defied comprehension.

Tenoch had been right to warn me against letting that half of myself fully out. Maybe there wasn't anything inherently evil about it, but that much power was dangerous when it didn't come with a normal conscience. It was like a bomb. Drop it on the right target, and it could save lives. Drop it on the wrong one . . .

"My lord!" Dagon cried. Then he fell forward, clutching his head the way I had when the Warden had let out that otherworldly roar. From the way Dagon rocked and moaned, it was as if he were hearing it directly into his head.

"What about Ian's soul?" I asked.

The Warden's gaze turned fathomless. For an instant, I felt the same mindless, helpless feeling I had in dreams when I was falling from a great height and knew nothing could save me. Then he blinked and I was staring into bright beams of silver again.

"He goes where he has sent himself, as does Dagon."

My emotions cleaved. Dagon would finally get the justice he deserved. Everyone I'd promised to avenge would be avenged. *I* would be avenged. Ian would, too, but he wouldn't be at peace. No, if I let my father do this, Ian would be worse off than he had been when he'd almost died in the Australian outback as a human.

Ever been lost? Ian had roughly asked when speaking of that time. *The worst part was knowing no one cared enough to save you. That's what you remember forever. Not the physical pain or the never-ending fear, but the despair of being utterly alone and knowing you'll die that way . . .*

Ian was lost like that now. He'd stay lost that way forever, unless I did something very reckless with the most powerful being I'd ever encountered. One who didn't feel a shred of love for me because his nature wasn't wired that way.

Given the choice, I'd always rather go down fighting . . .

So would I, I'd replied. Time to prove it. "No deal," I told the Warden.

He paused. No surprise that he'd already dismissed me and turned away. Now, he turned back, the angry twitch to his brow seeming to say, *Who the hell do you think you're talking to?*

"No deal," I repeated in a stronger tone. "Taking Dagon to whatever torment awaits him might make the two of *you* even, but it isn't nearly adequate compensation for me."

"Your additional compensation is not fearing any retribution for all the demon lives you have taken," the Warden replied. Then he pulled Dagon into his boat. He didn't struggle. Dagon didn't even seem to notice. He was still consumed by whatever had him shaking and clutching his head. The two of them and the river started to fade, wood fragments from the blown-up roller coaster now peeking through those dark currents.

Panic made me shout "Wait!" with all the emotion my father couldn't feel. Then I lashed myself. *Stick to terms he understands. Scales and balances, not feelings and needs.*

"Everyone who makes a deal with you has to fill your boat with adequate recompense or they forfeit their lives, right? Well, *my* boat is still empty because I don't want exemption from retribution over killing those demons. I only want Ian's soul returned to his fully healed body."

The Warden rematerialized, saying, "You cannot withdraw one soul from Dagon without freeing them all," in a tone that was as close to snapping as I'd heard from him.

"Then do that." I didn't want to cry, but I couldn't stop the tears that trickled down my cheeks. "Dagon only got them through deals he struck. Knowing him, none of them were fair."

"Fairness is up to another to judge, not me," the Warden replied in that borderline curt tone.

"Once again, you're giving me nothing!"

It tore out of me with all the pain I couldn't force down. I'd tried to reason with him using scales and balances. It hadn't worked. Now, even if it made no difference, he'd know every damn thing I'd been holding back, both now and in the past.

"You sent Tenoch to rescue me, but that was more to keep Dagon from getting too powerful than to save me, wasn't it? You only told Tenoch to look in on me afterward, to keep tabs on me, so I didn't do something similarly problematic with my powers. How else would he know to keep warning me about them? But Tenoch chose to help me heal. He chose to make me his family. You never did. I hope that's because of some cosmic prohibition. Whatever the reason, if you think we've even because you're finally punishing Dagon and you'll shield me from other demons' wrath, let me tell you how you're not even close."

I swiped at my tear-soaked face before getting right up in his. His arms folded across his chest. I ignored the subtle warning. He'd either kill me for this next part or he wouldn't, but he wasn't going to intimidate me into staying silent.

"You sired a half-mortal child. As such, I have emotional needs. You knew that, and you refused to meet them even when I was so broken, I wanted to die. Your *debt to me*, therefore, is enormous. I'm offering a way for you to settle it cheap. Restore Ian's soul back to his body. I don't care what you have to do to make that happen, just like you didn't care what *I* had to do to get the mortal-driven need for love, support, and companionship you denied me for the better part of five thousand years. If you don't, you are choosing to leave your debt unpaid. Whatever big deal you might be in this plane of existence, in my world, that makes you nothing more than another worthless, deadbeat dad."

The Warden's eyes were blazing when I finished, until I had to look away or risk being blinded by them. I waited, expecting something terrible to occur. Dagon bolting out of the Warden's boat wasn't it, but that's what happened.

The Warden caught him after only a few steps. Then he grasped Dagon by his long blond hair and put his hand flat over Dagon's chest, speaking in a language I'd never heard before.

"What are you doing?" Dagon hissed, saving me the trouble.

The Warden didn't reply. Multiple lights began showing through the tattered remains of Dagon's clothes. I sucked in a breath. *Please let those be what I think they are. Please . . .*

Dagon began to scream. The sounds grew into high-pitched shrieks. Then he tried to run again. The Warden lifted him by the hair until Dagon's feet were sawing at the air. All the while, those lights moved farther up Dagon's body. When they reached Dagon's throat, they glowed until his skin resembled a lamp shade thrown over a spotlight.

"What's happening?" I had to shout to be heard.

"The souls are eating their way out of him," my father replied in his normal, dispassionate voice. "The more of his essence they devour, the faster they can free themselves."

Devour his essence? That sounded ominous, but I'd worry about the ramifications later. I watched, hope building as those lights crawled ever higher. Then, like fireworks shooting out, they burst from Dagon's open, screaming mouth.

There were so many of them! I counted thirteen or fourteen before they vanished from sight. I whirled, looking back toward Ian's body, but I still couldn't see it. All I saw was the dark river flowing around me. My father dropped Dagon. He fell much the same way he had when I'd stabbed his eyes out, but he wasn't dead. His closed eyes were now as whole as my own. Both of them.

"It is done," the Warden said in a flat tone. "Your terms of reimbursement have been met."

I stared at him as I approached. Then I did something I never thought I'd have the courage—or desire—to do. I put my arms around him. "Thank you."

I'd be in less pain if I hugged a power station transformer shooting electricity from every wire, but I didn't let go even when his arms stayed loose and he didn't hug me back. Something flowed over me, though, breaching even the pain. A sensation that felt like an otherworldly caress.

Then it stopped as he stepped out of my arms. "Time is short. I must tell you the repercussions for this."

"Whatever they are, I'll deal with them," I promised.

"Yes, you will," he said darkly. "For now, Dagon must be returned to your world instead of being punished in mine."

The Warden held out his hand. Dagon was suddenly sucked away as if a giant vortex had opened up and swallowed him. I was still gaping after that when the Warden resumed speaking.

"Dagon will be weakened by what was torn out of him from the escaping souls. I have also taken away his ability to teleport, and I will ensure that he cannot go near your companion without paralyzing pain. Thus, he will not be able to seek vengeance against you by killing him. But Dagon will regain his strength in time. When he does, he will come for you."

Oh, yes. He'd see this as my stealing power from him twice: first, when he was forbidden to seek human worship; then, when losing the extra souls he'd hoarded to stave off his own death. He wouldn't rest until I was dead, no matter how long it took.

Let him come. I had no intention of backing out of my vow to kill him, either. I only hoped those I'd promised justice to could forgive me for delaying it a bit longer. Then again, they of all people should understand. If they could have saved a loved one from Dagon, I had no doubt that they would have.

"Some of the souls that were released are very dark," the Warden went on. "The oldest ones will be slowest to regenerate since their bodies have long been dust, but when they do . . . the power they consumed from Dagon's essence will make them formidable. You must hunt down the evil ones to limit the havoc they will wreak, since it was your demand that caused them to be freed."

I nodded. "Hunting down those who use their abilities to harm others is what I do. I won't fail." *Gods, please, let me not fail, since I was responsible for this . . .*

I took his barest inclination to the right as a returned nod. "Toward this end, I have removed all their memories connected to Dagon and their time spent trapped inside him. This will limit their knowledge of their new abilities. It will also spare them from being . . ." he paused as if choosing a word, "broken over what they experienced in their imprisonment," he finished.

I caught myself before I said something caustic. So, he *did* understand the concept of extreme mental and emotional trauma. He'd probably removed those memories only to limit the people's dangerousness, since a psychotic, powerful evil person was a bigger threat than a normal, powerful evil person. But whatever his motivation, it meant less suffering for Ian and the rest of them . . . wait. He'd removed *all* memories connected to Dagon? All of them?

"Will, ah, will Ian remember anything about these past few weeks, if all of it happened in direct connection with his deal with Dagon?"

My father stared at me, unblinking. "No. He will not."

*P*ain tore into me, as sudden and ferocious as the wraith attack. I forced myself to nod. To pretend that my father hadn't just ripped my heart out and scrubbed the side of his boat with it. Ian was alive. Nothing else mattered, not even the fact that his only memories of me would be as the law-worshipping bitch he'd thought had helped murder his friend's child.

It was for the best, I told myself. Dagon would be gunning for me, plus many other demons for my slaughter of their kind. I also had several powerful evil souls to hunt down before they became even more dangerous and deadly. Ian's best chance, now that he was finally free of Dagon, was to stay as far from me as possible. My father hadn't intended it, but he'd done me a favor. This would keep Ian safe better than I ever could. My pain was such a small price to pay.

Besides, Ian and I wouldn't have lasted. He'd said he *could* have loved me, but "could" and "did" were very far apart. Much like the distance between Ian saying I was his, but not saying that he was mine. He'd ended his life to stop me from making a deal with Dagon, but he'd probably known Dagon would kill him anyway, making his actions as much a "fuck you" to his old nemesis as they were a sacrifice for me.

In short, if I looked at it coldly, Ian had never promised me anything beyond the moment. Ian reveled in the here and now, and there *was* value in enjoying that. But I would always want more, and it was no doubt beyond him to give it to me.

"There is more," the Warden said. Of course there was, when consequences were the currency. "You are now as vulnerable to death as any vampire."

"What?"

Incredibly, he looked away as if unable to hold my stare. "It was never your power that resurrected you. You do have the ability, but you have not cultivated it. Every time you came back, it was I who raised you. Once word of what I have done here reaches others, I will be removed as Warden and will no longer be able to raise you. Thus, you must take care of your life. You, like Dagon, now only have one of them."

It wasn't hearing about my new mortality that made tears spring to my eyes. It was knowing he *had* been checking in on me all these years, just in a way I'd never suspected. He'd also admitted that he was sacrificing his position as Warden to do as I'd asked. This wasn't merely him satisfying a debt I'd forced him to acknowledge. This was much, much more.

"You do care for me, in your way." Wonder tinged my voice.

He looked back at me, that flash of emotion gone and his face the impassive mask I was used to. "Your companion is of Tenoch's bloodline." Once again, I was taken aback. He knew Mencheres had sired Ian, and Tenoch had sired Mencheres? "Tenoch could regenerate from a similar state of decomposition. I have activated that same power in your companion. Give him blood, and his body will fully heal within hours instead of weeks."

"Thank you, Father," I said, but found myself speaking to the air. The Warden, his boat, and the river had vanished.

A soft whine made me turn around. Silver lay next to Ian's body. He had a paw over Ian's head as if seeking to protect him from the damage that had already been done to it. The sight was heartbreakingly sweet . . . until I heard what sounded like twigs snapping and Ian's desiccated arm yanked Silver close. Then the Simargyl screeched as Ian's bony jaws clamped down on him.

"No!" I shouted, snatching Silver away.

Blood dripped from Ian's fangs. He snapped them at me, trying to tear into any available flesh again. His eyes were sightless, his body was more bones than skin, and his hair had turned pure white. I would have been terrified if I hadn't seen this sort of thing before. Tenoch could wither until he looked exactly like this. It had been a valuable trick that fooled his enemies into thinking Tenoch was dead when he wasn't, but it had also left Tenoch mindlessly hungry until he regenerated.

Now Ian had just gotten a mouthful of Silver's opiate-equivalent blood. That, plus his ravenous state and gods-only-knew what powers he'd absorbed from Dagon after devouring his way out of the demon, made him dangerous. Worse, it wouldn't be long until police arrived. All the explosions, even in this remote area, had to have attracted someone's notice. I had to get Ian secured and away from innocent people, all before he healed enough to realize who the hell I was.

I couldn't do this alone. I needed help. Fast.

I held on to Silver as I ran over and grabbed the heaviest piece of theme-park debris I could carry. Then I dragged it over to Ian, who'd already started to crawl in a mindless search for blood. I dropped it on top of Ian, wincing as I heard bones break. Then, still holding Silver, who wouldn't stop whimpering, I ran into the mirrored fun house.

Amid the wreckage, I found the mobile phone Ian had insisted I have in case of emergency. This definitely qualified. I scrolled through the contacts, glad he'd taken the time to fill some of them in. Once I found the name I was looking for, I dialed. *Answer*, I silently urged when it only rang. *Come on!*

"Ian?" a British voice said on the first ring.

"Tell me you're still in New Jersey!" I burst out, not bothering to return the greeting.

"We're on our way to you," was the answer I never expected. "Ian rang us from a different mobile half an hour ago and said he needed us. Where is he? And what are the ashes he told us we *must* recover if we saw them?"

The burning in my chest had to be my heart splitting apart. After vowing not to involve them because he couldn't bear to endanger them, Ian must have also called Bones when he went to get Rani and Fenkir's bodies. He'd made sure someone was coming to help me if the wraith ended up killing us both. Why else would Ian tell them to recover the ashes he knew I'd rise from? If Ian had thought he'd still be alive, too, he could have recovered my ashes himself.

"Ian needs blood." My voice was a rasp because my throat just closed off. "Buckets of it. And restraints."

"What happened?" Bones asked in an icy tone.

"I don't have time to explain." Damn it, did I hear sirens? How long could I hold off the police? "Just hurry."

"With the new stop to get blood, we'll arrive within two hours," he said crisply. "And if you're responsible for what's happened to Ian, you will regret it."

"Good enough," I replied, and hung up.

*A*n hour and a half later, dawn splashed the darkness with its first bright rays, highlighting the helicopter that had just landed. Bones jumped out, dragging several lengths of thick chains behind him. His brows barely rose at the destruction in the former theme park and the police I'd mesmerized into holding the perimeter, but he gave the skeletons scattered everywhere a longer look.

"They stink of sulfur," were his first words. "How many of them were demons?"

"All of them," I said, still struggling with the draped form beneath me. I'd frozen time around Ian for an hour, but had run out of strength to hold the spell these past thirty minutes.

"All?" Bones repeated in disbelief. "Then how—"

He stopped speaking when I drew back the tarp. Ian's face was a thing of nightmares, if you didn't have my unending gratitude that he was still alive.

Bones stared at him. "Bloody. Fucking. Hell."

"Less shock, more chains," I said wearily. "Don't let how Ian looks fool you. He's incredibly strong." And after everything that had happened, I was running on fumes.

"What happened?" Thankfully, Bones's question came with action. He sprang forward, slinging chains around Ian while avoiding the jaws that snapped at him. Once Bones had Ian encased from neck to feet, he picked him up as if he weighed nothing and carried him toward the helicopter.

"Silver!" I called out. "You can come out now!"

The Simargyl flew out of the fun house, one wing still bloody from Ian's fangs snagging it when I'd snatched Silver away from him. He landed right in my arms. Understandably, the events of the past night had left him very shaken.

"I didn't know your dog had *wings*!" a delighted voice called out. Then I saw a flash of drab brown hair as Cat jumped out of the helicopter. "Where did—oh, shit, who's that?"

"Ian," Bones replied shortly. "Open the cooler, Kitten. We'll need everything in it."

I climbed in after Bones, relieved to see vast quantities of bagged blood when Cat opened the cooler in the back. I set Silver safely out of Ian's reach and grabbed a bag, putting it to Ian's mouth. He tore into it so ferociously, half of it landed on us.

"Wait," Bones said. "I'll hold him." His power snapped out, invisible and potent. Ian's head froze and I emptied the next bag into his mouth without any splatters.

"What happened?" Cat asked, her head swinging back and forth between Ian, Silver, and the bodies outside the helicopter.

"Demon attack." Now that we were finally safe, all my weariness hit me, leaving me unable to speak in complete sentences. "Need some bone for weapons, but rest have to go."

"Here." Cat handed me a blood bag, then shoved it back in my face when I pushed it away. "You look *terrible*, Veritas. Don't worry. We've got plenty for Ian. You can take this one."

I took it because I didn't have the strength to argue. Drinking it made me feel slightly less like I'd pass out. "The bones," I mumbled again.

"I'll take care of them," Cat said, jumping out after giving Silver a quick pat on the head.

Bones kept feeding Ian blood bags. Muscle and sinews started slowly reknitting themselves in the glimpses I caught, though Bones's body blocked most of Ian from my view.

"How long until he can think normally again?" I asked.

Bones cast a glance at me. "Is this his first time regenerating? Or has he been hiding this ability from us for a while?"

"First time," I replied, leaving it at that.

"Half a day, at least," Bones stated.

I closed my eyes. "Good. That'll give me enough time."

"To do what?"

I didn't bother opening my eyes. "Set Ian up the way he last remembers." It wouldn't be in Poland, but I could keep the rest of my promise. "I'll tell you what to say so you can fill in his memory gaps."

"*What* memory gaps? And what about the ashes Ian is so keen that we collect?"

I ignored the sharpness in Bones's tone. "Don't worry about the ashes. All you need to worry about is repeating what I'm about to tell you."

"Why don't you tell Ian yourself?" Instantly.

I closed my eyes; a reflex against the truth. "He won't remember me."

"What?"

"Short version is he pissed off the wrong demon and lost his memory of the past few weeks." Now I opened my eyes so he could see how serious I was. "The demon got away and he'll be coming for me, so it's safer for Ian not to remember any of it."

Bones's dark gaze bored into mine. "You don't intend to even tell him you're his wife?"

"No, I don't!" It flung out of me with all the pain I was fighting not to feel. Then I sighed. "All of you were right. Ian didn't suddenly fall in love. Circumstances forced us to fake being married. The rumor spread and we used it to our advantage. Don't worry; I'll make sure everyone knows it wasn't real."

I'd have to convince Xun Guan and the Enforcers to recant their witness of the ceremony, but I'd faced tougher obstacles. Xun Guan might even be happy to help eradicate my marriage.

"Who is the demon that did all this?"

"Dagon." I hated saying his name, but Bones should know it so he'd know who to watch out for. "My father made it impossible for Dagon to go near Ian without paralyzing pain, but none of you get that safeguard, so watch your backs. Good news is, Dagon's very weak now. Bad news is, he'll heal."

Bones's brows went up. "Your father? Who is he?"

Dammit. I was so exhausted, I'd let that slip. "No one you need to worry about."

"Got the cops sweeping up the demon bones!" Cat announced, coming back in the helicopter. "We'll pick them up after we get Ian and you set up. Then we'll haul them to a crematorium and incinerate them. Can't take them now because we don't have room in the chopper, but we should have it all done by noon."

"Good," I said, closing my eyes again. "Thank you. In the meantime, take Ian to a whorehouse capable of throwing a carnival-themed orgy. Don't worry, I'm buying."

"What?" Cat gasped while Bones said, "Why?" in a steely tone.

"I made a blood vow." Now, I didn't open my eyes because I was afraid they'd see the tears welling in them. "Besides," I added with a flash of despairing humor, "if Ian *does* have any memories of the events before these past few weeks, that's where he'll expect to be."

"What about you?" Bones's tone was softer. Almost pitying. "What will you do now?"

"Don't worry," I said with a short laugh. Silver came over, putting his head beneath my arm as if to remind me that I wasn't alone. I petted him as I said in all truthfulness, "I have *plenty* of things to keep me occupied."

Epilogue

Ian

Someone needed to stop the bloody hammering or he'd murder whoever was doing it.

Ian opened one eye, startled to discover the terrible din came from inside his head. He ran his hand along it, feeling for wounds. Then both eyes opened when he felt nothing except the smoothness of his scalp beneath his hair.

That wasn't right. He'd been injured . . . hadn't he?

"Finally awake," a familiar voice said.

Ian turned, seeing Crispin lounging in a chair not far from him. Crispin's hair was a dreadful shade of dirty blond and he stank as if he'd been swimming in demon sweat. He was clothed, though, while Ian was naked as the day he'd been born. Then giggles drew Ian's attention to the rest of the room.

Women naked except for leonine body paint frolicked on the other side of the large area. Men wearing gazelle markings walked past them, avoiding the fire hoops that were in their path, and was that a car full of *clowns*?

"Where are we? And what are you doing here?" Ian demanded. "Cat will kill you if she catches you at a bordello."

"I'm not the one indulging," Crispin replied, eyeing him with an intensity that belied his languid tone. "I'm babysitting you after your hangover. Head hurt?"

"Like the very devil," Ian moaned, then found himself snapping, "The fire rings are there for a *reason*, or do none of you have a proper work ethic?" at the next group of painted whores who walked past them.

Crispin's brows rose. "Hardly their main performance objective, is it?"

No, it wasn't. Why did he care if they jumped through the fire rings? And why did he feel the urge to praise the clowns for showing markedly more enthusiasm for their roles?

"Don't bother," Ian called out when the faux lionesses and gazelles started to line up before the fire hoops. When they took that as an invitation to turn their attentions to him, Ian brushed their hands away. "Start without me. Go, play amongst yourselves."

"Something wrong?" Crispin asked, still in that mild tone.

Yes. Not only did his head ache as if Lucifer's hammer itself was pounding away at it, he had the near uncontrollable urge to check the back of it for wounds. And why was he utterly uninterested in the erotic spectacle going on in front of him? Not only did he have no desire to join, he could barely be bothered to watch. "How did I get here?" he asked Crispin.

A dark brow arched. "You don't remember?"

He remembered . . . blimey, not much. Had he been upset about something and decided to numb the pain with shagging? That sounded right, but being here somehow felt . . . wrong.

"What did I tell you about playing amongst yourselves?" he snapped when a faux gazelle and lion crawled forward and began stroking his legs. "Off you go, there's a good lass and lad."

They walked away, pouting. Ian turned to Crispin. "Are you *certain* I wanted to be here? In truth, I couldn't be less interested, and look at him." He shook his cock at Crispin for emphasis. "Limp as a dead snake, he is."

Crispin pointedly kept his gaze on Ian's face. "I can hardly offer my assistance."

"Eh, never fancied you that way. Good thing, too, since we turned out to be cousins. In all seriousness, though, Crispin, why am I here, why do you stink like demon, and why does my head feel as though it's been split open recently?"

Something filled Crispin's gaze. Ian's sense of unease grew. His friend was about to lie to him. Even if he couldn't see it in Crispin's gaze, he felt it all the way to his bones.

"I smell like this because we fought the very brassed-off owner of the Red Dragon source you stole," Crispin said. "Your recent drinking rampage wasn't enough, so you stole your own source, drank it until you decided lying about being married was the height of hilarity, then called me when the source's demon owner came after you. We killed him, you set the source free, and decided to celebrate at this whorehouse. I stayed only to make sure you didn't do anything else supremely stupid."

Crispin was lying. Ian's surety grew with every merciless hammering in his head. So why did parts of that story feel familiar?

"This isn't right," Ian said aloud. "You're lying and I'm not supposed to be here. I'm supposed to be . . ."

"Where?" At once, that intentness was back in Crispin's gaze. "Where are you supposed to be?"

"You tell me," Ian snapped. "And where is—"

He stopped. That sense of wrongness roared to the forefront, growing until Ian got up and began to pace. Something more was going on than Crispin's lies. He found his hands running over the back of his head again. His hair was white for some reason, but that didn't concern him as much as searching for wounds that still weren't there. Why was he so certain they should be? Why did it feel so wrong that he was here with Crispin instead of . . . somewhere else? *With* someone else?

"I was about to say a name," Ian said slowly, "but now I have no idea which one. Why was I about to say a name I suddenly can't remember? What the hell is going on?"

Crispin rose, his gaze flicking to the whores Ian had already forgotten about. "Leave," Crispin told them. "All of you."

Déjà vu had Ian whipping around to stare at the whores filing out of the room. This had happened before, but not with Crispin. Someone else. Who? *Who?*

A woman's voice whispered across his mind, her tone more amused than mocking. *Are you getting them out of the way because you're intending to fight me?*

"Where is she?" Ian found himself demanding.

He didn't remember moving, but suddenly, his hands were on Crispin's shoulders and he was shaking him as if he could rattle the truth out of him. Crispin's eyes went wide as he stared back at where Ian had been moments before.

"You teleported!"

It took a few moments for Crispin's stunned statement to penetrate. Then Ian scoffed, "More lies, mate?"

"*That* is no lie." Crispin shoved Ian back, then gave him a look of growing expectancy. "See if you can do it again. Where do you think you should be right now?"

"Shower," he found himself saying. *I don't need to tell you what you smell like . . .*

The words had barely formed in his mind when Ian was staring at old blue tiles and grout that had seen far better days. He burst out of the bathroom into the adjoining bedroom, shouting "Crispin!" when a feminine squeal stopped him.

"Who are you? How did you get here?" the petite brunette on the bed demanded. She wasn't alone, and her companion gave him a very annoyed look.

"Get out," he snapped. "I paid for an hour!"

Ian ignored them as he left the bedroom. "Crispin!" he shouted again when he reached the hallway.

A whoosh of power, then Crispin flew up the stairs. Ian had started down the hallway toward him when it suddenly dissolved into the blackest of rivers. A thin boat sailed over it, its single occupant appearing out of mists made of darkness.

Crispin's shout of "Angel of Death!" should have worried Ian. So should the cloaked skeleton turning its bony face toward him while raising its scythe. Instead, Ian found himself saying, "Don't fret. What you're seeing isn't what he really looks like. On this side of the veil, you see what you fear."

How did he know that? Were those his words? Or were they someone else's?

The figure's mouth stretched in a terrifying version of a smile. Then that skull dissolved into dark bronze skin, a handsome visage, hair the color of a cotton-candy mistake, and eyes that flashed with bright, silvery beams.

"You do remember," the thing said. "I told her you would not, to ease her pain in case you cared nothing for her, but when emotions run deep, they can never be fully erased."

Her. Someone *had* been stolen from him! "I don't remember much." Fear crept over Ian, but not fear of dying. He was afraid this creature would leave without telling him what he needed to know. "But I want to. Tell me what I lost."

"I cannot restore all that was removed. Even the little I can restore could break your mind," the creature said bluntly.

"Ian." Crispin had recovered from his shock enough to start edging toward him. "Don't. It's too dangerous."

His urgency skyrocketed. He *needed* the memories that had been taken from him. Risks didn't matter. Crispin's objections didn't matter. He'd knock his mate through the wall if he tried to stop him again.

"Give them back to me," he told the creature.

The thing put his hand on Ian's head. Images blasted through his mind, fragmented and without context. A tiny blonde Law Guardian fighting him before changing into a statuesque woman with the same platinum, gold, and blue hair as that creature . . . flashes of a waterfall . . . then a castle . . . why was he fighting to save a flying dog? And what was *this*?

By my blood, you are my wife . . .

Feelings ripped through the next set of images. Her body entwined with his. *Mine.* Her blood on his lips. *Mine.* So many demons. *Protect her.* Blood and salt strafing the air. *Must save her.* Silver eyes staring in his pleadingly. *"I can't just let you die."*

Then two knives ramming into his skull, one he'd never seen, the other he'd shoved through himself. Had he . . . had he died?

That stygian river suddenly rose up and swallowed him. He screamed but nothing came out. Then he tried to run, to move, to do *something.* He couldn't. He had no body. The darkness had devoured him whole, but he wasn't alone in it. Something else was here. What was it? It came nearer . . . no. No. NO!

He came back to reality on his knees, blood pouring from his eyes, mouth, nose, and ears. After a panicked moment, he realized the other world was gone. So was the creature who'd stuffed these memory shards back into his head. Crispin was beside him, while a few prostitutes and a disgruntled client clustered at the other end of the hallway.

"Ian," Crispin was saying. "Speak to me, mate!"

Ian wiped the blood off, endlessly relieved that he still had a body that could bleed. Then he paused, sniffing his hand. A quick lick revealed what he'd suspected. His blood now tasted like a milder form of Red Dragon. Why?

One person had the answers. He didn't know much, but he knew that. If the little vixen thought she could run away without telling him the rest of what he'd lost, she didn't know who she was dealing with.

Ian got up. "Your trousers," he told the annoyed customer, lighting his gaze up with green. "Give them to me."

The man took off his trousers and handed them over. Ian put them on. They didn't fit, but it hardly mattered. He went down the stairs, ignoring Crispin's fluttering behind him, and took a coat off one of the hooks by the door.

Crispin finally grabbed him hard enough to spin him around. "Where do you think you're going?"

"Where am I going?" he repeated, then laughed.

His memory was in pieces, his abilities might now include teleporting, his blood was wrong, and he was about to run headlong into a demon war, if he guessed rightly about the parts he *could* remember. But for some reason, he felt better than he ever had. In fact, if this feeling was a drug, he was never going to get clean.

"Yes, where are you going?" Crispin urged.

Ian laughed. "To get my wife."

Veritas and Ian's story continues
in the next Night Rebel novel,
WICKED PROMISES
Coming Summer 2019!